A Taste of

WHISKEY

The Whiskeys

Special Edition

MELISSA FOSTER

Cover Design: Elizabeth Mackey Designs

WORLD LITERARY PRESS
PRINTED IN THE UNITED STATES OF AMERICA

A Note to Readers

I have been excited to write Sasha and Ezra's story since I met them on the page a few years ago. Sasha is such a strong woman, and she has always known exactly what she wanted in life and in love. It turns out that Ezra has, too, though they both had many obstacles to overcome. These young lovers, and little Gus, have a lot of history, and I take great joy in finally bringing them to their happily ever after. I hope you adore them as much as I do. If this is your first introduction to my writing, all my books are written to stand alone and may also be enjoyed as part of the larger series, so dive right in and enjoy the sweet, sexy ride.

The Whiskeys are just one of the series in my Love in Bloom big-family romance collection. Characters from each series make appearances in future books, so you never miss an engagement, wedding, or birth. A complete list of all series titles is included at the end of this book, along with previews of upcoming publications.

Be sure to check out my online bookstore for pre-orders, early releases, bundles, and exclusive discounts on ebooks, print, and audiobooks. Remember to sign up for my bookstore newsletter to make sure you don't miss out on future releases or sales.

Shop My Bookstore
shop.melissafoster.com

WHISKEY/WICKED
FAMILY TREE

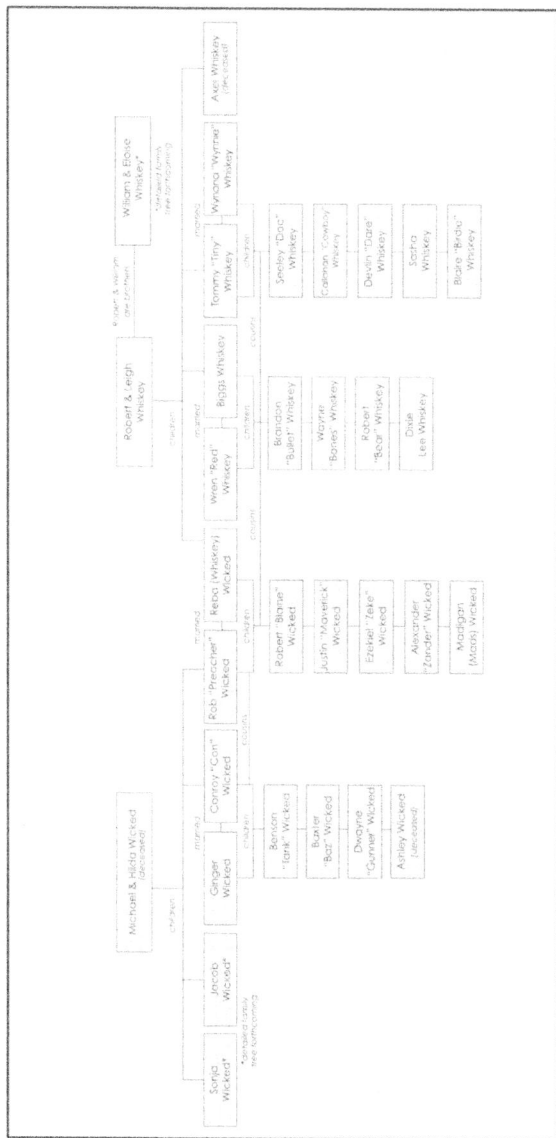

Michael & Aisha Wicked (deceased)

- Sonja Wicked* *tempted tartan tree forthcoming
- Jacob Wicked*

married → **Ginger Wicked** / **Clayton "Con" Wicked**

children:
- Brandon "Tank" Wicked
- Baxter "Bax" Wicked
- Dwayne "Gunner" Wicked
- Ashley Wicked (deceased)

married → **Rob "Preacher" Wicked** / **Reba (Whiskey) Wicked**

children:
- Robert "Blane" Wicked
- Justin "Maverick" Wicked
- Ezekiel "Zeke" Wicked
- Alexander "Zander" Wicked
- Madigan (Maddi) Wicked

Robert & Leigh Whiskey

married → **Wren "Red" Whiskey** / **Bullet Whiskey**

children:
- Brandon "Bullet" Whiskey
- Wayne "Bones" Whiskey
- Rush "Bear" Whiskey
- Dixie Lee Whiskey

Wilson & Eloise Whiskey *tempted family tree forthcoming

Robert & Wilson are brothers

married → **Tommy "Tiny" Whiskey** / **Wynona "Wynnie" Whiskey**

children:
- Seeley "Doc" Whiskey
- Callahan "Cowboy" Whiskey
- Devlin "Daze" Whiskey
- Sasha Whiskey
- Blaine "Birdie" Whiskey

Axel Whiskey (deceased)

New York Times Bestselling Author

MELISSA FOSTER

Gus

Sasha

Ezra

Playlist

"Shut Up and Drive" by Rihanna

"Kiss the Girl" by Brent Morgan

"Country Girl (Shake It for Me)" by Luke Bryan

"Rock and a Hard Place" by Bailey Zimmerman

"All Too Well (Taylor's Version)" by Taylor Swift

"Die from a Broken Heart" by Maddie & Tae

"I Can't Fall in Love Without You" by Zara Larsson

"Lose My Mind" by Dean Lewis

"In a Perfect World" by Dean Lewis and Julia Michaels

"I Fall Apart" by Post Malone

"More" by Hunter Hayes

"Stolen" by Dashboard Confessional

"Rumor" by Lee Brice

"Closer" by Nine Inch Nails

"Pour Some Sugar on Me" by Def Leppard

"In Case You Didn't Know" by Brett Young

"Love Story" by Taylor Swift

"Everything I Love" by Morgan Wallen

"How Do I Do This" by Kelsea Ballerini

"Lovesong" by The Cure

"Secret Love Song" by Little Mix with Jason Derulo

"Love You a Little Bit" by Tanner Adell

"Wannabe" by Spice Girls

"Lean on Me" by Bill Withers
"Complicated" by Avril Lavigne
"Fight Song" by Rachel Platten
"Keep Holding On" by Avril Lavigne
"Love You Anyway" by Luke Combs

Chapter One

ANOTHER DATE BITES the dust. *Story of my life.*

Sasha Whiskey climbed into her truck after yet another mediocre Saturday-night date. She mentally added *boring bankers* to the growing list of men she *wasn't* looking for. People said finding a good man was like hunting for a needle in a haystack, but she wasn't buying it. It was more like diving bare-ass naked into a haystack full of needles. She started the truck and "Another One Bites the Dust" came on the radio.

Are you freaking kidding me?

Even the universe agreed with her. She was jabbing at the screen on the dashboard to change the song when a call rang through from her younger sister, Birdie. Birdie was the only one of her four siblings who didn't work and live at Redemption Ranch in Hope Valley, Colorado, their family's second-chance ranch, where they rescued horses and gave troubled souls the therapy and support they needed to find their path in life. Birdie lived in Allure, a neighboring town where she co-owned a chocolate shop.

"Hey, Bird."

"Darn it! I was hoping you wouldn't answer."

"Then why did you call?" Birdie had always marched to her own beat. She was brilliantly creative, but her mind ran in a dozen directions at once, and while Sasha adored her, she was never quite sure where she was coming from.

"Because I was dying to know what happened on your date. If you didn't answer, I would've assumed you were finally getting laid. But I guess Randy wasn't so *randy* after all."

"Did you stop to think I might not answer because I could be in trouble? What if I'd been kidnapped or something?"

"As if there's that type of crime in Hope Valley? Besides, Randy's not exactly the kidnap—*Wait!* Did you role-play? That could be hot. But then you wouldn't have answered. So…what happened? Did he kiss like a seventh grader?"

"What does that mean?"

"You know. All tongue with his mouth open too wide? Or worse, barely opening his mouth at all. I hate guys who kiss like cracker boxes. They should really come with warnings. Like when you visit an animal shelter and the little cards on the cages say things like, *Not cat friendly* or *he's a chewer*."

Sasha laughed. "Wouldn't that be nice?"

"Yes, so give me the deets. Did he try to ring your doorbell, but he couldn't find it? Tell me he's not one of those guys who's hot and smart but has no idea what he's doing in bed."

That was big talk for a girl who didn't get much action, but Sasha loved that Birdie always knew how to lighten the air. She could also be nosy and annoying, like any younger sister, but having grown up with three overprotective brothers, they had to stick together.

Sasha drove out of the parking lot. "I hate guys who need a

road map, but I have no idea if Randy is one of them. We didn't even kiss."

"Not even a good-night kiss? Why? You guys had all of that great flirty banter every time you went into the bank."

"Once we got to talking, we had nothing in common. His life is banking and golf. He's very business minded. I imagine him checking off lists in his head while he has sex. Kissing. *Check.* Touching. *Check.* One orgasm. *Check.*" Being brought up in a biker family with rugged men who would stare down the devil himself to protect the people they loved, and working with men and women who had been in prison or were recovering from substance use, Sasha had been exposed to some dark situations, and she was drawn to men who could handle them. "Just once I'd like to go on a date and feel that zing of attraction that makes you crave everything about a guy, from his voice and his energy to his lips and—"

"Giant anaconda?"

"Yes, that, too. Why is it so hard to find a guy who's smart *and* passionate? Someone who exudes masculinity without crossing the line to toxic and can make you want him from across the room without saying a word?" *The way Ezra does.*

Ezra Moore was the epitome of Sasha's ideal man. He was a member of the Dark Knights motorcycle club, which her father had founded more than three decades ago, he loved his five-year-old son, Gus, with everything he had, and he had a heart of gold. He was also beyond beautiful. He looked like a Greek god, tall and dark with soulful eyes and olive skin, and he had an edge that he kept under wraps. An edge she'd like to set free. But he was also a therapist at the ranch, making him forbidden territory since they didn't allow intracompany dating.

"*Ugh.* Sasha, you're doing it *again*," Birdie complained.

"Doing what?"

"Comparing everyone to Ezra, and don't even pretend you're not. I can hear your brain twisting this back to him. You do it with every guy you go out with. You and Ezra shared one kiss when you were teenagers, and you've built it up to be this life-altering moment."

It *was* a life-altering moment.

Ezra had grown up in a different town, going to different schools than the Whiskeys, and he'd been such a rebellious teenager, his father had enrolled him in a program at the ranch for troubled kids when he was a senior in high school. But one night before Sasha and her siblings knew who Ezra Moore was, his and Sasha's paths had crossed, and she'd gotten a glimpse of the edge he now kept so tightly locked down and a taste of the lips she'd fantasized about ever since. She'd never forgotten the raw passion and primal hunger behind that kiss, the feel of his strong hands, or the confidence with which he'd taken that kiss. How could she when she had spent the last thirteen years searching for the equivalent—and regretting turning him down when he'd wanted more?

Not that it mattered. While their friendship had deepened over the years and he was playful and flirty when they were alone, he'd never given her any indication of wanting more since he'd cleaned up his act.

"You know I'm right," Birdie said, bringing Sasha back to their conversation.

"I never should have told you about that."

"You can thank your good friend tequila for your loose lips, and now *I'm* your voice of reason."

"That's a scary thought."

"Look, I get it. He's a hot single dad with a panty-melting

broody stare, but you guys have had years to scratch that itch, and he hasn't made a move. Do we need to watch *He's Just Not That into You* again?"

"*Birdie*, that was mean." Even if it was true, she didn't need it thrown in her face. She truly believed there was something more, something *real*, between them, and no matter how hard she tried, she couldn't turn her back on that belief.

"I'm not trying to be mean, but with Dare's wedding coming up next month and Cowboy getting engaged, I can hear your biological clock ticking, and you've wasted enough time on your teenage crush." Their brothers, Seeley, Callahan, and Devlin, were Dark Knights and went by their road names, Doc, Cowboy, and Dare. "You've gotten pickier the last few years. You find something wrong with every guy you go out with, and it's always the same things. They're not tough enough or smart enough or take-charge enough. It's like you want an Einstein biker or something. Have you even checked out the profile I made you on the Cowboy Cupid app yet? That's where you'll meet those kinds of guys."

"*No*, and stop making me one of your missions." Birdie was always on one of her made-up missions, but Sasha knew she wouldn't find what she was looking for on any app because it wasn't only about the man Ezra was. It was also about Gus, whom she loved with all her heart. And it had nothing to do with her biological clock. She wanted to be with her soul mate, and Ezra was the only person she'd ever been able to envision in that role.

"Someone has to wake your butt up. In every other aspect of your life, you're decisive, and you face things head-on. You never let things linger, except with Ezra. You know what we need to do?"

"End this call?"

"No. We need to break this stupid Ezra spell you're under. You need to go over there right now, knock on his door, and when he answers, just kiss the hell out of him. Then you'll see his kisses aren't what you've built them up to be, and you'll stop using him as your gauge for other men."

"You *know* I'd never do that." She gripped the steering wheel tighter. "I gotta go. I'll talk to you tomorrow."

"Just kiss him!"

"Good night, Bird." She ended the call.

Fucking Birdie. Just kiss him. Yeah, right. As if I could ever do that.

She tried to push those thoughts aside as she turned into the ranch, driving beneath the wooden beam with an iron *RR* across the top. The first *R* was backward. The ranch had been in her mother's family for several generations. Her mother was a psychologist, and after her parents were married, they'd expanded the ranch from solely a horse rescue to offer services as a second-chance ranch for people, too. They owned several hundred glorious acres with cabins for live-in clients and staff, offices for traditional therapeutic services, and a full veterinary clinic. Sasha had grown up on the ranch, and it was the only place she'd ever wanted to work or live. As she drove past pastures, riding arenas, and the barns where she worked as an equine rehabilitation therapist, she felt a sense of comfort. Usually that comfort could override any uneasy feelings, but as she turned off the main road, heading for her cabin, discomfort clung to her like a shadow.

She stopped at her crossroad, but instead of turning right and going home, she glanced in the opposite direction toward Ezra's cabin. The flicker of a bonfire in his yard had her pulse quickening, taking her back to that fateful night so long ago, when her friend Bobbie Mancini had begged her to go to a field party at Clayton Field in the next town over with a guy named John she'd met in town. Sasha had been the ultimate good girl, but at fifteen she'd started to develop a rebellious streak, and she'd told her parents she was sleeping at Bobbie's house that night. They'd snuck out, and John, who was seventeen, had driven them to the party. She could still see that night unfolding as clear as day.

Music blared, competing with Sasha's nerves, as she climbed out of the car in the dirt field, taking in dozens of cars and trucks and older kids drinking and dirty dancing by a bonfire. Excitement and fear battled inside her. She'd been to parties with older kids, but they were kids she'd grown up with, and her brothers were always there to protect her. She didn't know anyone besides Bobbie and John, and as John got out of the car, he howled like a wolf, causing cheers from the partygoers.

"Holy shit," Bobbie whispered excitedly. "This is so cool."

Sasha tried to hide her trepidation. "It's awesome."

Bobbie nudged her, motioning toward the fire. Sasha followed her gaze to the hottest guy she'd ever seen. He was wearing jeans and a T-shirt with the sleeves torn off. He had thick, longish jet-black hair and a smattering of whiskers, like her older brothers did. He was with three girls, but when he tipped a liquor bottle to his mouth, his eyes locked on Sasha, sending a jolt of electricity straight to her heart. She swallowed hard, unable to look away from his piercing stare.

"He's hot," Bobbie whispered. "You should go talk to him."

Was she nuts? "He's with three girls, and he looks like trouble."

"Exactly. Tonight's about getting into a little trouble."

"Let's go get a beer," John said as he slung an arm around Bobbie, leading them to the keg. He high-fived a few guys, said

hello to about a dozen girls, and finally handed Sasha and Bobbie red plastic cups filled to the brim with beer.

Sasha tore her gaze away from the hot guy by the fire but couldn't escape the heat of his stare. Bobbie and John left her alone to go dance, and Sasha tried to act cool as she nursed her beer. She talked to a few guys who came over to her, but she was totally out of her element and wished she could leave. But she had no way to get home. When a sandy-haired boy sauntered over, she prayed she didn't ramble like she often did when she got nervous.

"Hey, I'm Chad."

"Hi. I'm Sasha."

He lifted his hand, offering her a joint.

"No thanks."

"Come on. It's just pot."

"It's okay. I'll stick with my beer." She scanned the crowd for Bobbie and saw her sitting in the grass kissing John a few feet from where the black-haired boy stood by the bonfire watching her and Chad, his jaw tight.

Chad stepped closer, holding the joint up to her lips. "Go on. Take a hit."

"I don't want to." She pushed his hand away. She might be new to rebellion, but she wasn't a wallflower. She'd learned a thing or two from her tough brothers.

"What are you afraid of?"

"I'm not afraid of anything." She saw the black-haired boy stalking toward them.

"Then take a hit," Chad challenged.

"Dude, she said no," the black-haired boy said sternly.

"Chill, Moore. I'm just trying to get her to loosen up."

"There are plenty of other girls you don't have to ply with weed to get laid," Moore said.

"Whatever, man. She's a Goody Two-shoes anyway."

As Chad walked away, the other boy turned a dark stare on her. "He's got a point. What're you doing here?"

She narrowed her eyes, irritation mounting inside her. "What do you think I'm doing here?"

"I think Little Bo Peep lost her sheep and she wandered into a wolf's den."

She held his gaze, refusing to back down. "For your information, I came here on purpose."

"That's big talk for a Goody Two-shoes."

"I'm not a Goody Two-shoes."

He scoffed. "I know a Goody Two-shoes when I see one. I bet you've never even been to a party before."

"I have too." She wasn't about to let some hot, jerky boy get the best of her.

"Unchaperoned?" He cocked a grin.

"I go to parties alone all the time." It wasn't a lie. She arrived at parties alone and met her friends there.

"Yeah? Do they have pony rides and piñatas at your parties?"

She glowered at him. "I'm fifteen, not five."

He arched a brow. "Is that right?"

"Yes, and I'm not the goody-goody you think I am."

"You've been holding that same cup of beer since you got here. I bet you've never even drank before."

"Shows how much you know." She'd tasted beer before. She just didn't like it. To prove her point, she took a gulp of her beer, filling her cheeks before sucking it down, trying not to flinch at the bitter taste.

A rough laugh tumbled from his lips. "So you're not a goody-goody?"

"Nope." She was proud of herself for that little lie, which was *feeling more like the truth as she took another drink.*

His eyes narrowed, and he dragged his gaze down the length of her, causing a wild flutter in her chest. "I don't know, Bo Peep. I'm still getting that goody-goody vibe. I bet you've never even kissed a guy before."

"I have too!" She hoped her burning cheeks didn't give that lie away.

"Yeah?" He stepped closer, his dark eyes drilling into her.

She willed herself not to act any different despite his close proximity turning her skin to fire. "Yup. Lots of them."

"Prove it."

"What?" Was he serious? Could he hear her heart thundering like a herd of horses in her chest?

"I dare you to kiss me."

A nervous laugh bubbled out, but his expression didn't change. "You want me to kiss you? Like, right now?" Shitshitshit. She'd never kissed a boy before. But she'd never wanted to kiss anyone the way she wanted to kiss him, either, and that made no sense. He was the type of pushy guy her brothers warned her away from.

He grinned arrogantly. "Unless you really are a goody-goody, in which case—"

"I'm not."

"Prove it."

She froze. She didn't think he'd call her on it! But she couldn't back down now. She looked around to see if anyone was watching and was relieved that nobody seemed to be. Gathering all her courage, she went up on her toes, put her hand on his chest, and pressed her lips to his. His chest was hard and warm, but his lips were soft and oh so kissable.

"Just as I thought," he said as she sank down to her heels. "You've never kissed a guy before."

"What? Why do you say that?"

"Because you don't know how to kiss."

Mortified, she tried to save face. "Maybe I just don't want to kiss you with everything I have."

He leaned closer. "It's a damn shame that a cute girl like you doesn't know how to kiss, Bo Peep."

"I know how to kiss. But if you think you're so good at it, I dare you to kiss m—"

He grabbed her face with both hands, crushing his lips to hers before she even finished the sentence. He angled her mouth beneath his, and her lips parted with the movement. His tongue plunged and swept over hers, rough and insistent, sending thrills darting through her. He tasted like liquor and lust, and she couldn't get enough. She clung to him, pushing up on her toes, desperate for more. A moan escaped, and he must have liked it, because he made a deep, guttural sound that lit flames beneath her skin. One of his arms circled her, holding her tight against him. His other hand fisted in her hair, sending more electrifying sensations skittering through her as his tongue delved deeper, like he couldn't get enough of her, either. She felt him get hard, and he ground against her, bringing a whole new type of thrill. Heat seared through her, pooling low in her belly, and she felt her panties dampen. He palmed her ass, slowing their kisses, making hungry sounds that stole her ability to think.

As their lips parted, he kept her close. "What's your name, Bo Peep?"

Breathless and foggy brained, she managed, "Sasha."

"Sweet, sexy Sasha," he whispered huskily, sending her heart into another flurry.

Nobody had ever called her sexy before. She was known as her brothers' little sister, the studious one, the good girl who everyone thought was more interested in horses and school than boys. But this hot boy, with his ripped shirt and liquor breath, saw her as something more.

"How about we take this party to my car?"

Her high deflated like a popped balloon, her mind reeling. She was so turned on, part of her wanted to let go of the reins and let him lead her into that car and teach her all the dirty things she wondered about. But the scared-shitless part of her overrode that curiosity. "Actually...um." She stepped out of his arms, pointing over her shoulder. "I have to go...find my friend. Um, yeah. So. Thanks for..." Ohgod. Stop rambling!

Amusement rose in his eyes. "The kiss?"

"Uh-huh. Yeah. That. Ohmygod. I'm leaving. I have to go. Nice meeting you." Holy crap. Leave already! With a shaky wave, she said, "See ya," and hurried away, lips still tingling, body vibrating like a bundle of live wires, and her overwhelmed heart scooped up every detail of the kiss—the way he tasted, the sounds he'd made, the feel of his body against hers—and tucked that treasure trove away with the rest of her secrets.

Sasha sat at the crossroad, breathless from the memory, as Birdie's voice traipsed through her mind. *Kiss the hell out of him. Then you'll see his kisses aren't what you've built them up to be, and you'll stop using him as your gauge for other men.*

It would surely take an act of God for that to happen, but Birdie did have a point. She'd dated plenty of guys since that kiss, and she'd be lying to herself if she didn't admit to comparing every single one of them to Ezra.

"Okay, Birdie. Here goes nothing." She turned left, heading for Ezra's cabin.

Chapter Two

EZRA TOSSED ANOTHER log on the fire and looked up at the starry summer sky, thinking about how lucky he was to live and work at a place he loved, surrounded by so many wonderful people who had become family to him and Gus. He'd come a long way from the delinquent kid who'd spent years resenting his mother for abandoning him when he was fourteen and his father for being emotionally closed off and putting so much energy into the motorcycle club when Ezra had desperately needed him. He'd resented the club, too.

All these years later, he was still trying to understand his father, which wasn't easy when his old man wouldn't talk about the past, but as a member of the club, Ezra had nothing but respect for it.

Truck headlights lit up the road. There were a few cabins beyond his, and just as he wondered who it was, Sasha's truck came into focus. She was at the top of that list of wonderful people. He and Gus had moved to the ranch when Gus was barely one, when he'd separated from his ex-wife, with whom he now shared custody. Sasha had been there for him and Gus through his messy divorce, and in the years since, she'd become one of their closest friends. She often took care of Gus when Ezra's unreliable ex failed to show up for her scheduled nights with him and Ezra had to work or had club commitments. Sasha often stuck around afterward, and they'd talk, have a drink by the fire, or watch a movie.

He waved as she pulled into the driveway, trying to ignore the prickle of desire that had always been there but had become even harder to tamp down lately.

She climbed out of her truck looking like she rolled out of every country boy's wet dream, leggy and beautiful in a short floral dress and those fancy brown cowgirl boots with flowers on them that were so very *her*.

"Hey, Ez. I saw your fire and thought I'd stop by. I hope that's okay."

"You know it is. Get over here."

She laughed softly, her long blond hair falling in gentle waves as she walked over to the fire. She was all dolled up with smoky eyes and a soft shade of lipstick. *Damn*, she smelled good, too. Like vanilla and cocoa. A far cry from the fresh-faced, ponytail-wearing girl who usually smelled like hay and horses, which oddly enough, smelled really fucking good on her.

"Is Gusto sleeping?"

"Like a bear. He said to tell Sugar good night if I saw her." Gus had a big-time crush on Sasha. He called her Sugar, which he'd picked up from Dare's casual use of the endearment when speaking about his female friends. What Ezra didn't tell her was what Gus asked him to do nearly every time he kissed him good night. *If you see Sugar, give her a good-night kiss for me.* Ezra was strong but not strong enough to do that without wanting more.

Not even for his son.

"He's the sweetest. How many stories did it take tonight?"

"Only three." Gus had recently learned the art of negotiation and had been using it at every opportunity.

"You got off easy." She shivered and crossed her arms. "I didn't realize it was so chilly tonight." June evenings in Colorado could be nippy.

"Come here." He took her hand, bringing her closer to the fire, and shrugged off his zip-up hoodie. "Put this on." He held it up, helping her into it.

"Sure you don't mind?"

"Of course not. You look cute in it." He straightened it on her shoulders. "I always run hot anyway."

"Tell me something I don't know." She held his gaze a beat longer than usual and tucked her hair behind her ear, flashing the breathtaking smile that always did him in.

Everything about the woman made him want her in ways he shouldn't, from her alluring hazel eyes and caring nature to the hint of innocence she still gave off, which contrasted sharply with her innate sensuality. But that innocence wasn't naivete. It was a reflection of her pure, loving heart. Sasha Whiskey had become his biggest conundrum. She'd been the star of his spank bank when he was younger, and she'd become so much more. But she was the last person he should be thinking about like that for too many reasons to count, including the fact that her parents, Tiny and Wynnie, ran Redemption Ranch. Wynnie was his boss, and Tiny was also the founder and president of the motorcycle club.

So why, after all these years, am I still thinking about you that way? He'd been asking himself that forever, and the answer was still nowhere in sight.

"You look nice. Were you out with the girls tonight?"

"No, but that probably would have been more fun." She lowered herself into a chair by the fire. "I was on a date."

He needed a drink for this conversation. "Hold that thought. I'll grab us some drinks. I'll be right back." He went inside and got two beers for himself and a Truly hard seltzer and a bag of peanut M&M's for Sasha, shoving that wicked spear of jealousy down deep before he headed back out. He found Sasha rubbing her thighs, for warmth, he assumed. His mind refused to behave, trudging down a dark path, imagining *his* hands spreading those gorgeous thighs, and—

"You got more Truly," she said cheerily.

Silently berating himself for letting his mind wander, he opened the can and handed it to her. "I got you these, too, but I didn't take the time to make popcorn." Her favorite snack was popcorn with peanut M&M's mixed in.

"Thank you. You always know what I need."

She was doing it again, holding his gaze longer than usual. They had an easy friendship, and somewhere along the line, flirting had become a part of it. A part he looked forward to, and had to be careful with. But that lingering gaze was new.

He tried to quell the thrum of attraction rising to the surface. "It's the least I can do with everything you do for me and Gus." He set one can of beer on the ground and opened the other, taking a swig as he sat beside her, and because he was a glutton for punishment, he asked the burning question. "So, who's the lucky guy?"

"His name is Randy and he works at my bank, but he wasn't very lucky. There won't be a second date, and if I ever want to go out with someone from my professional realm again, please slap me."

And there it was, like a neon light. The warning he needed to back the fuck off. He was far deeper into her professional realm than any banker. "Slap you, huh? I didn't realize you were into that."

"I'm *not.*" Her smile suddenly faded. "Are *you?*"

He laughed and shook his head. "You're the one who asked me to slap you."

"Yes, but only because now it'll be weird when I see Randy, and I don't want to make that mistake again. Maybe I should change banks." Her brows knitted, and she tapped the side of the Truly can, like she was mulling over the idea.

He tightened his grip on his beer. "Did he try something? Need me to set him straight?"

"No, it's nothing like that. We just had no chemistry."

"I've been there a few times. That's never fun. But if you knew this guy from the bank, couldn't you tell whether there was chemistry or not?"

"That's the thing. He's usually fun to flirt with, but at dinner, there was no fun banter, and we didn't have anything in common to talk about."

Sasha was funny, interesting, and empathetic. He couldn't imagine anyone not finding something to talk about with her. He could talk to her all night and never get bored, and sometimes he did. He enjoyed those nights a hell of a lot.

"That sucks. But you must have guys lining up to take you out." Like him, she kept her private life under wraps. He assumed she dated, although as far as he knew, she'd never brought a guy back to the ranch. Which was probably smart, since her brothers wouldn't let a guy get far without a complete interrogation and a threat hanging over his head, which would crush any guy's hard-on. Except Ezra's. Her brothers didn't faze him, but her relationship with his son had always been precious enough to douse those flames. Unfortunately, his heart wasn't as easily dissuaded. Lately, seeing her with his little boy brought all of his emotions to the surface, making it that much harder to keep himself in check.

"Hardly. Maybe I *should* check out Cowboy Cupid."

"The dating app? The hell you should. That's dangerous, Sash. You don't know who's on the other end of that app."

"With my luck, it'd be Hyde or Taz."

Over my dead body.

Hyde and Taz were ranch hands and members of the Dark Knights. They were good men, and Ezra would always have their backs, except where Sasha was concerned. They were known for sharing women, and he wasn't about to let them get their hands on her.

"You're not really thinking about using that app, are you?"

Just fucking say no, because that's not something I can handle.

"I don't know. Maybe."

His jaw tightened. "Are you only looking to hook up with guys? Because that's what most of those apps are known for."

"I *know* what they're for," she said, running her finger around the rim of the can. She sat up a little taller, eyeing him defiantly, reminding him of the way she'd pretended to have experience with boys as a teenager. "What's wrong with playing the field? It would be nice to find a guy who knows where the doorbell is."

A rough laugh tumbled out.

Her eyes narrowed. "Why is that funny? I'm a healthy, young woman. I have *needs*."

"Doorbell?" What the hell was she trying to prove? It was one thing to sleep with a guy she'd dated for a while, but to just put herself out there for sex? That wasn't Sasha. She was a natural nurturer and a caring friend who had listened to him bitch about his cheating ex when he'd been too exhausted to know better than to unload on her. Sasha wasn't the kind of woman you fucked and forgot. She was the type you cherished, made love to, ravaged with pleasure, and introduced to your family, because once she let you into that sweet heart of hers, there was no way in hell you'd ever let her go.

"Stay off those apps, will ya?" He took a drink.

"Why? It's not like there are many hot prospects around here."

He bumped her leg with his. "Hey, I take offense to that."

"*Please.* You know you're hot. All the girls at the Roadhouse ogle you." The Roadhouse was a biker bar they all frequented. It was owned by Manny and Alice Mancini, Bobbie, and Dare's fiancée Billie's parents. Billie worked there full time, and Bobbie worked there part time.

"But not hot enough for you." He said it teasingly, because if he let his true feelings come out, his and Gus's lives would implode, and they could both lose her.

Sasha rolled her eyes. "You've known me forever. If you wanted me, I think I'd know by now."

"I made my move a long time ago, Bo Peep. You turned me down, and my ego took a hell of a hit." They'd never spoken about the night they'd kissed, and he didn't know why he was bringing it up now. As a therapist, he knew talking about past events could help put them into perspective, but as a man whose feelings for his friend had deepened over the years, he knew he was fucking with Pandora's box.

Her eyes widened. "*Your* ego? You told me I was a crappy kisser."

"No. I said you'd never kissed a guy before."

"*Whatever.* It wasn't nice." She took a drink, annoyance shimmering in her eyes.

"You're right. I was a self-centered dick back then. Full of piss and vinegar. But my ego *did* take a hit. I'd never been turned down by a girl *after* kissing her."

She rolled her eyes. "You probably forgot about me five minutes later and picked up some other girl."

"I wouldn't be so sure about that." It wasn't only the kiss that had left its mark. It was the sweet girl who'd refused to back down from him. He finished his beer and exchanged the empty can for the full one.

Her brows pinched again, curious hazel eyes searching his face.

"You had no business being at that party, and you know it. I was goading you that night, trying to get you to leave before you got yourself into trouble."

She pressed her lips together and looked down at the can in her hand, her cheeks flushing.

"I didn't expect you to kiss me," he said gentler, bringing her eyes back to his. "I didn't expect you to dare me to kiss you, either. You were a determined little lady."

That earned him a smile. "I wasn't about to let some cocky boy one-up me, and you know you would have been happy to defile me."

"Damn right I would've. I was a horny teenager."

"You can say that again. I remember when you were going through the program with my mom. You were a relentless flirt."

That was a rough time in his life. A year or so after his mother had left, his father had prospected the Dark Knights and had put so much of his focus and energy into becoming a member, Ezra had been left floundering. He was a hellion, and when he was a senior in high school, his father had enrolled him in a ninety-day program at the ranch for troubled teens. Most of the kids who were in the program lived and worked on the ranch, but his father had wanted him home at night. Ezra had gone to the ranch every day after school. He'd undergone therapy with Wynnie and had done manual labor around the ranch. What Sasha didn't know was that she was the reason he hadn't pitched a fit about going through the program. After she'd left that party, he'd asked around about her and found out she was a Whiskey and lived on the ranch. He'd have done anything to see her again.

"Do you blame me?" He took a drink of his beer. "You were hot, and you were the biggest challenge I'd ever met. All nose-in-the-air uninterested."

"I didn't put my nose in the air."

"My ass you didn't. You were a tease, too."

"I was *not*." She shoved him.

"Bullshit. You'd strut around in tight jeans or skimpy cut-offs and boots just to get my attention, and when you saw me checking you out, you'd tip your nose up to the sky and walk away."

"I didn't do that to get your attention. *God*, you were so arrogant. I was—"

"Teasing me. I know how you are." He winked, enjoying their banter. He had so much responsibility on his shoulders, he tended to be serious around most people. But Sasha brought out the rebellious kid in him, and he loved cutting loose with her.

"Shut up. I was *not*." She laughed, but her pink cheeks gave away the truth. "You were always getting in trouble, and I didn't want any part of that."

"I don't know how you resisted me. I was damn cute."

"Ohmygod." She rolled her eyes.

"Tell me I'm wrong."

"*Fine.* You were cute, but you were also trouble waiting to happen. You were *exactly* the type of guy my brothers warned me about, and as exciting as that was, you were also incredibly intimidating."

"I was not."

"To me you were. Don't you remember the first thing you said to me when you came to the ranch?"

"That's a moment I'll never forget. You were adorably embarrassed."

"I was shocked to see you. I didn't even know your name, and suddenly my mother is introducing me to the boy I'd kissed at a party that I'd snuck out to go to. I could've gotten in so much trouble, and the second she turned her back, you whispered, *Hey, Bo Peep. How about a roll in the hay?*"

He laughed.

"It wasn't funny. I just about died."

"Aw, come on. You might have been taken aback, but you were also intrigued. I saw it in your eyes."

"Would you stop?" She shoved him again.

"I know what I saw."

She tried to scowl, but the upturned corners of her mouth gave away her smile.

He sat back and took another drink, thinking about those three months and how he'd asked to work late every day and would take any job by the barns and horse pastures just to get a glimpse of Sasha. He'd watched her shadowing the woman who had worked with the rehabbing horses at the time and taking her schoolwork into the barn to sit with the injured animals while she studied. Over the course of those three months, he'd gained a hell of a lot of respect for Sasha, and when he'd realized she deserved someone who had their shit together, he'd backed off.

"All kidding aside, I don't blame you for keeping your distance. Your mother and the people on this ranch, and the work I did here, saved me from myself. I went into that program a delinquent kid with no respect for anyone and came out with a purpose and something to prove."

"I'd say you've done a good job of proving yourself."

"Thanks, but it's no longer about that." He nodded toward the cabin. "It's about making sure that little guy has an easier time growing up than I did." He'd hoped Gus would get through his childhood avoiding the pitfalls he'd had to navigate, but with his unreliable ex, that seemed impossible.

Her expression warmed. "You're a great dad, Ez, and look where he's growing up. Gus is surrounded by people who love him. We're not going to let him get into trouble."

"Says the girl who snuck off to a party at fifteen and almost got eaten by the hungry wolf."

She was quiet for a moment before responding. "We won't let him sneak out."

He couldn't remember a time when she didn't say *we* in relation to anything having to do with Gus's well-being, and tonight he realized how good that made him feel. He knew she meant *we* collectively, as in everyone on the ranch who knew and loved Gus, but it was Sasha and her family that had always made him feel like he wasn't a bumbling single father raising Gus alone.

"We can try, but teenagers are sneaky, and they do stupid shit. It's a rite of passage. I just hope I give him enough stability and confidence that he won't go looking for trouble he can't handle."

Her brows knitted. "I had stability and confidence, and I still went looking for trouble."

"I know. I'm sorry I was a dick when we were kids. I'd like to believe I wouldn't have gone through with banging you in the car at that party or taking you for a roll in the hay. Lord knows you were too damn innocent for the likes of me."

"Right." She sounded annoyed, and guzzled the rest of her drink. "I should go." She pushed to her feet, shrugged off his hoodie, and put it on the chair.

He stood, wondering what had ticked her off. "You okay?"

"Yeah, fine." She stepped to the right as he stepped to the left, accidentally blocking her way. She stepped in the other direction as he did the same. Her hand balled into a fist. "Sorry."

What the…? "Hey, Sash?"

"Hm." She didn't look up.

He lifted her chin, taking in the conflicting emotions in her eyes. "What did I say?"

"Nothing that wasn't true, but I don't need to relive how awkward I was."

"If you're upset because I said you were innocent, I didn't mean it to be derogatory. I meant that I was a total shit back then, and I'd hope I wouldn't have stolen your first time just to get my rocks off."

"I get it," she said sharply.

"Do you? Because you said you thought I forgot about you five minutes after we kissed."

She closed her mouth. That hint of innocence that she'd never fully lost rose to the surface, drawing him in like it had all those years ago, when it had been as blatant as the rising sun. He wanted to tell her that innocence was rare and good and demand she stay off that fucking dating app so some asshole didn't steal it from her. But that wasn't his place, so he tried to ease her worry with another truth.

"Like I said, I'd *like* to believe I wouldn't have gone through with it." He couldn't resist brushing his thumb along her jaw. "But after that unforgettable kiss, who knows what would have happened."

Her lips parted, and he swore he saw heat rising in her eyes, but in the next second, it was gone, and she said, "I guess we'll never know. I'll see you tomorrow."

Jesus. Was I seeing things?

He watched her climb into her truck and drive away, telling himself to lock that shit down before he got them both in trouble.

Chapter Three

AFTER A FITFUL night's sleep filled with too many thoughts of Ezra's lips on hers and too much disappointment in herself for not going through with Birdie's plan, Sasha was out the door at dawn, working off her frustrations before checking on the horses. Horses picked up on human emotions, and many of their rescues had been so badly abused, they suffered from anxiety. The last thing they needed was to feel her stress. Luckily, there was never a shortage of ways to work off her frustrations on the ranch.

She gripped the handlebars of the ATV tighter, speeding over rocks and ruts on her favorite trail, memories of last night peppering her. She'd really thought she could go through with kissing Ezra, but when he'd brought up the time she *had* kissed him, she was thrown right back to that mortifying moment when he'd called her on her inexperience. That had set her back, but when he'd brushed his thumb along her jaw, she'd gotten caught up in his touch, drawn in by those dark eyes that so often invaded her dreams, and she'd *almost* gotten up the courage to kiss him. She hated that she'd chickened out.

She wasn't a chickenshit, and she wasn't a quitter, either. Her brothers' overprotectiveness hadn't afforded her much privacy over the years, but that had driven her to be competitive and prove she could do anything they could do. Well, almost anything. Dare did terrifying stunts she'd never even thought about trying, and her brothers were Dark Knights, which was only for men, but short of those things, she could do anything.

Except kiss Ezra.

She accelerated, her frustration mounting anew. The tires kicked up dirt as she snaked between trees and around ruts, overthinking the situation with Ezra. Bobbie was always saying that guys wanted what they couldn't have. Sasha had never bought into that theory with Ezra, since she'd been off-limits for years and it hadn't made a difference. But maybe she'd never given him a reason to see her as anything more than a good friend who sometimes flirted with him. She'd always stayed on her own side of that invisible line in the dirt. Maybe she needed to treat him like any other guy. A little jealousy could go a long way in getting noticed.

She maneuvered around a branch and caught air over a hill, feeling a rush of adrenaline. The end of the trail appeared in the distance, and she opened the throttle. The engine roared. As she sped off the trail, flying into the long grass behind the main house where Ezra and the other therapists worked and everyone who lived and worked on the ranch gathered to eat meals together, her determination returned.

She wasn't that inexperienced little girl anymore.

She knew what she wanted, and it was time she either got that sexy single father on board or forgot him altogether.

SASHA SPENT THE rest of the morning in the rehab barns doing critical-care rounds with the horses. They took in rescues from all types of abusive and neglectful situations. Most of the horses probably wouldn't have survived if they hadn't been rescued and nursed back to health. Some had been malnourished and were on a refeeding program, others were recuperating from various surgeries, injuries, or illnesses, and the majority of them suffered from some level of anxiety. But on Redemption Ranch, the horses were treated with loving hands and promised a good life in which they would never go a day without food, shelter, or kindness. Like the people who went through their programs, every horse that came through the rescue became family.

Sasha gave the horses extra love as she monitored temperatures, gave medications, replaced bandages, removed stitches, turned out the horses that could be put in catch pens and paddocks, and took care of anything else they needed.

She was walking Gypsy, a four-year-old mare who was three weeks post-surgery on her left front leg, when she saw her oldest brother, Doc, the ranch veterinarian, coming down the hill from the main house. Doc was the deep thinker of the family, while Cowboy, the biggest and most overprotective of her brothers, managed the ranch hands, and Dare was a therapist and one of Ezra's closest friends.

Doc waved and raked a hand through his short brown hair. Her brothers had all inherited their father's height. Cowboy was six four, and Dare and Doc were just shy of that. Doc kept his thoughts close to his chest, which gave him a mysterious air.

Doc was six years older than Sasha, and he was the reason the ranch had a no-intracompany-dating policy. When Doc was nineteen, he'd fallen for a politician's daughter who had interned at the ranch one summer, and although Sasha didn't know *all* of the details that had led to their breakup and the new rules being put into place, she knew their relationship hadn't ended well. She'd watched Doc go from a cocky, rambunctious teen to more of a guarded observer. He could charm women with nothing more than a glance, but he never dated anyone for longer than a few weeks. She and Doc were close, and he was such a great guy, she hoped he'd allow himself to fall in love again someday.

"Doc's going to be so happy with how well you're doing," she said to Gypsy as they walked around the paddock.

"Her gait looks good," Doc called out as he came to the fence. "Any issues?"

"No. She's doing great. She's confident and responsive, and her wound healed up nicely." She petted Gypsy's neck. "Another couple of weeks, and she'll be as good as gold."

He gazed out at Hurricane, a beautiful gray thoroughbred with white socks and a white blaze they'd rescued from a breeder nine months ago. "Did he give you any trouble?"

"Not any worse than usual." Hurricane could be ornery, but she didn't blame him. He'd changed hands three times and had been suffering from a number of injuries when they'd saved him from a slaughter truck. He'd done well, but they feared he'd hurt himself if he was put with other horses, so he was kept in a catch pen in a paddock of a herd of geldings, safely getting the socialization he needed. "One of the cats left me a present in the office. Would you mind taking care of it for me? *Please?*"

He chuckled and shook his head. "I'll never understand how

you can deal with seeing awful wounds on the horses and still be squeamish about dead mice."

"And I'll never understand how you can be squeamish about relationships with women when so many of them vie for your attention, so we're even." That always shut him up.

His brows slanted. "Are you doing rounds after this? I'll walk with you."

"I already did them. I got up early and went for an ATV ride."

Doc's brows knitted. "You only ride the ATV when you're pissed or stressed. What's going on?"

"Nothing. I just felt like riding."

"Come on, Sash. We both know you don't take joy rides at the ass crack of dawn. What's bugging you?"

"I don't know. I guess now that Dare and Billie are getting married and Cowboy and Sully are engaged, I've been thinking about things." Dare and Billie were childhood best friends and Dare had been in love with her forever. They'd finally gotten together last summer, and they were getting married July Fourth weekend on the ranch. Cowboy had fallen hard for Sullivan Tate last fall, when she'd come to the ranch for protection after she'd escaped from a cult. They'd gotten engaged in April but hadn't set a wedding date yet.

"What kind of things?" Doc asked.

"Everything. Life. The future." She mulled over what she wanted to say as she walked Gypsy around the far side of the paddock. When they neared Doc, she said, "Do you ever get lonely?"

"It's hard to be lonely with all these horses to care for."

"You know what I mean. Lonely for a deep relationship. You're in your thirties. You've had time to sow your wild oats, and you're a great guy. Don't you want someone special to share your life with?"

"I've got the club and our family. My life is full enough."

"I get that, but you really don't want something real with a woman, beyond a few weeks of good sex? Someone you can share everything with? The good, the bad, the scary, the fun? Dare and Cowboy are happier than I've ever seen them. Doesn't that make you want the same?"

His jaw tightened. "They got lucky. Love like that is hard to find. But if that's what's on your mind, you need to be careful—"

"Save it. I don't need a lecture on the perils of dating from the guy who treats himself like an extended-stay motel." That's what her brothers said about him because he never dated women for longer than two or three months. "I'm sorry I asked."

Doc grinned and splayed his hands. "There are too many fish in the sea to swim in one pond forever."

She rolled her eyes. "If I said something like that, you guys would fit me with a chastity belt."

"We've already got one ordered."

"Shut up," she said with a laugh. "Forget I said anything. Let's stick to horses."

After a few more minutes of teasing, she gave him an update on the horses, and when he left, she finished walking Gypsy and then took her back to the barn. She was latching Gypsy's stall when Gus and Ezra, wearing a snug T-shirt that hugged his biceps, faded jeans, and black leather boots—*Yum*—walked in, sending her heart into overdrive.

"Hi, Sugar," Gus said in a loud whisper, flashing an infectious grin. She had taught him not to yell or run in the barns.

His mass of wild dark curls bounced around his adorable face as he dragged Ezra toward her.

"Hey, Gusto." She ruffled his hair, sharing a smile with Ezra as they made their way back out of the barn. Gus was good around the horses, but at five, he was also a bundle of unpredictable energy. "What are you up to this morning?"

"We're going on a trail ride to the meadow," he said excitedly. "Wanna come?"

Gus came to see her all the time, and he never failed to invite her to do whatever they had planned, but she knew how much Ezra treasured his time with his son. As much as she'd like to jump on every opportunity to spend time with them, she always gave him an out in case Gus was speaking out of turn. She crouched in front of Gus. "That's really nice of you to ask, but I don't want to interrupt your time with your dad."

"Daddy doesn't mind. He said I could ask you." He looked at Ezra. "Right, Dad?"

"That's right, buddy, unless Sasha has to work or has other plans."

"I don't have plans." As she pushed to her feet, Ezra's grin set her nerves aflame. Maybe she could tell him how she felt today. "And I'm done here, so I have time."

"Yay. Dad, she'll come!" Gus exclaimed.

Ezra laughed. "I heard her."

"Come on, Sugar." Gus slid his hand into hers. "I wanna ride Moxie with you!"

Moxie was Sasha's horse, a gentle ten-year-old Percheron cross they'd rescued six years ago.

As they headed for the other barn, where they kept the healthy horses, Ezra said, "We missed you at breakfast."

She was glad he'd noticed. "I went for an ATV ride and

wanted to get an early start on morning rounds."

Ezra's brows knitted. Like Doc, Ezra knew what that ATV ride meant.

"So you could come riding with us!" Gus said.

"You caught me." She gave his hand a squeeze. "I was hoping you'd come by and sweep me off my feet."

Ezra flashed an easy smile, warming her from the inside out.

She thought about how special their friendship was and how moments like these might not come as easily or as often if she put her heart on the line and Ezra didn't reciprocate. The thought sent her stomach into a nose dive. She needed to feel him out a little more before jumping in with two feet.

"Come on, Daddy!" Gus grabbed Ezra's hand and started running, pulling them both toward the barn.

They all laughed, her and Ezra's gazes connecting over Gus's head.

"I think my boy's got that sweeping-you-off-your-feet thing down pat." He winked, turning that nose dive into a gust of hope.

IT WAS A beautiful, sunny morning as Ezra's horse ambled behind Moxie, following Sasha and Gus along the well-worn trail, winding through brush and grass and rocks. They'd been riding for half an hour, and Gus, sitting in front of Sasha, had been chattering the whole time. Sasha was as patient as ever, answering his questions and asking her own. She was always teaching Gus, reminding him to use soft hands on the reins, pointing out certain trees and bushes and dangerous slopes where he should never take a horse. As if he'd be off riding on his own next week and would remember every little thing she said.

She'd been that way with Gus since he was a baby. She'd fawn over him, like her mother and Birdie did, but she'd always treated him like he was a sponge who could learn everything and anything. Ezra would like to believe his son was a sponge for knowledge and love, but there were plenty of things he hoped his son might forget. Like the times his mother hadn't shown up on her visitation days or made plans that didn't include him on holidays. Gus had gotten so used to his mother's unreliability, he appeared to take it in stride. But Ezra knew that could be the beginning of attachment issues, and he was keeping his eyes on him.

The meadow came into view, and Gus cheered, "There it is! Dad! There's the meadow!"

"I see it, buddy." It was days like this, when Gus was incredibly happy, that made Ezra wish he had full custody, so Gus would never be overlooked again. But he knew firsthand how that came with a host of other complications, and as he did so often, he pushed those thoughts away.

Sasha glanced over her shoulder, her eyes gleaming at him from beneath her cowgirl hat, before she turned back to Gus. She took as much joy in his son's happiness as he did. He had been up half the night thinking about that and a dozen other things. Like how he and Sasha had ended up where they were. After he'd cleaned up his act and had put Sasha in a hands-off category, he'd gone to college and had worked over the summers at the ranch. They were busy years for both of them, spent focusing on school, striving toward their careers, interning, working, and living their separate lives. But they'd remained connected through the ranch, and she was *always* on his mind. He'd eventually gotten his master's degree, and the night they went out to celebrate had changed everything.

He'd been dating Tina at the time, and she'd never been as fond of the Whiskeys as he was. She'd opted not to join them to celebrate at the Roadhouse. She was a beautiful, fun party girl and a good distraction from the stress of school but not somebody he thought he'd be with long term. That night at the Roadhouse, Sasha had asked Ezra to dance with her. When he'd held her in his arms, she'd set those hazel eyes on him and said, *I'm so freaking proud of you. But I think you should know that while you may be a professional therapist in everyone else's eyes, you'll always be my wolf in sheep's clothing.* All the emotions he'd been holding back had come rushing forward. Years of silly flirting and blossoming friendship had become so much more. They'd become *everything.* Sasha had become everything. He'd done it. He was finally worthy of Sasha Whiskey. That was when he'd realized he'd been biding his time since he was seventeen, and he needed to end things with Tina so he could finally make the move with the woman who had taken up residence in his heart all those years ago.

Excited to have come to the realization that felt righter than anything ever had, he'd stopped by Tina's house on the way home to end their relationship. But before he could get a word out, she'd told him she was pregnant. The news hit like a bullet to the chest. He'd been so close to having what he'd wanted. But he couldn't turn his back on a child the way he'd felt his parents had with him. He'd married Tina, hoping to give Gus the stability and love he'd missed out on.

That hadn't worked out as planned, and Sasha had become the woman Gus trusted and cared about most in the world. Ezra was right there with him. When he saw her with Gus like this, he caught himself entertaining the idea of what could have been if their situation were different. But he couldn't risk jacking things up for his son. As much as he hated the idea of it, he'd had no right trying to convince Sasha not to use that dating app. She deserved to be happy, even if it couldn't be with them.

When they reached the meadow, wildflowers sprouted up through the long grass, around rocks, boulders, and shrubbery, as far as the eye could see. It was absolutely breathtaking. They rode to a group of trees by the stream and climbed off their horses.

Sasha set Gus on his feet, and as they tied the horses to a tree, Gus said, "Can I run?" just as he did every time they went there.

"Sure, buddy, but don't go in the water." The stream was only a few inches deep, but Gus liked to traipse through it, and he always ended up falling on his butt and getting soaked.

"I won't!" Gus yelled as he sprinted through the long grass.

"Watch out for rocks," Sasha called out.

"I know!" Gus yelled.

They finished tying off the horses, and Sasha planted her hands on her hips, watching Gus run. "He loves this place as much as I did as a kid."

Ezra pictured her as a little towheaded girl in a cowgirl hat and boots, chasing after her brothers and Birdie. "I bet you were adorable."

"Well, *duh*." She laughed as they followed Gus. "Although I have to admit, Birdie was even cuter than me. She's got that whole impish thing going on."

Birdie was petite and impish, with an outlandish style all her own. She was a trip, always up to something. But she had nothing on Sasha, who was as competitive and fierce as she was sweet and feminine. She could kick anyone's ass in paintball, muck stalls, and play in the dirt with Gus, and she never complained about working in the freezing cold or blazing heat. But she also liked to cuddle under cozy blankets wearing her favorite soft gray sweatpants and pink sweatshirts with her hair in a messy bun and no makeup, as she'd done with Gus many times.

"Birdie is cute, but I doubt she was cuter than you."

"You, my friend, have all the best answers," she said cheerily and gazed out at Gus heading for a boulder.

"Sorry if Gus talked your ear off."

"You know I don't mind."

He watched Gus climb onto the boulder and jump off. "Listen, Sash, I was thinking about last night."

"You're not going to embarrass me again and make me relive what a teenage dork I was, are you?"

"You were *not* a dork, and I'm sorry if I embarrassed you. I was going to say, I shouldn't have discouraged you from using that dating app."

Her brows knitted. "*Oh.* It's okay. You were right about that. It doesn't seem very safe. I was thinking I'd look closer to home, anyway."

"Yeah?"

"Mm-hm. Flame texted me last night. I'm thinking about going out with him."

Fuck. Finn "Flame" Steele was a smoke jumper and a Dark Knight. Ezra couldn't say a bad thing about him, except that most of his female friends came with *benefits*, and he despised the idea of Sasha becoming one of them. It should probably make him feel better to see her with one of his trusted friends, but it was easier to pretend she wasn't with anyone at all if he didn't have to look at the man she was sleeping with every damn week.

He tried to play it cool. "Oh yeah?"

"Maybe. We've been friends for a long time, and I know I can trust him because he'd never do anything to jeopardize his standing with the club. And, well, he is hot and definitely interested. What do you think?"

I think you should give up dating altogether and continue hanging out with me and Gus, because I'm a dick like that and I want you all to myself. "He's got a dangerous job."

"That makes him even more intriguing."

Of course it does, compared to a therapist whose biggest danger is tripping on his way into the office. "He's got a lot of experience with women. He'll have expectations."

She lifted her chin. "Good. I like a man who knows what he's doing."

Was it his imagination, or was she getting more brazen by the day?

"Daddy, Sasha, watch!" Gus threw a stone into the stream.

"Nice one, buddy."

"Good job, Gus." Sasha looked at Ezra curiously. "Enough about my dating life. What about you?"

"What about me?" He crossed his arms, watching Gus.

"Where do you meet women?"

This was not a conversation he wanted to have. "Around."

"Around? Like at Gus's camp? What do you do, date the single moms?"

"*No.* You really think I'd troll his camp?"

"I don't *know.* Maybe you do."

He glowered at her and lowered his voice. "You know me

better than that."

"Then where do you meet the women you date?"

"I wouldn't classify what I do as dating."

She tilted her head to the side with a playful expression. "How would you classify it?"

He narrowed his eyes, gritting out a warning. *"Sasha."*

"What? If you're not dating, what are you doing? Hooking up? Do you use a hookup app, like Tinder? Or do you meet women at coffee shops? The Roadhouse? And how does it work, exactly, if you're not dating? Do you agree on what you're doing ahead of time? Do you go back to their place or to a hotel? I really need to figure this out."

No, you don't. "I'm not having this conversation with you." He stared at Gus, teeth grinding.

"That's not fair. I was honest with you. I told you that I had needs, and I assume you do, too. Why can't you tell me? We're both adults."

He shook his head, tension pulling his shoulders higher.

"Forget it," she said. "I'll ask Flame."

The fuck you will. He took her by the arm, leaning in close, seething, "What do you want to hear? That I pick up women and fuck them senseless and never see them again because I've got too much shit on my shoulders to get tangled up with anyone?" What the hell was he doing? He never lost his shit around her. *Fuck it.* Better she knew the truth about him. "That makes me a dick in your eyes, doesn't it?"

"No." She swallowed hard, eyes serious. "It means we're both filling needs, and we're not so different after all."

"We sure as fuck better be different." Because now he was imagining her with nameless, faceless men, and he wanted to kill every one of them.

"Daddy! Sugar!" Gus was running around the meadow

again. "Come play with me!"

"We're coming!" Sasha said enthusiastically, a mischievous grin curving her lips. "Daddy was just telling me how much he likes to *play*." She ran after Gus.

Fucking right I like to play.

"He loves it!" Gus shouted. "Right, Dad?"

Sasha looked over her shoulder, eyes twinkling with amusement.

What the hell are you doing to me?

It took everything he had to force those thoughts away and flip his internal switch to daddy mode. "That's right, buddy." He sprinted after them, scooping up Gus.

Gus squealed with delight. "Sugar! Help me!"

"I'll take him down, Gusto!"

Sasha ran toward them, and her hat flew off. Her blond hair flowed like a mane behind her as she threw her arms around Ezra, and Gus shrieked with laughter as they all tumbled to the ground. Ezra landed on his back, cradling them against his chest. Gus scrambled off, yelling, "Bet you can't catch me again!"

As his son darted across the meadow, Sasha's beautiful face came into focus. She was still sprawled on top of him, hair tousled, supple breasts pressing against his chest, hips on his. She felt too damn good to ignore. His cock took notice, and the heat in Sasha's eyes told him she did, too.

"Mm. Feels like Daddy *does* like to play."

He narrowed his eyes. "Since when are you such a trouble-maker?"

"Maybe I've always been a troublemaker and you just never noticed." With a flirtatious giggle, she got up and went after Gus, leaving Ezra lying in the grass thinking of all the dirty things he'd like to do to her.

Chapter Four

"LET'S GO, GUS," Ezra called out Monday morning as he finished making Gus's lunch and put it in his backpack for summer camp. He checked to make sure the child's smartphone watch was in the front pocket. He'd gotten the easy-to-use watch for him six months ago, after Gus told him he'd wanted to call from his mother's house when he'd had a bad dream, and Tina wouldn't let him. Ezra had given Tina hell about that, because while Gus should be able to count on his mother to soothe his fears, Ezra didn't trust she would. He'd programmed his phone number, along with his father's and Sasha's, into the watch in case Gus couldn't reach *him* in an emergency. He'd gone over what constituted an emergency with Gus until he knew the rules by heart. For example, bad dreams were not emergencies. He'd explained that while it was okay to call Ezra after a bad dream, he shouldn't call the others. Thankfully, his little boy respected his rules about its use and had only used it once when he'd woken up with a fever. Tina had been happy to let Ezra come pick him up that night.

"Ready!" Gus ran out of his bedroom shirtless, wearing only his cowboy hat, shorts, and boots.

"Buddy, where's your shirt?"

"I don't need it."

"Yes, you do. Please go put your shirt on."

"But Dare says girls like boys who don't wear shirts."

Ezra made a mental note to have a talk with Dare. "Not at camp they don't, unless you're at the pool. Come on." He put a hand on Gus's back and headed into his bedroom. He pulled a T-shirt from Gus's drawer, took off Gus's hat, and slipped it over his head. "Who are you trying to impress anyway?"

Gus shrugged.

Ezra crouched so they were eye-to-eye. "Buddy, is there a girl at your camp who you like a little more than the others?"

He shook his head, his curls bouncing adorably.

"Then whose attention are you trying to get by going shirt-less?"

His big brown eyes sparkled with excitement as he whispered, "Sasha's."

What kind of torture was this? He felt a prickle of guilt for what he'd said to Sasha yesterday, and for getting aroused when she was on top of him, despite the fact that she'd acted like her normal, bubbly self for the rest of the afternoon and at dinner last night, while *he* was losing his fucking mind over it.

"Gus, you don't have to try to impress Sasha. She loves you exactly the way you are."

"I know, but Dare says he gets extra treats from Billie when he takes his shirt off."

"I think you need to stop hanging out with Dare so much." The words were out of his mouth before he could stop them.

"Why? I *love* him!"

"I was only kidding. I love him, too, buddy, but if you're not careful, you'll end up with a ton of cavities from all the sugar. You don't want that, do you?"

Gus shook his head.

"Good, then how about you keep your shirt on?"

"Okay," he said reluctantly.

"Let's get breakfast so we're not late."

Ezra drove to the main house and parked in front of the massive stone, wood, and glass building, which looked more like a resort than offices and residential space where everyone who worked and lived on the ranch gathered for meals. Everything about Redemption Ranch promoted the concept of family and support, right down to the homey environment. The main house boasted a large two-story gathering area, a movie room, offices and conference rooms, a large open dining area with several farmhouse-style tables and a pass-through to the enormous kitchen. On the second level there were bedrooms for younger clients who were going through their programs. Adult clients stayed in cabins on the property.

Ezra pocketed his keys as they walked up to the door.

"Dad, there's Sully's bike! When can I learn to ride a bike?" Gus asked.

Sully had missed out on a lot of typical childhood activities because she'd grown up in a cult, and Cowboy made sure she got a chance to experience them all. She'd been as happy as a kid at Christmas when she'd learned to ride a bike, and she'd been riding one on the ranch ever since.

"Soon, buddy," he said as they headed inside.

They were greeted by a cacophony of conversation and laughter coming from the dining area. Having grown up as an only child, the noisy, banter-filled mealtimes were among Ezra's favorite things about the ranch. But today he couldn't shake the feeling that he needed to talk to Sasha and clear the air. The sinful dream he'd had about her last night hadn't helped. Especially since he could still see it in vivid detail. He doubted he'd ever forget the images he'd conjured of her luscious mouth wrapped around his cock as he came down her throat, and lying beneath him naked as he pounded into her, his name sailing from her lips like a fucking prayer.

"Come on, Dad!" Gus ran down the hall to their right toward the dining room.

Cursing himself for getting lost in that damn dream again, he called after Gus, "Slow down," but his little boy was already making his way around the dining room, as he did most mornings, calling out hellos to everyone by name. Between the Whiskeys, the ranch hands, the other staff, and their current live-in clients, the place was packed, and they all responded to his eager little boy with *Hey, Gus,* or *Good morning, buddy,* followed by greetings for Ezra.

"Hi, Tiny! Whatcha got?" Gus climbed into Tiny's lap.

Sasha's father, Tommy "Tiny" Whiskey was a big, bearded biker at about six four with a pendulous belly, arms full of ink, weathered skin, and keen eyes. He had long gray hair, which he always wore in a ponytail with a bandanna tied around his forehead. Ezra had never seen him without his black leather vest, proudly displaying Dark Knights patches on the back. Tiny looked hard despite his soft physique, and he was one of the physically and emotionally strongest, most loyal, no-bullshit men Ezra had ever met.

Ezra owed Tiny a hell of a lot, and he felt another stab of guilt for fantasizing about doing filthy things to his daughter. Once Ezra had gotten past his teenage rebellious anger and had finally *listened* when people spoke, Tiny had taught him more than a thing or two about *how* to love, and about family, loyalty, and brotherhood. Tiny wasn't much of a talker, but his words always mattered, and you could feel his emotions from across a ravine. Ezra learned by watching him show Wynnie affection every time he walked by with a wink, a touch, or even a smile, by the way he pulled out chairs for her and supported her in her every endeavor. Even the way they argued when their opinions differed reflected love and respect. The way Tiny watched out for his family and friends was equally tangible. Ezra knew his father loved him even if he wasn't good at expressing it. He also knew his mother had loved him when she'd lived with them. Maybe she still did—he couldn't be sure. If she did, it wasn't a type of love he wanted to emulate. But he knew one thing for certain. He never would have learned how to express his love, how to forgive, or how to move on without Tiny's and Wynnie's help.

He caught Tiny's eye and motioned to Gus, silently asking, *Want me to get him?*

Tiny waved a hand dismissively, his mustache and beard twitching with his grin as he handed Gus a piece of bacon.

Ezra headed for the buffet and saw Sasha chatting with Sully at their usual table with Dare, Billie, Doc, and a few ranch hands. Beside Sasha were his and Gus's empty seats. There was so much comfort in that, and in the whole family atmosphere, sometimes he couldn't believe he was the same person who had felt like he didn't fit anywhere. That was even more of a reason he needed to clear the air with Sasha. He didn't want anything to come between them.

Doc's black Lab, Mighty, brushed against Ezra's leg, drawing him from his thoughts. He petted him. "How's it going,

Mighty?"

"Mighty!" Gus scrambled off Tiny's lap, and the dog trotted over to him. Gus's giggles filled the air.

Sasha looked over, her eyes connecting with Ezra's. He lifted his chin, and she smiled, holding his gaze so long, it felt like it was becoming their new normal. He couldn't think about that too much, or he'd start to question his decision to respect the fact that she was off-limits.

He stopped by the table where Taz, Hyde, and Sasha's cousin, Rebel—who didn't live or work at the ranch, but like Birdie, often showed up for free meals—were joking with some of the other ranch hands and residents, including two of Ezra's clients: Paul, a thirty-eight-year-old woodworker who had spent the last twelve years incarcerated for selling drugs and was trying to make amends with his family and regain his footing in society, and Mike, who at twenty-four was eight months clean and sober. He had a two-year-old son and a wife whose trust he was trying to regain. Good men who had gone through hard times. Thankfully, they were doing well in the program.

"Morning, guys." He looked at Paul and Mike. "Are these guys giving you a hard time?"

"Nah, mate," Taz said. "We're only messing around with them."

"Everything's cool," Paul said, and Mike nodded in agreement.

"A'right. I'll see you guys later." He joined Cowboy and Wynnie at the buffet, which was stocked with delicious foods. He grabbed a plate for himself and one for Gus. "Looks like Dwight outdid himself this morning." Dwight Cornwall, a retired navy commander, had been the resident manager and cook for as long as Ezra could remember.

"Doesn't he always?" Cowboy bit into a biscuit and put two more on his plate. He was as tall as Tiny but as solid as stone, and he'd earned those muscles and that appetite from the endless hours he spent toiling on the ranch. "Are we still on for eleven?"

"Sure are." Cowboy oversaw the therapy clients who worked in the field, and he met with Ezra weekly to go over their progress.

Cowboy nodded. "I'll see you at the table."

"Honey, don't forget, you and Dare said you'd start cleaning out the big barn this afternoon for the wedding," Wynnie reminded him. She hadn't changed much over the years. She still wore her blond hair in a short shag, favored jeans and cowgirl boots over skirts or dresses, and was as warm and straightforward as a person could be.

"We're on it, Mom," Cowboy said. "Ez, how late are you working?"

"My last meeting is at three. I can be out of here by four fifteen. Why?"

"Mind giving us a hand with the barn when you're done?" Cowboy said.

"Sure. I just have to pick up Gus by six."

"Great. Appreciate it." Cowboy headed for the table.

"That was nice of you," Wynnie said.

"It'll feel good to get my hands dirty." Especially after comparing himself to Flame. He bit back that uncomfortable memory. "How are *you* this morning, Wynnie? Getting excited about the wedding?"

"I'm beyond excited about it. Knowing my boy is marrying the woman he's been in love with since they were kids is a great feeling."

"I bet it is."

"You'll see when Gus gets older. But as far as today goes, it definitely feels like a Monday to me. Does it feel like that for you, too?"

"You tell me," he said as he filled his and Gus's plates. "Gus wanted to come to breakfast without a shirt on to impress your daughter, because he heard Dare say he gets extra treats from Billie when he's shirtless."

"Oh, Lordy." Wynnie laughed. "I guess growing up around all these rowdy men has its pitfalls."

He saw Gus talking with Dwight by the kitchen door. "He couldn't grow up around better people, and I don't mind setting him straight when he needs it. But I think I'll have a talk with Dare so he's aware of how closely Gus listens."

"Good luck, honey. I've been trying to rein him in for thirty years. I thought when he became a therapist, it'd get easier. But he didn't buy into that old saying about the goose and the gander." Wynnie laughed softly. "Enjoy breakfast, honey."

She headed over to Tiny, and Ezra headed for his usual table. As always, there were several conversations going on and some whispering between Cowboy and Sully. "Good morning," he said as he set Gus's plate next to Sasha.

"Hey, *Ez*," Sasha said with a playful lilt in her voice. "How was your night?"

Full of fantasies about you. "Not bad." He leaned down, speaking for her ears only. "I'm sorry about what I said yesterday."

Her brows knitted. "Why? We all need a roll in the hay sometimes." She picked up a sausage link and took a bite, her finely manicured brows rising with amusement.

What was this new hell he was living in?

He looked for Gus and saw Dwight handing him something in a napkin. Gus cradled it in his hands as he headed for Sasha.

"Hi, Gusto. What do you have there?"

"It's for you." Gus beamed as he lowered his hands.

Sasha opened the napkin and gasped. "Where did you get my favorite cherry Danish?"

"Dwight made it for you," he said in his chirpy little voice.

She put her hand over her heart. "Gus, did you ask him to make this for me?"

Gus nodded, shocking Ezra to no end. "I asked him the other day, but he didn't have time until today."

"Aw," Sully said. "Gussy, you're so sweet."

"Do you want one?" Gus asked.

"No, thank you. I'm stuffed." Sully leaned forward, putting a hand beside her mouth as if sharing a secret. "Don't tell Callahan there are more, or he'll eat *all* of them." She was the only one who called Cowboy by his given name.

Gus giggled. Cowboy was doing a great job of pretending not to hear them.

"Thank you, Gus." Sasha put the Danish on her plate and lifted Gus onto her lap, hugging him tight. She looked at Ezra over his boy's shoulder, dreamy eyed.

He'd never been jealous of his son before.

"Your little dude has *game*," Dare said.

And good taste in women.

"You could learn a thing or two from him," Billie added. "Sasha's a catch."

"Thank you, Billie," Sasha said sassily.

"Are you trying to get him in trouble?" Doc asked, his gaze moving between Billie and Ezra.

Billie looked nonplussed. "What? She *is* a catch."

"Relax, Doc," Ezra said. "She's not telling me anything I don't already know, and neither are you."

"Good morning! The bachelorette party planner is here!" Birdie announced as she breezed into the dining room, drawing everyone's attention. She was wearing heart-shaped sunglasses and waving something white in one hand and a sparkling crown in the other. Her dark hair was piled on top of her head and held in place with a bright yellow clip. Her lips were painted hot pink, which matched her belly-baring, off-the-shoulder ruffled top. Her cutoffs had a *Teenage Mutant Ninja Turtle* patch on one side and a stick-figure person flipping the bird on the other, and her strappy sandals had long pink ribbons that wound up her calves and were tied in bows below her knees.

"Hi, honey!" Wynnie called out. "You're just in time for breakfast."

"No time to eat, Mom." Birdie strode across the room toward Billie. "I have a bachelorette party to plan, and I have to be at the chocolate shop in an hour." She put the crown on Billie's head.

"*What* did I tell you?" Billie yanked it off her long dark hair. She wasn't a jeweled-crown type of girl. She'd been a daredevil and a professional motocross racer before her and Dare's best friend, Eddie, one of the three *Daredevils for Life*, as they'd called themselves, had been killed in a dare gone wrong. She'd given up the sport and just about everything else that had brought her joy, until last year when she and Dare had gotten together and he'd somehow brought those parts of her back to life. Now, in addition to bartending at the Roadhouse, she taught kids how to ride motocross bikes. Dare had recently finished having a new racetrack and clubhouse put in for her on the far side of the property.

Birdie took off her sunglasses and planted a hand on her hip. "You said you wanted to play paintball and have a bonfire instead of having a party, but that's ridiculous. Every bride needs a last hurrah, and it's up to the maid of honor and bridesmaids to put it together. Bobbie, Sasha, and I have a great plan. Sasha, back me up here."

"I think paintball is a great idea!" Sasha exclaimed.

Cowboy threw his arms up, shouting, "*Paintball*," and high-fived Sasha across the table, causing cheers and commotion. They were the queen and king of paintball. They'd spent weeks expanding the paintball field, and when they were on it, they were as competitive as Olympians.

Birdie rolled her eyes. "Seriously, Sasha? What about our plan?"

"Sorry," Sasha said. "I didn't know paintball was an option."

"Cowboy and I are Dare's men of honor, and I'm with Cowboy on this one," Doc said.

"*Ugh!* Of course you are," Birdie complained.

"Can I play paintball with you guys?" Gus asked around a mouthful of Danish.

The Whiskeys had always used paintball as a way to bring people together. It allowed the staff and their resident clients to work off steam, and they had always included Gus in their paintball games. Some of Ezra's fondest memories were of Gus toddling around on the paintball field at three years old, protected by the adults as he hid with them and called out the people he saw. He even had his own neon-yellow paintball suit with reflectors, so everyone could see him.

"Of course you can," Billie said. "Everyone can play. We were thinking of doing it the weekend before the wedding."

"But I bought you a sash and a crown!" Birdie complained.

"I'll wear the crown," Simone, a feisty auburn-haired woman, chimed in from the other table. "It's probably the only crown I'll ever get." She'd come to the ranch two and a half years ago from Maryland, when, after she completed rehab, her ex-boyfriend/drug dealer had come after her and it had become unsafe for her to stay in the area. She'd been working at the ranch ever since and was taking classes to become a counselor.

"No, it isn't," Sully said supportively. "You'll find your Prince Charming just like I did."

"I can charm your panties off, Simone, and you can wear a crown if you'd like," Hyde hollered, causing laughter to ring out.

"Hey, now," Ezra said. "Little ears are listening."

"I was kidding, Gus," Hyde said.

"Wait, does this mean Dare's not getting a bachelor party?" Rebel asked from across the room.

"No strippers?" Taz asked.

"The only one stripping will be Dare when he dances for *me*," Billie announced.

"You tell 'em, sweetie," Wynnie called out.

"You'd better stock up on dollar bills, baby," Dare said as he pulled Billie into a kiss, earning whistles and shouts.

"How about strip paintball, mate?" Taz shouted, inciting a round of laughter.

"What's strip paintball?" Gus asked.

"Nothing that's going to happen," Sasha said.

"Bikini paintball?" Hyde asked.

"I'm related to half of these women. Can we recruit a few of their friends?" Rebel asked.

"That still leaves half of them," Taz pointed out, inciting

more jokes and comments.

The banter continued throughout breakfast, and when everyone got ready to leave, Gus took Sasha's hand and sweet-talked her into walking him out and strapping him into his booster seat. He looked like he'd won a trip to Disney World. Ezra didn't blame him. He'd be wearing that goofy grin, too, if the sweetest girl he'd ever met were holding his hand and looking at him like he'd hung the moon.

She buckled Gus in and kissed his cheek. "See you soon, cutie."

Ezra shut Gus's door and leaned on the car. "Sasha Whiskey, stealing hearts and taking names."

She smiled. "I think it's the other way around. He stole my heart when he was a tiny baby, and he just keeps stealing more of it."

Ezra knew the feeling. He hated himself for what he was about to ask, but he had to know the answer. "So, have you firmed up a date with Flame?"

A mischievous glint sparkled in her eyes. "You want to know if I've *firmed up* Flame?" She leaned closer, whispering, "I don't firm up and tell."

"*Jesus*, Sash. That's not what I meant."

"No?" She feigned wide-eyed innocence.

"You know it's not." *What kind of games are you playing lately?*

"Do I?" She shrugged. "Have a good day, Ez, and let me know if you need firming up, too."

Fuck. He curled his hands into fists to keep from hauling her back and telling her if she were firming him up, there would be no "too" about it.

SASHA WORKED STRAIGHT through lunch to late afternoon. When she finally finished, she was starved and headed up to the main house to raid the refrigerator. She saw Sully riding Beauty, a horse she'd helped rehabilitate last year, down from the pasture between the main house and the paintball field. They'd both come a long way since arriving at the ranch. Sully was confident and happy and had created a niche for herself illustrating children's books. When she had time, she helped Sasha with the rehab horses. She had a gift for connecting with and calming anxious horses, and Sasha believed that innate ability was exactly what her once-surly brother had needed to allow someone into his heart.

Just like I'm exactly what Ezra and Gus need. Even if Ezra doesn't realize it yet. She didn't know where that *firm up Flame* comment had come from, but she'd seen a glimmer of jealousy in Ezra's eyes, and she wanted to see more of that interest.

She waved to Sully and headed around to the kitchen door. Dwight was pouring something over trays of chicken. He was a big man, with a shaved head, never a hint of whiskers, and a deep V that appeared permanently etched between his brows. He'd worked there since Sasha was ten or eleven, and he was as much a part of their family as the rest of their staff.

He looked over as she walked in. "I figured you'd show up sooner or later. You missed lunch."

"Two of the horses we rescued last week were having a difficult day. It took a while to get them settled."

"They're lucky to have you." He opened the fridge and took out a platter of sandwiches. "Help yourself."

"Thanks. Were these left over from lunch?"

He cocked a brow. "Have you seen the crew eat? Those are fresh. Dare asked if I could bring some sandwiches and water to the big barn for him and the guys. They're working on cleaning it out."

"Oh. I'll grab an ATV and take it down, if you want. I'm heading that way anyway." She and Birdie had stored some things in the barn from when they were kids, and Dare asked her to stop by and show them what they could throw out.

"I'd appreciate that."

"Thanks for letting Gus swindle you into making me that Danish this morning."

"That boy's got a charm all his own, and it was for you." He shrugged. "Win-win. I boxed up the rest and gave them to Birdie to take over to the chocolate shop."

"I wonder if any made it there." Birdie might be petite, but she had an appetite about as big as Cowboy's. Sasha watched Dwight preparing their dinner as she ate a sandwich. He looked as serious as he acted, but beneath that drill sergeant exterior was a tenderness that had helped her through some tough situations, like breakups and losing her first horse. When she was younger, she'd sneak out of her parents' house and into the big house at midnight to drown her feelings in ice cream or whatever they had on hand. Dwight always wandered into the kitchen within minutes of her arrival with stories at the ready. He didn't know it, but he'd helped her rebuild her confidence when she'd returned home feeling uncomfortable in her own skin the morning after she'd kissed Ezra. She wondered if he could help her with her current situation. She'd have to be careful. Dwight was also a Dark Knight. The last thing she needed was for her father to get wind of her feelings.

"Can I ask you a personal question?" she asked as he washed his hands.

"Depends what it is." He put the dish of chicken in the fridge and began pulling potatoes out of a bag and putting them in the sink.

"Have you ever liked someone you worked with?" She knew he'd never been married, but beyond that, she knew very little about his personal life.

He started washing the potatoes. "I like everyone I work with."

"No, I mean, have you ever had feelings for someone you worked with?"

The V deepened between his brows, and his jaw tightened. "Once. Why are you asking?"

"My friend works at the bank, and she likes one of the tellers," she said as convincingly as she could. "I want to be sure I'm giving her good advice. How did you handle it?"

"There was nothing to handle. I was her superior. It wasn't allowed, so I kept my feelings to myself."

"You never told her?" She couldn't imagine not telling Ezra how she felt. It was all she could think about.

"Nope. I knew it would come down to my career or hers, and that wasn't a decision I wanted either of us to have to make."

"Did you like her a lot?"

"You could say that," he said gruffly.

That made her sad for him. "Do you know if she liked you?"

The muscles in his jaw bunched. "It doesn't matter."

"But what if she was the love of your life?" When he didn't respond, she said, "Do you regret not telling her?"

"I don't believe in wasting time on regrets." He continued scrubbing the potatoes. "But if I had one, that would be it."

"Then my friend should go for it? I mean, to make sure she doesn't have any regrets later."

He scowled. "I didn't say that. I don't know your friend or what she's feeling. There's a big difference between lust and love, and make no mistake, both come at a price."

"I think it's more than lust. She's liked him for a really long time."

He studied her so intently, she felt like he could see the truth behind her lie and quickly tried to redirect the conversation back to him.

"Maybe you can look up that woman now."

"She got married a few years later and left the military."

That made her feel even sadder for him. "Oh. I'm sorry."

"Don't be. I had a great career."

"But what about outside of work? Was there ever anyone else you liked as much as you liked her?"

He shook his head. "Nope."

She could feel his sadness hanging between them and knew she had to find a way to tell Ezra how she felt, because she couldn't go her whole life without ever knowing what might have been. "Maybe you'll meet someone else."

He scoffed. "I'm not about to saddle some woman with the likes of me. Now, let's load up that ATV so you can get outta here before those boys come looking for food and traipsing dirt into my kitchen."

When she pulled up to the big barn, it was surrounded by displaced hay bales, an old tractor, ancient horse tack, boxes from her and Birdie's old bedrooms, broken skateboards, old tools, and a plethora of other junk. She parked the ATV and followed her brothers' voices around to the other side of the barn.

"I could do this all day long," Cowboy hollered.

"Sully says otherwise," Dare called out.

"I'm going to beat you both," Doc said.

She stopped cold at the sight of each of them stretched between two hay bales facing the ground, with their hands on one hay bale, feet on another, and Hula-Hoops around their waists, their hips moving in a humping motion. Kenny Graber, a teenager who had gone through their program and had stayed on to work at the ranch part time and train with Billie on motocross was filming them on his phone.

"*What* the heck are you doing?" she asked. "Why are you *hula-humping* with our Hula-Hoops?"

"They're trying to beat my best time," Dare said proudly.

"He's got them beat by twenty seconds. I've got it all on video," Kenny announced.

"You guys are nuts," Sasha said. "Keep our Hula-Hoops out of your cowboy stunts."

Doc looked over and lost his balance. *"Shit!"* The guys cracked up as he fell to the side, bitching about Sasha ruining his concentration.

Their voices turned to white noise as beyond where Doc had been perched, she saw Ezra stretched between two hay bales. He was shirtless, jeans riding low on his hips, the hard planes of his body glistening with sweat, muscles flexing as he humped the hell out of the air, the Hula-Hoop swirling around his waist. Her mind sprinted down a dark trail, imagining how good it would feel to be lying beneath him, naked, as he drove his hard cock into her. Heat rushed through her. He looked over, a slow grin crawling across his handsome face, and her mouth went bone dry.

Doc strode over. "Did you bring water?"

"Yeah, I need water," she said absently, unable to look away from the man who was currently feeding her fantasies.

"*Sasha*," Doc snapped, startling her out of her reverie.

"Sorry. *Yes.* It's on the ATV. I brought sandwiches, too." She started to go with him around the barn, hoping he didn't notice she'd been gawking, and couldn't help taking one last look at all the hotness that was Ezra Moore.

"Quit staring," Doc said.

Shit. "I was just admiring his Hula-Hoop technique," she said as they strode around to the front of the barn.

"Yeah, right," Doc grumbled.

As he chugged a bottle of water, she heard Dare and Cowboy bitching a blue streak. A minute later they came around the corner of the barn with Ezra. Her gaze was drawn like metal to magnet to his glistening broad chest and to those muscles that made girls stupid. The ones by his hips that formed a V and disappeared beneath the waist of his low-slung jeans.

"Hey, Sash. You got some water for the champ?" Ezra's fists shot into the air.

"Here." Doc tossed him a bottle.

She blinked away her lust-induced stupor. "I can see these fools hula-humping." She hiked a thumb at Dare and Cowboy. "But how did they get *you* two to do it?"

"We goaded them into doing it," Dare answered.

"They called them chickenshits," Kenny added.

"That's not why I did it." Ezra flashed a cocky grin. "Someone had to show these boys how a man moves."

"I'd say you accomplished that." Sasha fanned her face, earning glares from her brothers.

"Yup. I've still got it." Ezra guzzled some water.

"You don't have shit," Doc said.

"Don't be jealous because I am the master humper," Ezra said, and Cowboy and Dare cracked up.

I bet you are.

"You're lucky Sasha messed me up," Doc said. "Otherwise I'd still be going strong."

"Your reputation says otherwise, bro," Cowboy teased.

"Yeah," Dare agreed. "Women taking off after a few weeks definitely doesn't say you're strong in the sack."

Doc glowered at them. "That's my choice, not theirs. They'd all give me a ball and chain if I let 'em."

As they heckled each other, Ezra stepped aside to answer a call, annoyance stealing his smile. There was only one person Sasha knew of who could change his mood that quickly. Tina Fucking Moore or, as she liked to refer to Gus's mother, the Selfish Witch of the West. The witch had never liked Sasha. The few times she'd seen her, she'd given Sasha the stink eye or made snide comments. Sasha didn't care what Tina thought of her, but she hated how she treated Gus and took advantage of Ezra.

"Thanks for bringing this stuff down," Cowboy said, drawing her attention as he ate half of a sandwich in one bite.

"No problem."

"Can you go through these boxes and let us know what you want to keep?" Dare asked.

"Sure." She started going through the boxes as her brothers and Kenny finished eating and went back to emptying the barn. She watched Ezra pacing, his every move riddled with tension. When he finally ended the call, he strode over with a pinched expression. "Everything okay?"

60

"Tina can't take Gus tomorrow night."

"Again?" Tina had never been fully reliable, but she'd gotten worse about spending time with Gus over the last year. She was supposed to take Gus on Tuesday nights and every other weekend, but she missed half of them. Last Thanksgiving she didn't even bother telling Ezra she couldn't take him. He'd shown up to drop Gus off, and she wasn't there. "I have no idea how that woman sleeps at night when she's continually disappointing her own son. Gus should be *all* that matters to her, and she treats him like an afterthought."

"No shit, but it is what it is."

She knew he struggled with this as much as she did or more, but sometimes he was so damn good at not rocking the boat for Gus's sake, she wanted to shake some sense into him. But now was not the time. "I know. I'm sorry, but you know my claws come out where Gus is concerned. I can watch Gus while you're at church tomorrow night." Church was what the Dark Knights called their club meetings.

"Thanks, Sash, but I hate to lean on you all the time. Gus isn't your responsibility."

"I know, but you can't miss the meeting. So would you rather go searching for a sitter or let Gus stay with his favorite person on this ranch besides you?"

"You know the answer to that."

"Then it's settled," she said, excited to spend time with Gus.

"Are you sure you don't mind?"

"I never mind spending time with my favorite little man, but be careful what you ask for. Your bare chest might be affecting my decision-making skills."

He cocked a brow. "Gus did tell me that girls like boys who don't wear shirts."

She laughed as her brothers carried boxes out from the barn, bantering about Doc's rotating bedroom door. "I'd ask where he heard that, but I think I have a fairly good idea. In all seriousness, you know I love Gus, and there's nothing I'd rather do than hang out with him tomorrow night. But you need to put your shirt on right now, because I have boxes to go through, and"—she waved to his naked torso—"all of that is a bit distracting."

He chuckled and walked away, shaking his head.

The view of his jeans-clad butt was equally distracting, and she enjoyed every second of it before he disappeared around the side of the barn.

Chapter Five

EZRA SAT WITH Sasha's brothers and a few buddies in the Dark Knights' clubhouse Tuesday night. He'd never been a religious man, and the club wasn't religiously affiliated, but there was something spiritual about the connection the men in that room shared. Many of them had saved his father when he'd joined the club in much the same way they'd saved Ezra several years later, when he'd become a member. Like the Whiskeys, the club had given him a sense of belonging and support he'd desperately needed. He was proud to be a member of the Dark Knights brotherhood.

All other eyes were on Tiny, who was sitting at the head table beside Billie's father, Manny Mancini, the vice president of the club, as they went over club business with the group. But Ezra's attention was on Flame, sitting with Hyde and Taz at the next table, thumbing out a text. He couldn't help but wonder if he was texting Sasha. She'd looked sexy as sin when she'd shown up to watch Gus, wearing cutoffs, a cute clingy long-sleeve top, and one of her many pairs of cowgirl boots. He didn't blame the dark-haired smoke jumper for going after her. Flame didn't have the complications Ezra did where Sasha was concerned. He didn't work for her parents or live on their property, and he didn't have a kid whose heart would break if he tried to make things work with her and screwed it up.

"If you haven't signed up to volunteer at Festival on the Green, we still need a few more guys to help with security at the event," Tiny said, drawing his attention back to the meeting. "As usual, Wynnie and Alice will be coordinating volunteers." Alice was Billie's mother, and Festival on the Green was a weeklong event with sidewalk sales, live music in the park, and a host of vendor tents. Redemption Ranch and the Dark Knights set up tables every year to raise awareness about who they were and what they did.

Ezra had attended community events with his mother when he was a boy, but that had ended after things started going south between his parents a few years before his mother left. His father had only sporadically attended with them and eventually had stopped attending altogether. But since joining the club, his father had never missed one. He was glad his father had found a sense of community and family, though Ezra had to wonder why he hadn't put that effort into his own family.

He looked across the room at his father, Samuel "Pep" Moore. They'd once shared the same jet-black hair, sharp features, and broad, six-two frame, but now his father was mostly gray, his jowls were heavy, and his rounded shoulders made him appear smaller than he was. Ezra hadn't been surprised to learn his father had been given the tongue-in-cheek road name "Pep" because he was the least peppy member of the club. He was tight lipped and rarely smiled for anyone other than Gus.

"As the last order of business, we're moving forward with

our Reindeer Ride and rally to benefit Hope Valley Hospital in August," Tiny said, drawing Ezra's attention away from his father. "In addition to the ride through town, we'll be holding a toy drive for the kids at the hospital. Everyone who can be there should show up, not only for the ride and the event but to help deliver the gifts. Remember, some of these kids may not make it to the holidays."

That reality had hit harder since Ezra had become a father. There were so many levels of helplessness as a parent. He couldn't save Gus from his mother's unreliability any better than he could keep him from skinning his knees or going through his eventual first heartbreak. He hurt when Gus hurt, and he was sure as a parent he wasn't alone in that. When he was a kid, he'd felt like his father had been able to separate himself from Ezra's pain. He'd learned enough about human emotions and trauma to know better, even if his father wouldn't talk about it.

He was also fully aware that those situations paled in comparison to the helplessness parents of terminally ill children must feel. He didn't want to imagine that inescapable pain and focused on Tiny talking about the Reindeer Ride.

"We'll be decorating our bikes, and we're asking everyone to dress festively. Wynnie and I will be dressed as Santa and Mrs. Claus."

"You've got the gut for it, old man," Doc called out, causing a rumble of laughter.

Tiny leaned back in his chair and patted his stomach. "This took years of hard work to develop. If you're lucky, one day you'll be worthy of a Santa suit, too."

"Doc would have to rig his dating schedule so he's not between women, or he'll be the first single Santa," Rebel shouted, causing more laughter.

"A'right, boys, settle down. We've got more to cover," Tiny said, and the din quieted. "If you need suggestions for bike decorations or what to wear, talk to Wynnie or Alice. They've got some good ideas. Wynnie's going to try to get Sasha and Birdie to dress as elves…"

Ezra's mind took off running with that tidbit, picturing Sasha in a sexy little green-and-red elf outfit, and that's where his mind remained for the rest of the meeting.

As everyone got up to stretch their legs, grab drinks, and play pool or darts, Ezra checked in with Sasha. He never worried about Gus when he was with her. Not even when Gus had been a baby and Tina had been having one of her *off* mornings, leaving Ezra to take Gus to work with him. On those trying days, when Ezra had clients to meet with, everyone offered to help, and Sasha was at the front of that line every chance she got. So why was he checking in with her when he'd been gone only a couple of hours? Because he'd spent the last twenty minutes fantasizing about her in a skimpy elf outfit after wondering if she was texting with Flame, and while he couldn't claim her as his own sexy elf, he could sure as hell make sure he remained on her mind.

Ezra: *How are things going?*

Sasha: *Great! We threw back a few beers, and now we're heading over to Billie's racetrack to nail a few jumps.*

He chuckled to himself. It was almost nine, and Gus was more likely sleeping or half-asleep, snuggled up with her as she read him stories. The latter an image Ezra lingered on before responding.

Ezra: *Awesome. Make sure he doesn't wear a pesky helmet.*

Sasha: *No worries. I gave him a spiky mohawk, and we dyed it red. A helmet won't fit over it anyway. Are you going out to a strip joint after the meeting?*

Ezra: *Don't I always?* He added a devil emoji.

If he could have gotten into strip clubs when he was seventeen, he probably would have lived at them, but as an adult that had never been his thing. He did enjoy having a beer now and then at the Roadhouse with the guys, but tonight he wanted nothing more than to get home and spend time with Sasha. He pushed to his feet and pocketed his phone.

"Hey, man. Are you coming to the Roadhouse with us?" Flame asked.

"Not tonight. Sasha's at my place with Gus. I want to get back to her."

"Cool. Tell her to head over to the Roadhouse afterward."

"I will, but I wouldn't count on it. We usually hang out for a while." The bonds of brotherhood were unbreakable, but that didn't mean when jealousy reared its ugly head, he couldn't be an arrogant ass.

"Lucky you," Flame said as Dare, Doc, and Cowboy joined them.

"You getting lucky tonight, Ezra?" Dare asked.

"If he is, it's with your sister," Flame said, and walked away laughing.

Dick. "Don't pay attention to him."

"I never do. We're thinking about heading out to Rocky Point on Sunday's ride. You in?" Doc asked.

They did a club ride every weekend, and Ezra joined them when he could. "Yeah, as long as Tina doesn't flake again. What about you, Cowboy?" Cowboy had missed several of the last rides and always claimed to be too busy with Sully to get away. "Or is Sunday now officially Sexy Sully Day?"

Cowboy snickered. "Every day is Sexy Sully Day."

Doc clapped him on the back. "Then get that ten seconds in early. I'm sick of you missing Sunday rides."

Everyone laughed.

"Have fun tonight. I'm going to catch up with my old man before I take off." Ezra headed across the room to where his father was talking with Otto, an affable guy whose wife, Colleen, was a fellow therapist at the ranch. "Hey, Pep. Otto." He hadn't called his father *Dad* since he went away to college, and the truth was, mentally putting his father into a less connected role had helped him expect less from him.

"Hi, son," his father said, dark eyes serious. "How're you tonight?"

Son. He longed to be pulled into an embrace or something—*anything*—to make him feel like that endearment meant something more than a simple word to separate him from all the other guys his father kept at arm's length. "I'm good. You?"

"Can't complain."

"Hey, Ezra. How's your boy doing?" Otto asked, as boisterous as always.

"He's great. Getting bigger every day."

"You going out with the guys while he's with Tina?" his father asked.

"No. She couldn't take him tonight. He's with Sasha."

His father's brows slanted, but he didn't say a word.

Ezra was used to the uncomfortable silences with his father in situations that might evoke certain emotions and conversations with other people. Every time he'd tried to talk with his father about relationships, whether it was theirs, his parents', or his relationship with Tina, his father shut down. Even when he and Tina were going through their divorce, his father had never offered any advice or even condolences. It had gotten so frustrating, Ezra had finally stopped trying to talk to him about it. Now he and his father existed in some sort of middle ground that his father found safe or comfortable, and Ezra simply found a shame. He knew Pep wasn't good at handling his feelings, but he also knew their relationship would never fully heal until they talked about what had gone wrong in their own family.

"Par for the course with that one," Otto said. "It's a shame her priorities are so messed up. How'd Gus handle it?"

"He's been through it so often, he takes it in stride." But it was getting harder for Ezra to turn the other cheek.

"You're a better man than I am," Otto said. "I would've given her hell by now."

"You think I haven't?" He had, many times, but he had to be careful, because he'd always believed that it was better for Gus to have some time with his mother than none at all.

"Well, if she can't take him this weekend, you bring him to Grandpa's house," his father said. "I'd love to have more time with him."

"Will do. Need anything, Pep?" Ezra always asked, despite the response always being the same. He didn't begrudge Gus's time with his grandfather, but at times like these, he'd give anything to hear, *Yeah, son. Have time for a talk?* He knew that day would never come, but he couldn't get himself to stop trying.

His father shook his head. "Everything's good."

"I'm glad to hear it. I'd love to treat you to lunch or a drink sometime."

"No need for that. We'll get together with Gus," his father said.

"Right. Have a good night." Ezra headed out the front door.

Rebel was standing by his motorcycle, looking down at his phone. His dark hair shielded his face, but he bit out a curse as Ezra walked by.

"Hey, everything okay?" Ezra asked.

"Yeah," he grumbled. "It's just my brother Dallas warning me that my family's coming for Dare's wedding. I don't need their pressure right now."

Rebel's father was the founder of a Dark Knights' chapter in Upstate New York, and Rebel had married the vice president's daughter, Sailor Wicked, when he was too damn young to be saying *I do*. He'd come to Colorado to stay with his cousins a few years ago, after going through a messy divorce. He'd bent Ezra's ear about the situation from time to time, and two things were clear. He still wasn't over his ex, and his family wanted him back on home turf.

"I've got the time if you want to talk," Ezra offered.

"Thanks, but I think I'd rather fuck or drink this frustration away." He pocketed his phone.

"All right, but if you drink it away, don't climb back on that bike. Call me if you need a ride."

Rebel cracked a grin. "I plan to go with option number one, but if that fails, I'm not dumb enough to drink and drive. I'll get a ride, or you'll get a call. Thanks, man."

"Anytime." As Ezra climbed onto his bike, he wondered which was worse, having a family like Rebel's, that was always up in his business, or a father who wanted nothing to do with it at all.

Chapter Six

WHEN EZRA GOT home from church, his two-bedroom cabin smelled feminine, sweet, and too damn good. It was a scent he knew well. One that had permeated his life for years. It was the scent of Sasha, and it instantly revved him up and calmed his soul. He put his helmet in the closet by the door, taking in the crayon drawings and Lego dinosaurs on the coffee table, which Sasha and Gus must have made, and Gus's tiny guitar lying next to Sasha's larger one on the couch. She'd surprised Gus with that guitar last year, when he'd begged her to teach him how to play. Gus's bedroom door was closed, and he heard the clink of silverware on a dish coming from the kitchen. As he made his way to the kitchen, he felt a familiar tug in his chest. This was the homelife he'd envisioned for his son. Being raised by two people who adored him in a home where he felt safe, surrounded by more family than he could ever want. But while Gus had most of those things, Ezra and Sasha were an impossibility.

He found Sasha standing at the counter in those sexy shorts, wearing one of his zip-up hoodies, eating a piece of the spinach and feta spanakopita he'd made Sunday night.

She looked over, cheeks full, eyes wide, like a kid caught with her hand in the cookie jar. "Hi. I thought you were going out for a drink with the guys."

"I decided to come home instead."

She glanced at the last bit of spanakopita left on her plate. "I hope you don't mind that I dug into this."

He loved that she helped herself to his things without feeling a need to apologize. "Do I ever mind?"

"No, thank God, because you really outdid yourself. This is the best thing you've ever made. Want a bite?" She held up a forkful.

Either he was seeing what he wanted to, or she was looking at him with a seductive glimmer in her eyes. Either way, it drew him closer. He put his hand over hers, guiding the fork into his mouth.

"So good, right?"

I can think of something much tastier. "It's not bad."

"Bullshit, *not bad.*" She poked him with the fork, then ate the last piece. "*Delicious.* Other than the whole inability-to-bake thing, you're going to make someone a great husband one day."

He couldn't bake worth shit. He burned cookies every time he tried to make them for Gus. "I think I've already proven otherwise."

"I call bullshit again."

He hadn't given his all to Tina or their marriage, but he wasn't about to get into that. "How was Gus tonight?"

"Good. We had fun. We took a walk and played guitar and Legos and colored. He asked me if I would sleep over again."

"My boy has good taste."

"I'm glad you noticed," she said with a sweet smile.

"Did he say anything about his mother?"

She shook her head. "He never does, but as always, he said he was excited to see Daddy in the morning."

"Really?" That made him feel good all over.

"Yes. I've told you that before. And as far as Tina goes, you *know* how I feel about her. She doesn't deserve either of you."

She was as protective of him as she was of Gus, and he fucking loved that about her, too.

"I know it's none of my business," she said as she carried her plate to the sink and began washing it. "But I still don't understand why you continue to allow her to see Gus when she lets him down all the time."

"I allow it because I don't want him to feel like I did when my mother left."

She set the dish and her fork in the dish drainer and turned to face him. "You've never really told me how you felt, but I can imagine how awful it was. I would've been devastated if my mother took off and left me behind, not knowing where she went or why."

"I told you I was fucked up for a long time."

"Yes, and you told me it was a big part of why you were so rebellious, but that doesn't tell me how you *felt*. I care about you and Gus, and I want to understand what you're really trying to protect him from."

He hated admitting to what had felt like a weakness for so many years. As a trained therapist, he knew it wasn't a weakness but a trauma response he'd dealt with and overcome years ago. But that didn't take away the unease of sharing it with a woman he admired, or the fact that given her relationship with Gus, she had a right to know.

"A mother is supposed to love her kids unconditionally,

above everything else, the way your mother does. When mine left, she made me feel like I wasn't worthy of that kind of love, and my father shutting down and shutting me out didn't help."

"I think that's how anyone would feel in that situation. I'm so sorry you felt like that."

She hugged him, and he soaked in her comfort. But she felt too damn good, and when she looked up at him with warmth in her eyes and said, "I hope you know you're worthy of the best kind of love," it felt like an invitation, and he forced himself to step back.

Feeling worthy was no longer a problem. But having the love he wanted? That was another story. "It was a long time ago, and I'm well past those bad feelings. I just never want Gus to feel like that, and I guess I've always felt like some time with his mother is better than none."

"Now that I know where you're coming from, I can understand that. But I'm not going to lie. Tina still pisses me off." Her expression turned serious. "Is that what the spanakopita was about? Your mother and Tina?"

There were downsides to Sasha knowing him so well. He only made that particular dish, which his mother had made often, when he couldn't settle his mind. But he hadn't made it because of his mother or his flighty ex. He'd made it Sunday night because of all the shit that had gone down with Sasha over the weekend. Although he wasn't about to tell her that.

"No, it's nothing."

"That's a whole lotta malarky, Moore. You don't spend two hours cooking when that mind of yours isn't stuck on something."

"Let it go, Sash."

"Nope." She stepped closer, standing right in front of him.

"I'm not moving from this spot until you tell me what's up."

She was too cute and too damn persistent. He shook his head, trying to school his smile. "Drop it."

"You know me better than that. What's got you *all* tied in knots?" Those last four words dripped with seduction, and she punctuated each one with a poke to his chest.

"*Sasha*," he warned.

"Was it because you're worried about Gus?"

"No."

"Is it a girl?"

He gritted his teeth.

"It *is*," she said in a singsong voice. "Well, *this* is interesting."

"Sasha, *stop*."

"Why? We've already established that we're both adults and we have needs. After what you said in the meadow, I think you know you can tell me anything."

"*Jesus.* Can we not go there?" She had him so tightly wound, he was getting turned on remembering how good she'd felt lying on top of him.

"Oh, we're"—she poked him again—"going"—*poke*—"there." She lifted her finger to poke him again, and he flattened his hand over hers, trapping it on his chest.

"*Stop.*" He stepped forward to emphasize his command.

"No," she challenged, pressing her body against his. His damn cock stirred. "Do you need me to stay with Gus a little longer while you go out and work off some frustration?"

"*No*," he growled, pissed that she'd even offer to hand him over to anyone else when the only woman he wanted was standing right in front of him. He knew damn well he should put space between them, but he was unable to stop himself from stepping forward and backing her up against the counter. "I don't even fucking like one-night stands."

"But you said—"

"I know what I said. I do what I have to because, yeah, I've got needs, and sometimes the only way to get out of my own head is to fuck until I can't see straight. But that doesn't mean I like it."

Her eyes flamed, and hell if that didn't make him want her even more.

SASHA DIDN'T KNOW how her legs were still holding her up, but this was *it*. She somehow knew in her heart that *she* was the woman he'd been thinking about, and she wasn't about to back down or run away scared this time. His restraint vibrated between them, and she was determined to sever it. His palm grew hotter on her hand as her fingers moved along his corded chest muscles and brushed her thumb over his nipple. His jaw tightened. He was always so in control, she felt him teetering, on the verge of losing control. She wanted to shatter it, to make him lose his mind and show him she was no longer a frightened or naive *good girl*.

She fisted her hand in his shirt, pressing her body harder against him, wanting to be *his* bad girl. "What is it about this girl that's got you all hot and bothered?"

He grabbed her wrist, tugging her hand from his chest, and pinned it to the edge of the counter. "I can't stop thinking about her."

"She must be awfully special to make you this crazy."

His eyes narrowed. "She's one of a kind."

She put her other hand on his chest, holding his gaze. "Bet you could use a little relief right now."

He snagged that wrist, too, pinning it on her other side. "It doesn't fucking matter."

"Doesn't it?" When she licked her lips, his eyes followed the slide of her tongue. "Isn't that *all* that matters?" She rocked her hips, rubbing against his cock. He growled, spurring her on. "Taking what you know we *both* want?"

"Fuck it—" He crushed his mouth to hers.

It took a second for her to realize the kiss was real, and then *holy shit.* There was no holding back. Years of repressed emotions came charging out. She pushed up on her toes, eagerly meeting every swipe of his tongue with one of her own. He grabbed her head as he'd done years ago, angling her mouth so he could take the kiss deeper, tongue thrusting, hips gyrating. He tasted like man and lust and was even more powerful and confident than she remembered, greedily devouring her. She was right there with him, wanting—*needing*—everything he had to give. His hand dove into her hair, and he made a gruff, hungry sound, sending bolts of electricity searing through her core. She opened wider for him, wanting to consume his sounds, feel every rumble in his chest, every grind of his hips, until each one became a part of her. His kisses were all-consuming, making her tingle from the tips of her fingers to the ends of her toes. She was on fire, utterly lost in him, grinding and moaning, her nipples burning, her entire body aching for more.

"Fuck, Sash," he rasped against her mouth.

He groped, bit, licked, and *sucked,* driving her wild. His teeth scraped against her jaw, and he reclaimed her mouth, rough and possessive, shattering her ability to think. He lifted her onto the counter, barely breaking the kiss as he grabbed her ass with both hands, hauling her to the edge, wedging his big body between her legs, grinding so exquisitely, her panties were wet. Their kisses grew messy and urgent, their breathing rampant. His hands skimmed up her thighs, and her breath hitched in anticipation. He pushed them beneath her shorts, thumbs teasing her through her panties, making her dizzy with desire. She panted out, "*Yes,*" and reached for the button on his jeans. He stilled, and the air rushed from her lungs—*Nonono*—as he gritted out, "*Fuuck.*"

She squeezed her eyes shut, clinging to him, and buried her face in his neck. "Don't say it."

"Sasha—"

She shook her head, hearing the restraint in his voice, feeling it return to his body. She wanted him to lose the battle again, to want her more than whatever was making him stop. Her heart breaking, she forced herself to meet his gaze. The torturous emotions staring back at her had her putting her fingers over his lips. "Don't say it. Please *don't.*"

He wrapped his hand around hers, kissing her fingers before drawing them away and taking her face between his hands. She tried to memorize the feel of them on her cheeks, knowing it would be the last time she ever would, as he touched his forehead to hers.

"I'm so fucking sorry. I want you. There's no one I want *more* than you. *You* are the one I can't stop thinking about. But we can't do this."

"Why?" came out as strangled as she felt.

"Gus. Your parents. This place. My *job.* There's too much at stake."

She averted her eyes, embarrassment and hurt battling for dominance as she pushed away and slid off the counter, heading out of the kitchen on wobbly legs. He wasn't wrong, but her thoughts were spinning. She couldn't process anything beyond the disappointment sinking into her bones.

"Sasha, we should talk about this."

She shook her head. "I can't."

"But—"

"No." She picked up her guitar and lifted her chin, trying her best to hide her devastation before looking at him. "It's fine. You're right. There's too much at stake." *But there's only so much heartbreak a girl can take.* "Pretend it never happened."

She headed for the door, and as she reached for the doorknob, he said, "Sash, I'm sorry. Gus loves you, and I hope I didn't screw things up for him."

"He'll never know the difference." She hurried out the door and down the road, refusing to give in to the tears vying for release.

How could her sister have been so wrong *and* so right? She hadn't built up their kisses to be more than they were. They smoldered, sweeping her into a world she never wanted to leave. But he'd forced her out, cut her off at her wobbly knees. She tried to swallow past the lump in her throat and looked up at the stars, telling herself this was exactly what she needed.

Now she knew where he stood, and she could move on.

So why did it hurt so damn much?

Chapter Seven

EZRA TRIED TO concentrate as Gus filled him in on his day at camp on their way home Thursday evening. He nodded and said "Uh-huh" here and there, but his mind was on a certain blonde whom he hadn't seen since yesterday morning at breakfast. As promised, Sasha had been her normal bubbly self toward Gus, and while she hadn't been cold toward Ezra, she hadn't been warm, either. She hadn't even looked him in the eye and had left the breakfast table faster than a bat out of hell. It sucked, and it was his own damn fault for giving in to his desires instead of staying on the safe side of that invisible line in the dirt.

She hadn't shown up for lunch at the main house yesterday, and when he'd gone down to the rehab barns to see her before picking up Gus after camp yesterday, she'd already left for the day. He'd stopped at her cabin, but her truck had been gone. She'd missed dinner last night, and when he'd texted saying they needed to talk, she'd replied with, *No need. We're good.* He'd followed it up with, *Haven't seen you lately*, and she'd responded with, *Been busy.* She'd added a smiling emoji, which he'd taken as a good sign. But then she'd missed breakfast and lunch again today. She was clearly avoiding him, and he fucking hated it.

"Can we, Dad?" Gus asked from the back seat.

"Sorry, buddy. Can we what?"

"Roast marshmallows after dinner?"

"Sure." As he turned into the ranch and drove to the main house for dinner, he gave himself hell for being distracted around Gus.

"I'm gonna ask Sasha to do it with us. Do you think she'll be at dinner tonight?"

He fucking hoped so. In trying *not* to fuck up things for Gus, he'd done exactly that. "I guess we'll see."

"I want to find a Y stick. Cowboy said they're the best for roasting marshmallows because you can roast *two* marshmallows at once. Do you think Cowboy and Sully will want to roast them with us?"

"I don't know, bud. You can ask them." He turned into the parking lot in front of the main house, wishing he could be as oblivious as his son was to what had gone down with Sasha.

"Sasha's here! And so is Sully! Park, Dad! *Hurry!*"

Ezra's chest constricted as he parked. Sasha and Sully were talking by the front doors. Sasha looked as gorgeous as ever with her hair loose and a little tousled over the shoulders of her V-neck top, jeans that accentuated her curves, and those flowered cowgirl boots she'd worn on that date with the banker.

"Come on, Dad!" Gus unhooked his booster seat straps and bolted out the door, hollering, "Sugar! Sully!"

Fuck. Ezra climbed out of the Bronco and made his way toward them as Sasha scooped up Gus. His little boy threw his skinny arms around her neck, obviously missing her as much as Ezra did. He'd been going over what he'd done Tuesday night, and no matter how he cut it, he knew he was doing the right thing by backing off to protect Gus. But doing the right thing had never felt so fucking wrong.

"How was camp?" Sasha asked.

"Fun. We went swimming, and guess what?" Gus said excitedly as Sasha set him on his feet.

"What?" Sasha and Sully asked in unison.

"I swim faster than everyone else!" he exclaimed.

"That's amazing, Gusto," Sasha said, smiling at Ezra. But it wasn't the same flirtatious smile she usually graced him with. It was the kind of smile he'd seen her give people she knew but wasn't close to.

That slayed him. It wasn't only the special smile he missed. It was what it said about their friendship. Hell, he missed hearing her laugh during meals, listening to his little boy chatter excitedly with her about whatever his five-year-old mind conjured, and the easy way she always made Gus feel special and heard. He didn't know how it was possible after only two days, but he just fucking missed *her*.

"Wow, Gus, that's impressive," Sully said.

"Guess what else I did." Gus shoved his hand into the front pocket of his jeans and pulled out a balled-up piece of paper. "I made you a picture!" He thrust the crumpled paper toward Sully, roasting marshmallows forgotten.

"You made it for *me*?" Sully asked enthusiastically.

Gus nodded, his curls bouncing over his forehead.

Ezra's heart took a hit, thinking about the drawings Gus had made Tuesday night with Sasha. He'd drawn two horses, which looked more like fat-legged monsters with spiky hair, with two stick figures on one and one on the other. There was no missing who he'd drawn. Sasha had long yellow hair, and flowers that were too big for the boots he'd drawn on her stick feet. He'd drawn himself sitting in front of her, with curly dark hair, and he'd drawn Ezra on the other horse, with big bumps for biceps and black hair. His little boy still thought he was godlike. But he had a feeling if Gus knew how he'd hurt Sasha, he'd want to kick his ass.

Don't worry, buddy. Dad's been kicking his own ass for days.

Sully tucked her shoulder-length golden-blond hair behind her ear as she straightened out the paper.

"Sorry, Sasha," Gus said. "I didn't make you a picture."

Sasha ruffled his hair. "That's okay. I have a ton of your drawings."

"On your fridge!" Gus exclaimed.

"That's right, and in my Gusto box."

Ezra's heart was taking a beating tonight. Sasha kept a box of cards and drawings Gus had given her over the years. She and Gus had decorated the box when he was three.

"Oh, Gussy. I love it! Thank you." Sully hugged Gus. "Look, you guys." She showed them the adorable drawing of a stick figure riding a bicycle, her stick feet aiming up toward a big yellow sun.

"That's Sully on her bike," Gus explained. "When I grow up, I wanna draw like she does."

"You're already a great artist," Sasha said, her gaze fixed on the drawing. "It looks just like Sully."

She was obviously trying *not* to look at Ezra, and that bugged the hell out of him. He already missed their shared glances over Gus's cuteness. "It sure does. Good job, bud."

Sully pressed the drawing to her chest. "I will treasure this forever. I'm going to take it inside right now and show it to Callahan."

As Sully headed inside, Gus reached for Sasha's hand. "Let's go! Before Cowboy eats all the good stuff."

"You'll have to go without me, Gusto. I have plans tonight."

"Okay!" Gus ran to the door and tugged it open. "Come on, Dad! I want to ask Sully and Cowboy about the marshmallows!"

"I'll be right in." He was grateful his son was oblivious to the stare down taking place between him and Sasha and to the heat and hurt thrumming between them.

"Okay!" Gus shouted, and ran inside.

"Are you planning on avoiding me forever?"

"I'm not avoiding you," she said flatly. "I just said I have plans."

"With Flame?" The question was out before he could stop it, and he knew it made him an asshole. He held up his hands in surrender. "Sorry. Don't answer that. It's none of my business. I'm sorry I hurt you. I shouldn't have let myself get carried away."

"Let it go. I already have." She turned and walked away.

He watched her climb into her truck and drive away. He'd fucked plenty of women and walked away without giving them a second thought. A few kisses with Sasha, and his heart felt like it was being ripped from his chest. If he was his own client, he'd dissect the hell out of that and make himself face every aspect of it and what it meant. But he shoved that pain down deep, burying it beneath his youthful rebellion, beneath his mother's abandonment, and beneath his failed marriage. The marriage he'd chosen over his feelings for Sasha with the hopes of giving his son what he'd never had.

That was the biggest mistake of his life.

He'd chosen the wrong woman six years ago, and he'd put all his energy into building an amazing life for Gus. A life that was now so connected with the ranch and Sasha's family, he'd forever pay the price for his decisions.

He headed inside with a little better understanding of why his father avoided talking about his past like the plague.

Chapter Eight

EARLY FRIDAY MORNING Sasha threw on a hoodie—hers, *not* Ezra's—jeans, and sneakers and headed out on an ATV. She wound up the jagged trail toward her favorite thinking spot, high on the crest of a hill. Everyone in her family had their favorite spots, and she knew where most of them were. She'd been a crafty kid. When her brothers would take off on ATVs or dirt bikes, she'd saddle up a horse and follow their trail. She'd had to in order to find her own place to hide from the world, which she'd done at twelve years old. It had taken several weeks of scouting, getting up at dawn, and riding the trails on horseback, until she'd found the right spot.

The trees gave way to a dirt clearing, and she slowed down, driving across the dusty ground to the base of *her* rocky ledge, and cut the engine. Filling her lungs with the crisp mountain air, she climbed the largest boulder to the highest point and sat down, drinking in the view of the ranch as she pulled her knees to her chest and wrapped her arms around them. Ribbons of reds, oranges, and yellows decorated the bluing sky like disappearing ink fading at the edges as the morning sun bathed the ranch, and all of its magnificent glory, in its light.

The land was as much a part of her as each of the horses that came through it. She'd learned to walk on that dirt, to ride horses on those trails, and to see every living thing for who they were on the inside. She'd learned about love and loss, fortitude and friendship. She'd learned *all* of the life lessons that mattered on that property and had even imagined getting married on it one day, like Dare and Billie were planning, and, she had a feeling, as Cowboy and Sully would do someday, too.

The trouble was, ever since Ezra had moved to the ranch, she'd held on to the hope that he would be her *someday*. She knew it might take years, but in her heart, it was always him. Now, for the first time in her life, part of her wished she didn't live there, having to see him and Gus every day. She'd hated telling Gus she had plans for dinner, but it turned out two days was nowhere near enough time to get over what had happened with Ezra. Coming face-to-face with him had brought back all the excitement and passion of their kisses and an onslaught of frustration and heartbreak that had made it hard for her to breathe. She'd *had* to get out of there, and while she'd been keeping busy at work and had met Bobbie for margaritas Wednesday night, she'd spent last night hanging out with Birdie at the chocolate shop to avoid being at the ranch, which why not living there was starting to look more appealing.

The sound of an ATV in the distance broke her concentration.

She listened more intently as it neared, wondering who would be out riding this early. Dare was her guess, although he was not one to rush out of bed when Billie was beside him. She didn't blame him. He was so in love with Billie, he reeked of it.

The sound of the ATV was growing closer. She didn't think anyone knew where her thinking spot was. She'd always taken a roundabout way to get to it, so there would be no well-worn paths for her family to follow. She went up on her knees and looked back toward the clearing just as an ATV came off the trail, and her mother came into focus. Her mother cut the engine and climbed off the ATV wearing jeans and a T-shirt, with a sporty red flannel overtop.

"Mom? What are you doing here?" She went to the edge of the boulder to climb down.

"I came to see my daughter. Stay there, darlin'. I'm coming up."

Her mother scaled the boulder as if she climbed for a living. Sasha shouldn't be surprised. Her mother was fierce. She hadn't grown up in a biker family, but growing up on the ranch had made her strong and unflappable. She'd learned to wrangle tough, unruly men early on and had since raised five strong children.

Her mother pushed to her feet and wiped her hands on her jeans. *"Whew."* She looked out at the sun rising into the sky. "It sure is pretty this morning."

"It is. How did you know where I was?"

Her mother arched a brow. "A mother always knows where her children are."

"That's a scary thought. Does anyone else know about this spot?"

"Only your father. Let's sit down."

"Dad knows where my thinking spot is?" she asked as they sat down.

"Who do you think showed me? You know how much your father loves you. Do you think that man would ever let you go out at dawn without knowing where you were heading?"

"Wait. Are you saying he's known about it since I first discovered it?"

"I'm afraid so." She patted Sasha's hand. "Nothing happens on this ranch without your daddy knowing about it."

"But *how*? I would have seen him following me, or at least heard him."

"Your father might be a big man, but he's as stealthy and as clever as the day is long. He armed himself with binoculars and a thermos of coffee, and he'd watch you sneak out, saddle up, and take your rascally self into these hills."

"I guess it's a good thing I wasn't sneaking out to meet a boy."

"If that'd been the case, you'd have definitely known he was there." Her mother put her arm around her, hugging her against her side. "Want to tell me why you've been making yourself scarce around the ranch lately?"

"I'm just busy."

"It's not like you to be too busy to eat a meal or two with everyone. Do you need some help with the horses?"

"No. I have plenty of time for the horses." She pulled her knees up and wrapped her arms around them. "I guess I've needed a little space."

"I can understand that. Working where you live can be difficult, and around here, you don't get much privacy."

"Apparently I get even less than I thought." Sasha bumped her mother with her shoulder. "Does Dad *still* follow me?"

"No. But I can't vouch for your brothers." She laughed softly.

Sasha could only smile and shake her head. "Did you ever want to get away from the ranch?"

"Sure, or at least I thought I did. When I went to college, I thought I was all about finally being free. Out from under your grandfather's thumb and from the endless chores. But after the first couple of months of school, I missed home."

Sasha remembered feeling that way when she'd gone to college, too.

"I'm a ranch girl at heart," her mother said. "There's something about this land that gets in your blood. I couldn't wait to come back, and when I did, fate stepped in, and I met your father."

Her parents had met at the Roadhouse, when her mother had been celebrating her college graduation, and her father, who was from Peaceful Harbor, Maryland, had been on a cross-country bike trip with his brother Biggs. He'd fallen hard, and instead of returning to Maryland, he'd gotten a job on the ranch working for Sasha's grandfather while her mother went to graduate school. A few years later, her parents had married, and eventually they'd expanded the ranch and her father had started the Dark Knights.

"I'd've followed that man to the moon if that's what he wanted. But, honey, that was *me*. It doesn't have to be you. There's a big world out there. We love that you're here with us, but if you're feeling restless or stifled in your career, you don't have to stay just because we're family."

"I know. I don't feel that way. I love working here, and you give me free rein to do what's best for the horses. I don't have any complaints."

"Good. I try not to pry into your personal life, but is that where the stress is coming from? Is there a new beau on the horizon who has you a little off-kilter?" she asked hopefully.

If Ezra were any other guy, Sasha could talk with her mother about it, but she knew better than to go there. "*No.* There's no new guy in my life."

"Okay, well, is *that* the problem? Because I might have some suggestions. Birdie tells me that dating apps are quite popular these days, and there's that cute young man who works at the feed store."

"Mom, please stop." She was going to kill Birdie.

"I was just trying to help, but don't worry, honey. You're a beautiful, smart girl. You'll meet Mr. Right when you're good and ready, and I might have a great opportunity for you to do so."

"I don't need to be set up."

"This isn't a setup. There's a networking dinner at the Broadmoor in Colorado Springs next month that's going to have some very important people in attendance, and they've asked us to speak about the ranch. It's a great opportunity to spread the word and even bring in some donations. You know how your father avoids dressy functions, and this one is five hundred dollars a plate. I was hoping you could go and tell them about the rescue and the work we do with the horses."

"Sure, I'd be happy to." She enjoyed talking about the rescue, and it would be nice to get away. "Is it black tie?"

"No, but it's fancy."

"Okay. I'll go shopping for a dress." She wasn't in the mood to shop, but at least it would get her away from the ranch.

"Well, you have plenty of time to find one. I'll have Maya email you the details." Maya Martinez ran the offices and kept the schedules for the ranch. She'd worked there for a few years, but she didn't live on-site.

"Colorado Springs is so nice, and you never know who you'll meet at the dinner. If you want to make a night of it, a hotel room is a write-off."

"Thanks. I might do that. I could use a night away. Doc said the guys are doing a Reindeer Ride and toy drive for the kids at the hospital and that you and Dad are going to dress up as Santa and Mrs. Claus. Is that true?"

"Yes. I wanted to talk with you about that, too."

"I *love* the idea. You and Dad will be so cute. The kids will go crazy for it."

"We're hoping to brighten their day. Alice and I were thinking you girls might want to dress up as elves or reindeer or something."

I need something to keep my mind off Ezra. "Sure. That sounds fun."

"Wonderful." She looked at her watch. "I'd better get back for breakfast. Are you coming?"

"I think I'll enjoy this view for a little while longer." At least until Gus and Ezra were safely inside the big house for breakfast. She didn't want to chance running into them on her way back.

"Okay. Should I have Dwight hold a plate for you?"

Sasha shook her head. "No thanks. I'm not hungry. Thanks for coming out here to find me."

"I've missed having alone time with you." She hugged her again, then pushed to her feet.

"Do you need help getting down?"

"Baby, I've been doing this since before you were born." Her mother climbed down, and as she got into the ATV, she said, "I'm going to talk to Ezra about speaking on behalf of our side of the business at the networking dinner. Maybe you two can drive over together. See you later, honey."

Sasha's stomach sank.

A week ago, driving to Colorado Springs with Ezra would have been like a dream come true. But now? She couldn't even sit through a meal with him without hurting. As her mother's ATV disappeared down the trail, she tried to pull her thoughts together. She didn't really want to move away or avoid Ezra forever. The idea of a life without him and Gus in it, even as friends, was worse than trying to pretend she wasn't walking around with a hole in her heart.

She'd just have to pull up her big-girl panties and figure out how to move forward. It was hard to believe only three days ago he'd been on the verge of pulling those panties down.

SASHA POPPED ANOTHER piece of candy into her mouth Friday evening at Divine Intervention, Birdie's chocolate shop, listening to Birdie sell the benefits of truffles to a middle-aged health-conscious customer. Divine was right. What was it about chocolate and peanut butter that made everything better?

"Truffles are low fat and cholesterol free," Birdie raved. "They're also loaded with fiber and protein, *and* they contain a lot of important vitamins and minerals that our bodies need. You really can't go wrong."

Unless you eat a dozen, like me.

As Birdie and the customer headed up to the register, Sasha bit into another piece of candy and carried the nearly empty sample tray to the far end of the counter, away from Birdie. She heard the door to the kitchen open and saw Quinn Finney, Birdie's chestnut-haired bestie and employee, carrying another tray of chocolates toward the display case.

Sasha put the rest of the piece of candy in her mouth and hurried over, blocking Quinn's way. "*Mm*, fudge," she whispered. "My favorite."

Quinn cocked a brow, looking more like a hot disapproving librarian with her black-framed glasses and pencil skirt than a full-time chocolate pusher. "I thought the chocolate-peanut butter truffles were your favorite."

"They *were* five minutes ago. What kinds of fudge are these?"

Quinn giggled, pointing out the flavors as she said, "Rocky road, Kahlúa and cream, potato chip pretzel, which is amazing when you have your period or you're in a bitchy mood, and my favorite, sugar cookie."

The bell above the door jangled as Sasha plucked a few off the tray. "I'll just try one of each." She bit into a piece of sugar-cookie fudge, and the sweet treat melted in her mouth. "Holy cow. This is amazing."

"Sasha Whiskey, back away from the fudge."

Sasha's eyes widened at Birdie's serious tone. She shoved the rest of the fudge into her mouth.

Quinn stifled a laugh, and as she headed up to the display case, she said, "Go easy on her, Birdie."

"*Stop* enabling her." Birdie planted a hand on the hip of her Hawaiian-print wraparound shorts that had Moana on them and pinned a dark stare on Sasha. "You've been hiding out here for two days, eating everything you can get your hands on."

Sasha chewed fast and gulped down the four pieces of fudge she'd shoved into her mouth. "It's *your* fault. You said to go for it with Ezra, and I did."

"I thought you'd get your answer and move on," Birdie said emphatically.

"That would be a lot easier if he'd said he wasn't into me or if his kisses had sucked," Sasha snapped. "But he is into me, and his kisses were *so* freaking good, and he's so passionate, I was ready to get naked right there in his kitchen. And the worst part about it is that it felt so unbelievably *right* to be with him, despite knowing it was wrong."

"I get it, Sasha," Quinn said. "I'm sorry you guys can't be together, and I hate to say this, but he does have a lot at stake. You both do."

"I *know* he did the right thing by stopping us," she admitted in a pained whine. "But that doesn't mean I don't *hate* it and it doesn't hurt like hell."

"I know it hurts," Birdie said. "But it's not like you to wallow like this."

"I'm not wallowing. I'm…taste testing."

"I hate that you hurt so badly, but you need to taste test something else to get your mind off Ezra once and for all," Birdie said.

"She needs to taste test another man," Quinn interjected.

"*Yes.* That's exactly what she needs to do. The Roadhouse is hopping on Friday nights. We'll go ride a bull, *and* she can save a horse!" Birdie was the best mechanical bull rider around and was always up for that.

"I don't want to ride a bull or a cowboy, thank you very much," Sasha said.

"Then skip the bull," Birdie said.

"She's right." Quinn sauntered over. "The best way to get over a guy is to get under a new one."

Sasha crossed her arms. "Bobbie said the same thing the other night when we were having drinks."

"Because everyone knows that's the best way to do it," Birdie said.

"Well, it doesn't work for me. I've been with plenty of guys since Ezra and I first kissed way back when, and he's still the one I see when I close my eyes at night. It's *so* frustrating. It's like he's always there, even when he's not. I hate being in this position."

"Then do something about it," Quinn said. "You're the only one who can fix this."

"She's right," Birdie said. "We can give you ideas until we're blue in the face, and you can eat chocolate until you're stuffed to the gills, but until *you* decide it's time to do something to get over him, it's never going to happen."

Sasha crossed her arms, looking between them. "Being schooled by you two is annoying, but you're right. I don't need to bury my feelings in chocolate. I need to get out there and figure out a way to get over the only man I really wa—"

"No!" they said in unison.

"You can't think of him that way," Birdie said carefully. "It'll make it harder."

Why is this so difficult? It's not like pining over him will change anything. She didn't want to feel like this forever. *I can do this. I have to do this.* She took a deep breath, determined to make the pain go away. "I am going to get out there and figure out a way to get over Ezra Moore."

"Darn right you are," Quinn said.

"Yes!" Birdie did a fist pump. "Roadhouse it is."

Suddenly their small town seemed *too* small. "I'd give anything if there was another fun bar in Hope Valley, so we didn't have to go to the one where the Dark Knights hang out." At least Bobbie was working tonight. She was a full-time elementary school teacher and a part-time bartender.

"Well, there's not, so deal with it," Birdie said. "You have to let us pick out your outfit. You need to look super sexy and available."

"*Fine*, but nothing hot pink or crazy like you wear." Birdie had a unique throwback style that might look ridiculous on anyone else, but she owned it, and it worked for her.

"I don't dress crazy," Birdie insisted.

Quinn and Sasha exchanged an amused glance.

"You're right," Sasha said. "You never know when you're going to be invited to a Disney luau."

Birdie shrugged. "It could happen, and I'd be fully prepared."

"Don't worry. I won't let her go full-on Birdie with you," Quinn reassured her.

"I wouldn't anyway," Birdie insisted. "I know my sister. She's *good girl meets rebellion, but don't tell Daddy*, and I have the perfect outfit in mind for her." She took Sasha by the shoulders and turned her toward the door. "Now, go home and shower. Meet us at my place at eight, and be ready to get your flirt on!"

Chapter Nine

SASHA STRUTTED INTO the Roadhouse with Birdie and Quinn, feeling confident and sexy in a crinkled cotton-and-lace ivory tank with a plunging lace neckline and a wide band of lace beneath her breasts. They'd paired it with stringy cutoffs, white cowgirl boots, and a few gold necklaces. When she'd shown up at Birdie's apartment, her overzealous sister had filled her in on what she'd deemed OPERATION FORGET SEXY SINGLE DAD. The plan included an Uber, plying Sasha with alcohol, a mechanical bull, which Birdie swore was the best kind of foreplay, and a night of flirting. Sasha didn't think the mechanical bull thing would work, but she'd try anything to redirect her heart.

Music blared through the rustic bar, and they took a moment to assess the crowd from the raised entrance. Every table was taken, and the dance floor was packed. A crowd cheered on a guy riding the mechanical bull to their right, and a few shouts came from the people gathered around the bar and pool tables. They were surrounded by dozens of good-looking, flirt-worthy men, and there were just as many attractive women. Sasha was glad Birdie had worked her magic on her hair, making the waves fuller than usual, and Quinn had shared her makeup expertise, giving Sasha just enough smoky eyes and crimson lipstick to make her feel a little vampish. She needed that extra dose of confidence if she was going to flirt the way they'd been urging her to—without first being flirted with. She wasn't usually that forward, but tonight was anything *but* usual. She was determined to get her mind off Ezra, and while she didn't need to sleep with a guy to do it, she definitely planned on getting her groove on.

"Tourist season has its benefits," Quinn said.

"I'll say. How about one of them?" Birdie pointed to a group of guys talking a few feet away.

"The dark-haired guy is hot," Quinn said. "But the blond is too smarmy-looking for Sasha."

The dark-haired guy *was* good-looking, but he didn't do it for Sasha. There was nothing special about him. He didn't have the broody stare or the Greek god thing going on that Ezra did.

Ugh. I'm not playing the Ezra game tonight.

"I think I need a drink," Sasha said, and descended the entrance steps.

As they headed for the bar, she noticed quite a few guys checking them out. It was anyone's guess which of them they were looking at. Quinn's hourglass figure always drew attention, and in a red silk tank top and black miniskirt, she was all that and more. Then there was Birdie in her black-and-white checked shorts, black bralette, and red ankle boots. She was the only person Sasha knew who could pull off an outfit like that without looking like she was either trying too hard or should be serving drinks at a racetrack.

Bobbie sidled up to them on their way to the bar. Her

blond hair was pulled up in a ponytail, and a twinkle of excitement danced in her eyes. "Damn, you girls are on fire tonight,"

"We're on a mission to get Sasha laid," Birdie announced.

"Oh? Has the mission changed?" Bobbie looked curiously at Sasha.

Sasha had texted her on the way over and filled her in on their plan. Bobbie was a great wingwoman. She'd told her that Billie wasn't working tonight, which meant Dare probably wouldn't be there. Hopefully Cowboy would be staying in with Sully, and Sasha would only have to worry about Doc showing up and getting on her case. "No, it has *not*. We're just flirting."

"Okay, well, the coast is clear," Bobbie said. "No sign of your brothers yet."

"Let's hope it stays that way," Sasha said.

"With this crowd, they'd have a hard time keeping track of you anyway," Quinn said as they approached the bar. Kellan, a part-time bartender, full-time law student, and a shameless flirt, lifted his chin in greeting as he served a drink to a customer.

"What are we starting with tonight?" Bobbie asked.

Sasha knew she was asking about drinks, but she felt sassy and said, "Hopefully someone tall, dark, and gorgeous."

"Yeah, baby," Birdie exclaimed as Bobbie headed around the bar.

"I've got all the tall and gorgeous you need, darlin'," Kellan said.

Sasha smiled. "Those dimples could knock a girl to her knees, but does that line ever really work for you?"

"You tell me. If it doesn't, I'll come up with a dozen more because, damn, girl. You look *fine*. That's a killer outfit. Are you meeting someone special here tonight?"

"I sure hope so," she said.

"Yes, she is," Birdie said.

"But it's *not* you, Kellan," Bobbie said, giving him a playful shove. "Go drool on customers at the other end of the bar."

He chuckled and made a *call me* sign with his hand as he walked away.

"Want your usual drinks?" Bobbie asked.

"Nope. Tonight I don't want my usual anything," Sasha said, getting into the spirit of the night. "How about a round of tequila shots?"

Birdie and Quinn cheered, and Bobbie filled their order.

Quinn held up her shot glass. "To girls' night."

"To an *amazing* girls' night," Sasha said hopefully.

"To Sasha getting some D," Birdie added, earning a laugh from Quinn and a deadpan stare from Sasha. They clinked glasses and drank their shots.

Two shots later, Bobbie was back to serving drinks on the floor, and Sasha was feeling good as they scoped out the crowd for her first flirtation victim. Birdie nudged her, motioning to the entrance, where Flame was walking in with Taz and Hyde.

"Flame looks *hot*," Birdie said.

He did, all big and brawny, with short dark hair and blue eyes that Sasha knew left a trail of melted panties in their wake. Flame was funny and sexy, but when his eyes locked on Sasha, she didn't get butterflies or feel that tug of desire low in her belly like she did with Ezra. She sighed inwardly, feeling pathetic for comparing him to Ezra. That one-way train had already left the station, and she was standing on the platform alone.

Stop being a fool, and get your head together. Just as the thought hit, the door to the bar opened again, and Ezra walked in, sending Sasha's heart into a tailspin. She'd counted on Tina blowing off Gus this weekend and Ezra needing to stay home with him. *Shitshitshit.*

Ezra's eyes found hers like homing devices. The edges of his lips curved into a devastating smile, bringing back the way those lips had felt on hers, the feel of his big, strong hands pawing at her, and the sexy sounds he'd made as they'd feverishly made out. In the space of a few short seconds, her body heated. In the next breath, his expression morphed to a more troubled one, as if he'd been happy to see her but then reality came rushing in. She told herself to look away, but she was still as entranced by him as ever.

"Be strong." Birdie grabbed her wrist, reminding her of the way Ezra had done the same a few nights ago. "Stop staring at him."

"Easier said than done," she said absently.

Quinn stepped in front of her. "Stop it. You are *not* going to let him toy with your emotions. Enough is enough."

As if she could stop her heart from trying to claw its way out of her chest to reach him?

"Stick to the plan!" Birdie moved beside Quinn, making it impossible for Sasha to see around them. "If you don't shift your attention to the hot smoke jumper in the next five seconds, I'm going to give you a titty twister."

That jerked Sasha from her reverie. Birdie would totally do it. She took a few deep breaths and forced herself to look at Flame. He lifted his chin in her direction. She felt the heat of Ezra's stare but didn't allow herself the pleasure—or pain—of meeting it. Her heart was racing for all the wrong reasons. She had to get control or she was going to make a fool of herself.

"Flame's looking at you like he wants to gobble you up. Go

check out his fire hose," Birdie urged.

"What? *No*," Sasha said. "I'm here to flirt, not make a spectacle of myself."

"You don't want to touch that man's equipment?" Quinn asked. "Ezra really has screwed with your head. Look at Flame. He's all rock-hard man, and he's hungry for a sexy snack." She bit her lower lip. "I'd let him nibble on me *a-ny-time*."

"As if Cutter wouldn't hunt him down and tear him apart?" Sasha said. Cutter Long was a big, strapping cowboy and a longtime friend of theirs. He and Quinn had been dancing around the heat between them forever.

"I don't belong to that possessive cowboy, and he's not even here," Quinn said. "But Flame *is*, and you've obviously friend-zoned him, so he's fair game."

Was *that* what the trouble was? Had she put him so deep in the friend zone that she felt nothing but appreciation for his good looks and friendship? Sasha mentally flipped through the times they'd hung out, texted, and casually flirted and realized with a painful twist in her belly that Quinn was right. She'd been so hung up on Ezra, she'd friend-zoned the entire male species.

Holy shit. How long had she been doing that? Maybe she *did* need to do more than flirt tonight. Maybe if she kissed Flame, *really* kissed him like she meant it, she'd get butterflies and would shove Ezra deep into the friend zone, where he so clearly belonged. A stab of longing and guilt moved through her. She told herself she had no reason to feel guilty. Ezra had made no bones about where he stood.

Or how much he wants me.

No. She wasn't going to do that to herself. She couldn't wait in the wings forever. Before she could overthink it, she said,

"He's not fair game. I think you're right and I inadvertently friend-zoned Flame. He's tall and dark, and I'm going to find out if he's delicious." That was much harder to say than she thought it would be, but she was determined to get over Ezra once and for all, no matter how much it hurt.

"My job here is done." Quinn tossed her hair over her shoulder with a little shimmy.

Birdie high-fived Quinn and said, "We're such a good team."

Sasha looked at them incredulously.

"Get that shocked look off your face," Quinn said. "It's time to get your flirt on. Flame's making a beeline for you."

"Holy shit. I need another drink."

"I've got it!" Birdie leaned over the bar. "Hey, Kellan! We need another round, *stat!*"

"Coming right up!" Kellan winked at Sasha as he refilled their glasses. "I don't know how I feel about you turning all that hotness on strangers when I'm right here in front of you."

She opened her mouth to respond, but a large hand landed on her lower back. Hope soared inside her. She looked over her shoulder, deflating as she realized it was Flame's hand, not Ezra's. *He* was standing beside Flame, jaw tight, eyes locked on her.

"We're hardly strangers," Flame said. "Right, Sasha?"

Quinn and Birdie were looking at her with hopeful expectance, silently urging her to flirt her heart out. With a gulp of courage, she met Flame's steady gaze. "We're definitely *not* strangers."

A slow grin slid across Flame's face. Ezra's jaw clenched so tight, it had to hurt.

Good. You should be jealous. You had your chance, and you

sent me away. He'd drawn his line in the sand, and he was right, so she needed to rip off the Band-Aid once and for all and see if she'd friend-zoned every other man, or she'd never move on.

"I see where I stand," Kellan teased. "What can I get you guys? A couple of beers?"

"*Yeah,*" Ezra gritted out.

"Sure, sounds good," Flame said, oblivious to the tension mounting between Sasha and Ezra.

Sasha went all in, trying to act normal with Ezra and maybe a little extra flirty with Flame because Ezra's refusal still stung. "Hey, Ez. I guess Tina showed up for Gus tonight?"

"Yeah," he said gruffly.

"That means Daddy came out to play," Birdie chimed in.

"We all have needs to fill, and this seems to be the place to do it," Sasha said, trying to ignore the green-eyed monster clawing at her.

Ezra's expression didn't change. "I came for a *drink.*"

She wanted to grab hold of that comment for all it was worth, but that wouldn't help either of them move on. She had to stick to the plan. "A drink, a sexy dance. A little…" She waggled her brows, turning a seductive smile on Flame. "You'd better save me a dance tonight, big guy."

Flame's gaze smoldered. "Baby, I'll save all my dances for you. Does this mean you're going to finally let me take you out sometime?"

"I guess we'll see how the dance goes," she teased.

He put his hands on her hips, and she felt Ezra's stare burning into her as Flame said, "I guarantee I've got all the right moves."

"I bet you do." She felt guilty leading him on, but she needed to figure out if she'd unknowingly friend-zoned herself out of butterflies or not.

"What's going on over *here?*" Taz asked as he and Hyde joined them.

Sasha didn't miss the curious—approving?—glances they shot Flame.

"We're doing shots," Birdie announced. "And they're flirting."

Ohmygod.

"I can see that," Hyde said.

"Uh-oh, double trouble is here," Bobbie said as she walked past and went around the bar.

"You should try us out sometime, beautiful." Hyde lifted his chin. "We're not double trouble. We're double your pleasure, double your fun."

Bobbie scoffed. "In your dreams. I don't want one of you, much less both of you."

"*Wait*, does he mean…?" Birdie's eyes widened, moving between Hyde and Taz. "You two *and* Bobbie? A threesome?"

"Or a foursome, if you want to take us for a ride, too," Taz suggested.

"Watch yourselves," Ezra warned gruffly.

Sasha liked his protectiveness over Birdie far more than she probably should, but she didn't need him fighting their battles. "Unless you want Cowboy to rip your heads off, Dare to shove them up your asses, and Doc to hide your bodies. I suggest you shut your mouths."

"Yeah, that wasn't cool," Flame said.

"Chill out," Taz said. "I'd never take Birdie into my bedroom."

"Why not? I'm hot," Birdie insisted.

"*Birdie*," Sasha chided her, but she knew it would do no

good. Birdie was as fierce as she was petite, and she never let anyone dismiss her.

Birdie planted a hand on her hip, eyes narrowing. "What? I *am* hot."

"You're smokin' hot, babe," Hyde said.

"See?" Birdie said defiantly, and turned a curious gaze on Hyde. "So, do you and Taz…?" She made kissing noises. "And…*you know*?" She waggled her brows.

"*Birdie.*" Sasha grabbed her by the arm. "Time to ride the mechanical bull." She heard Ezra and Flame giving the guys a hard time as she dragged Birdie away. "What were you thinking, egging them on like that?"

"I'm curious. Aren't you? I mean, Hyde *and* Taz?"

"No, I'm not curious, and stop thinking about them like that."

"Wait up!" Quinn hurried after them. "Why'd you drag her away? I wanted to know the answer."

"You guys are going to drive me nuts," Sasha said, exasperated. "They're into shit you don't need to know about." She'd heard things, and while she believed to each his own, she wasn't about to get into it with Birdie and Quinn.

"How do you know?" Quinn asked coyly.

Birdie gasped. "Have you been with them?"

"*No.* In case you haven't noticed, I've been a little preoccupied with *one* man, not two." Sasha and Birdie got into line for the mechanical bull, and Quinn stood off to the side. She never rode the bull. Sasha wasn't as good as Birdie, but she could hold her own, and right then, she'd take any reason to get out from under Ezra's watchful eyes.

"Maybe two *is* better," Birdie whispered. "If one isn't into you, the other might be."

"No more tequila for you." Sasha tried to divert Birdie's attention to the people around them. "Which one of these guys do you think will beat your time?"

Birdie eyed the men and women in line in front of them. "These city folks have no clue what they're in for. I feel sorry for their butts tomorrow." A clean-cut guy wearing a dress shirt, jeans, and shiny black shoes climbed onto the bull, and Birdie hollered, "*Woo-hoo!* You've got this." She lowered her voice. "He totally doesn't have it."

They cheered everyone on as men and women tried to one-up one another, each lasting only a few seconds before tumbling off, cracking up, or cursing. When it was Sasha's turn, Birdie and Quinn cheered her on as she mounted the bull.

Sasha couldn't resist scanning the crowd for Ezra. She spotted Flame walking over. He cupped his hands around his mouth, hollering, "Ride 'em, Sasha!" That's when she saw Ezra standing at the edge of the crowd, eyes trained on her, jaw tight as a vise. Something inside her snapped, twisting all that hurt and guilt into anger. *Why should I feel bad about having fun? He's the one who drew the line in the sand.*

She sat up taller, meeting his gaze. *Eat your heart out. I could have been yours.*

As she tightened her thighs on the sides of the mechanical bull, an errant thought about doing the same to Ezra flitted through her mind. Refusing to let it take hold, she shoved that thought away, slid her left hand under the leather strap, and wrapped her fingers around it—hating that her mind went straight to doing the same with a certain body part of Ezra's. It was definitely time to end that fantasy. She closed her eyes for a few seconds, inhaling deeply and exhaling slowly, doing her best to clear her mind and relax her upper body. Opening her eyes, she lifted her right hand for balance and gave Hardy, the bull operator, a nod, praying he wouldn't go too hard on her, and proceeded to put her all into showing Ezra what he was missing out on.

The crowd cheered as the ride started, slow and easy, giving Sasha time to get acclimated. *Thank you, Hardy.* It had been a while since she'd ridden the bull, but riding horses, some of whom liked to try to throw her off, gave her an advantage. As the speed increased and the violence of the bull's movements became more erratic, the crowd went wild. Sasha rode their high, adrenaline surging through her as the bull bucked and spun. She moved with it, earning more whoops, cheers, and whistles. She was vaguely aware of Flame's voice rising above the others and furiously aware of wishing it was Ezra's. She struggled against that thought, holding on for all she was worth as the speed increased even more. She didn't lose her balance or her concentration, and it felt fucking fantastic. She was elated, giddy with delight, as the crowd exploded into shouts and whistles. The bull spun faster, and that giddiness tripped her up. She keeled to one side and tumbled to the padded floor. Applause thundered around her, giving her another adrenaline rush as Birdie hollered, "Woo-hoo! That's my sister!"

Sasha was laughing as she came off the padded floor. Birdie and Quinn hugged her, and then Flame lifted her off her feet. "You were fucking awesome!"

She *felt* awesome. "I was, wasn't I?"

"Damn right you were." His eyes took on that hungry look guys got right before they kissed her.

Oh God. She wasn't ready. Thinking fast, she said, "We have to cheer for Birdie," wriggled out of his arms, and spun around to watch Birdie. Her eyes caught on Ezra on the other side of the crowd, looking like he wanted to kill someone. *Shitshitshit.*

"Let's go, Birdie!" Flame hollered, his body brushing against Sasha's back.

Sasha's mind ran in a dozen directions as they cheered for Birdie. She convinced herself to kiss Flame as many times as she convinced herself not to. If Birdie or one of their friends were in the situation she and Ezra were in, she'd tell them the guy was right to stop them before things got too complicated. So why was she having such a hard time accepting it?

After Birdie blew everyone away on the mechanical bull, they headed up to the bar for a round of shots. Birdie and Quinn veered off to talk to a couple of cute guys.

"Guess it's just us," Flame said. "Hey, Doc and Rebel made it."

She followed his gaze to Doc, Rebel, and Ezra, chatting with a group of women. Could tonight get any more uncomfortable?

Doc waved them over.

Yup. It sure can.

They joined them, and Sasha tried to act normal and keep up with the various conversations, while the attractive brunette Ezra was chatting with practically draped herself all over him. She wasn't a glutton for punishment. "I need a drink. I'll be right back."

"I'll get it," Flame offered.

"No, that's okay. Keep talking to the guys. I'll be right back."

Doc touched her arm, stopping her from walking away. "How're you getting home?"

"Uber," Sasha said.

"I've only had one beer, and I've got my truck," Flame said.

"I'll be sure she gets home safely."

Ezra looked like he had smoke coming out of his ears.

The nerve of him. Sasha flashed a flirty smile at Flame. "Thanks. I'll be right back."

She stewed as she made her way to the bar and was relieved to see Bobbie bartending.

Bobbie gave her a curious glance. "You look like you could use some tequila."

"A whole bottle might do it."

As she filled Sasha's glass, she glanced over Sasha's shoulder. "I can see why."

Bobbie walked away, and Sasha turned just as Ezra reached her. He stepped in so close, the air felt supercharged.

"What the hell are you doing?" he asked low and gruff.

"Getting a drink." She picked up her glass and showed him, as if she weren't at all affected by his close proximity or, she realized with a start, turned on by the jealousy rolling off him.

"You *know* what I'm talking about," he growled.

"I'm sorry, but I really don't. Maybe your latest conquest does." She lifted her chin and strode back to Flame, downing her liquid courage on the way.

Over the next half hour, she forced herself to focus on Flame. Not that it was a hardship. He was attentive, attractive, and sinfully good at flirting in a way that wasn't blatant enough to raise Doc's hackles. She was having a good time, but it was Ezra's eyes on her, not Flame's, that had butterflies swarming in her stomach.

"Country Girl (Shake It for Me)" came on, and she heard Birdie squeal seconds before Birdie and Quinn ran over to her.

"Come on!" Birdie exclaimed. "It's our song."

"Sorry, *Flame*," Quinn added pointedly.

They linked arms with Sasha, and the three of them rushed to the dance floor.

"What is going on over there?" Birdie asked as they danced. "That woman's all over Ezra, but he's looking at you."

"I wouldn't know. I'm with Flame tonight." Sasha sounded way more confident than she felt, but what was that saying? *Fake it until you make it?* That was her freaking motto tonight.

Quinn danced closer. "So you're going for it?"

"Maybe." She twirled around, unable to believe she'd said it, much less believe she was thinking about kissing Flame so she could finally get her answers.

"Ezra and Flame are *both* watching you," Birdie said. "Time to turn up the heat!"

They fell into their own version of dirty dancing. One that drew a lot of male attention and usually drove her brothers mad. The tequila had done its job. Sasha was in a rebellious mood, and she put everything she had into that dance, moving her hips and shoulders seductively. She flipped her hair over one shoulder, turning a lustful gaze in Flame's and Ezra's direction, letting them decide who it was meant for.

They danced to a few more songs, and when "Rock and a Hard Place" came on, Flame strode toward the dance floor, looking mighty fine.

"Excuse me, ladies." He took Sasha's hand, pulling her in close. "I believe you asked me to save you a dance."

"Yes, I did." She wound her arms around his neck, swaying to the music.

She saw Ezra walk past the dance floor, hands fisted, eyes blazing, causing the hurt, guilt, and anger inside her to coalesce with the tequila, making her all sorts of confused. She closed her eyes, focusing on the feel of the man she was dancing with and not the one making her heart hurt. Flame tightened his hold on her, and she felt every inch of his hard frame. He was a sensual dancer, his big hands moving up and down her back as his hips swayed against her. This was a man who knew how to use his body. Her pulse quickened. He was a good man and a good friend, and this was her chance to see if they should be more.

She gazed up at his chiseled, clean-shaven jaw, telling herself it was now or never. But when he gazed down at her with those sea-blue eyes and lowered his lips toward hers, her heart won out. "I need to use the ladies' room," she said, causing him to stop short of kissing her. "Sorry. Too much tequila."

"That's all right, darlin'. I'm not going anywhere."

"I'll be right back."

She hurried off the dance floor and saw Ezra watching her as she headed toward the hall that led to the ladies' room. Her pulse quickened as he fell into step beside her. He didn't say a word, but he didn't have to. Tension crackled in the air around them, hot and sharp and strangely intriguing. His fingers wrapped around her upper arm, tugging her past the entrance to the ladies' room, to the end of the hall, into a tight alcove that had an old pay phone attached to the wall.

She yanked her arm free, and he was *right there*. So close she could see fire in his eyes. "What do you think you're doing?"

"I was about to ask you the same question," he seethed, his chest brushing hers as her back met the wall.

Angry Ezra was so hot, her traitorous nipples rose to greet him. But that didn't matter. It was his fault her head was so messed up about other guys, and she was pissed. "What I do is *none* of your business."

"The fuck it isn't."

"In case you've forgotten, you had a chance with me, and

you didn't want it."

He leaned in, his mouth an inch from hers. "The fuck I didn't. I made my desire for you perfectly clear."

"That doesn't mean shit when you follow it up with *We can't do this.*"

He gritted his teeth, the muscles in his jaw bulging. "You don't belong with *him.*"

"You have some nerve telling me who I should be with. *He* doesn't turn me away or toy with my emotions. *He* will kiss me and *keep...on...going.*"

"Goddamn it, Sasha. You know I want you," he said through clenched teeth. "I just can't act on it and risk everything Gus has and needs."

The mention of Gus had her thundering heart hurting again. It took everything she had to say, "And I would never ask you to, so there's our answer. Good night, Ezra." She pushed past him and walked back to Flame.

Chapter Ten

AS EZRA NEARED the end of his four-mile trail run, his skin felt too tight, his head was too fucked up to think straight, and his goddamn heart felt like it had been put through a meat grinder. He wasn't a violent man, but if Flame were standing in front of him right now, he'd fucking tear him to pieces. Or die trying.

Sasha didn't come home last night.

He knew that because he'd been just fucked up enough to sit out front, watching for Flame's truck. He wasn't proud of that, but he couldn't have stopped himself if his life had depended on it. He ran faster, sprinting the last half mile, thinking about everything that had gone down last night for the millionth time. He was a prick for going off on Sasha the way he had, but a man could only take so much. It was one thing to see her flirting with Flame. He'd thought she was doing it to get under his skin, but when he'd seen her in Flame's arms on the dance floor, letting him touch her in that sexy outfit, he'd been too angry to be rational. Even now, in the light of day, that thought hit like shards of glass.

This was crazy. He prided himself on being a calm, rational person. He'd never even lost it or felt possessive of his own wife when she'd cheated on him. Then again, he'd never felt anything like he felt for Sasha toward Tina. He needed to get ahold of himself and fix this mess with Sasha before he fucked up things for Gus.

He slowed to a walk as he came to his pull-up tree at the end of the trail. He did thirty pull-ups, but they did nothing to loosen the knots in his chest. He dragged his forearm across his sweaty brow and walked off the trail. Dropping to the grass, he did fifty push-ups and a hundred sit-ups, hoping they might take the edge off, but he knew better. He'd done a grueling weight workout before his run, and he was still fit to be tied.

Pushing to his feet, he took off his shirt and wiped his face and chest with it as he made his way across the grassy knoll toward the road where he and Sasha lived. As he came up the hill, Sasha's truck came into view in front of her cabin.

Gripping his shirt in his fist, he headed up to her porch and knocked, ready to face the music. His pulse raced as minutes ticked by like hours. He had the uncomfortable thought that she could be in the shower, washing off Flame's scent. Fury boiled inside him, and that made him an even bigger prick, because he wasn't only angry about Flame. He didn't want her with *anyone* else. He knew he should get his arms around that before going looking for her, but fuck it. He headed down to the barn, where he really fucking hoped he'd find her.

As he traipsed across the grass, he told himself not to be an asshole. He'd had the same thought when he'd come to the ranch as a teenager, but the minute he'd seen Sasha, all his good intentions had gone out the window, and *Hey, Bo Peep, how about a roll in the hay* had rolled off his tongue. How could one woman wreak havoc with his sanity for so many years?

He saw horses in the smaller rehab paddocks and a couple in catch pens and knew Sasha had to be there. She loved the horses as much as she loved Gus. His chest constricted with thoughts of his son. Part of him wished Tina hadn't picked Gus up for the weekend. Then he could have been oblivious to Sasha's whereabouts last night. Hell, part of him wished they'd never kissed, so they could go back to the friendship he cherished.

He headed into the first rehab barn and found Sully standing in front of a stall, talking to a horse. "Hey, Ezra. Is Gus with you?" She peered around him.

"No," he said curtly. "He's with his mother for the weekend."

"I wanted to tell him that we framed the picture he drew for me and hung it up in the living room." Sully and Cowboy's walls were filled with Sully's sketches and photographs of their families and close friends on the ranch.

"He'll be thrilled to know he's made your wall." Their love for Gus was a great reminder of why he needed to keep his emotions in check. "I'm looking for Sasha. Is she around?"

"Yeah. She's in the other barn."

"Thanks. I'll see you later."

His nerves kicked up as he headed into the other barn, but he was determined to apologize and make things right. Stifling the urge to call out for her, knowing it might startle the horses, he scanned each stall as he walked past and was saddened by the poor state of some of the rescues. He knew they would thrive under Sasha's care.

Just like Gus and I did when we came to the ranch.

The tack room door was ajar. He saw Sasha standing on her tiptoes in those cute maroon boots, her T-shirt inching up as she stretched to reach a shelf. Her hair was loose and a little tousled, and she wore his favorite cutoffs. The ones that were a little too big and hung low on her hips. They had a rip above the left back pocket, revealing a sliver of skin. But those cutoffs reminded him of last night and the way Flame's hands had moved along her back. That reminder unleashed another surge of emotions. Jealousy and desire went head-to-head with his rational thoughts. He tried to maintain control as he stepped into the room, but when she turned around, her hair swinging over one shoulder, surprise and a glimmer of lust shimmering in her eyes, all bets were off.

"Ezra" flew breathily from her lips, her gaze falling to his bare chest.

"We need to talk." He closed the door and turned the lock, dropping his shirt to the floor. He didn't want any distractions.

"Why did you lock the door?"

"Because we're not leaving this room until we figure this out." He left no room for negotiation, closing the distance between them. He didn't miss the way her gaze trailed down his body as he neared. "Sorry I was an ass at the bar."

She nodded and licked her lips as if her mouth suddenly went dry.

"You didn't come home last night."

Her gaze flicked up to his. "How do you know?"

She didn't deny it, and jealousy slammed into him like a bullet train, obliterating any chance at rationality. "Did you fuck him?"

"We're not doing this."

"Yes, we are." He needed answers or he was going to lose his fucking mind, and it wasn't fair to ask, much less demand, but he was *done* being the guy who did the right thing with her. He pressed in closer, holding her gaze. "Did you *fuck* him?"

"*Ezra*," she said pleadingly.

"You know you don't want anyone else touching you but me. I see it in your eyes. I felt it when we kissed." He didn't know where that claim came from, but she swallowed hard, and the wanting look in her eyes told him it was true. "Did he fill your *needs* last night?" he gritted out. "Did you let him touch you the way you want *me* to touch you?" He skimmed his hand up her torso and brushed the side of her breast, feeling her shudder as "*Ez*" fell from her lips. "Did you let him do this?" He slid his hand along the nape of her neck and grabbed a fistful of her hair, tilting her face up to his.

She was breathing hard, her eyes darkening with desire.

He lowered his lips closer to hers. "Did he kiss you deep and hard the way I did? Did you moan and writhe for him the way you did for me?"

"*Ezra, please*," she whispered.

Fighting the urge to kiss her, he cupped her face with his other hand, brushing his thumb along her cheek. "You're too damn beautiful. You fucking kill me, Sasha." He pressed his thumb to her lower lip. "Did you let him *fuck* your pretty mouth?"

Her jaw dropped, and something between an appalled and curious sound fell out.

He knew he should stop, but he was too far gone. Tightening his grip on her hair, he lowered the hand from her cheek and palmed her breast, teasing her nipple through her shirt. "Did you let him put his mouth on these gorgeous tits the way you want *me* to?"

A needy moan slipped from her lips.

He dropped his hand, trailing his fingers up her inner thigh.

"Did he make you wet like I do?" The longing in her eyes spurred him on, and he teased the sensitive skin beneath the hem of her shorts. "I bet you're wet for me right now."

Her breathing hitched, and she touched his chest, her trembling fingers playing over his nipple as she whispered, "*God...*"

"Like what you feel, Bo Peep?" He leaned closer, brushing his scruff along her cheek, rasping, "Do you ache for me the way I ache for you?"

"*Yes*" fell needily from her lips, her eyes closing.

"Open your eyes. I want you to see the man who's going to make you come." Her eyes opened, so full of desire, his cock ached for her.

"*I see you,*" she said in one long, heated breath. "I *want* you."

He was hanging on to his control by a thread, but he needed to make sure they were on the same page. "I can't promise you more than a good time, and if anyone finds out, our lives could go up in flames."

"I never asked for more, and what goes on between us is nobody else's business."

"If I touch you, no other man does for as long as we're doing this. Is that clear?"

"*Yes. That's what I want.*"

He opened her shorts, holding her gaze as he pushed his hand into her underwear. His fingers slid through her arousal, earning a sexy moan from her and a growl from him. He cupped her sex. "This is *mine.*"

She nodded. "*Yours.*"

He pushed his fingers inside her, and a sensual sound fell from her lips. Thoughts of her doing that for Flame gnawed at him. He tried to push them away as he teased her clit and dragged his tongue along her lower lip. "This mouth is *mine*. No one tastes my Whiskey but *me*."

"*Yes.*"

He crushed his mouth to hers, kissing her roughly and possessively, trying to chase away the need for answers, but as he worked her into a moaning, writhing frenzy, all those unanswered questions hung over his head as dark and thunderous as a mounting storm. She was clinging to him, moaning and rocking, so fucking close to coming he could taste it. He stilled his hand, tearing his mouth away to demand an answer, but before he could, she said, "Ezra, *please*."

His need to pleasure her, to feel her lose control for *him*, overrode his need for answers. He grabbed a fistful of her hair, tugging her head back, and then remembered where they were and gritted out, "Don't scream too loud, Bo Peep." He slanted his mouth over hers, devouring her as he gave her what she needed.

What they both craved.

He was high on the taste of her luscious mouth and the feel of her tight heat riding his hand. He ached to bury his cock deep inside her. When she went up on her toes, on the verge of her climax, he tore his mouth away and sank his teeth into her neck. "*Ezra—*" flew from her lips loud and untethered. It was music to his ears, but knowing it could be death to his job, he reclaimed her mouth, swallowing the rest of her sounds as she bucked and writhed, her pussy pulsing around his fingers. He stayed with her, easing their kisses as she came down from the peak, and growled, "*Again*," and lowered his mouth to hers.

"Sasha?" a male voice called out from somewhere in the barn.

They froze, Sasha's eyes blooming wide with worry. *Fuck.*

Ezra quickly pulled his hand out of her shorts and buttoned them. She watched him suck his fingers clean, hunger battling with the worry in her eyes. Her hair was a mess from his hand, her cheeks flushed, her lips pink and swollen from their kisses. He smoothed her hair, whispering urgently, "You're gorgeous, but you look freshly fucked."

"Shit." As she shook out her hair. "Ez…?"

"Yeah?"

She pointed to his erection.

"Fuck." He grabbed his shirt from the floor and put it on, but it wasn't long enough to hide his raging cock.

"Sasha?" the male voice called out again, nearing the door.

"It's *Doc*," they whispered in unison.

She shoved Ezra toward the bathroom and unlocked the door to the tack room, whispering, "Go. Quick."

He hurried into the bathroom and heard the tack room door open.

"Hey. What're you doing in here?" Doc asked.

"I was putting tack away, but I knocked stuff off the shelf, and it took forever to put it back. I need to check on the horses. Walk with me."

Smart.

Ezra leaned his palms on the sink, staring at himself in the mirror. The rebellious bad boy she brought out in him grinned like a fucking beast, but the responsible father and therapist told him he was playing with fire.

Chapter Eleven

SASHA TRIED TO pay attention to the conversations going on around her at dinner, but her heart was racing, and her stomach was all knotted up. She'd been on edge all day, hoping to see or hear from Ezra so they could talk. But he hadn't sought her out, and now, while she could barely eat, he sat beside her acting totally normal, eating barbecue ribs like he hadn't said dirty things to her and made her come just a few hours earlier. *This* was the Ezra she knew. The calm, sensible, unflappable single father and therapist, so different from the jealous, lustful, *hungry* beast she'd gotten a delicious taste of in the barn. She hadn't even known she'd like a guy who was that aggressive and said filthy things that made her panties melt. Maybe she wouldn't like it if he were anyone else, but sitting so close to him brought it all rushing back.

How did he turn off his desire so easily? Was it because he was experienced with meaningless hookups? *Oh no.* Was what they'd done in the tack room a onetime thing?

Was all that talk about what he was going to do to her just to rev her up for what he'd been hoping to do to her in the tack room before they were interrupted? Was that why he'd really locked the door?

Great. Now she was thinking about him doing those things to her. She chugged ice water and glanced around the table to see if anyone noticed she was frying from the inside out.

Cowboy tore a piece of meat off a rib with his teeth and arched a brow at Doc, who was cutting his meat off the bone with a fork and knife. "What the hell are you doing?"

"What does it look like I'm doing?" Doc said.

"Afraid of ruining your manicure?" Cowboy asked.

"No, asshole. I have a date, and I don't want to get my shirt dirty."

Ezra leaned forward to see around Sasha and said, "Where are you taking her?"

How could he act so normal when she was losing her mind? She remembered what he'd said about fucking women senseless and never seeing them again and couldn't help but wonder if in his mind this was the same kind of situation despite what he'd said about nobody else touching her. Those knots in her stomach tightened.

"We're going"—Doc glanced around the table at the girls—"*bowling.*"

"Yeah, right," Billie said sarcastically. "It's a hookup." She bit into a rib.

"Bowling is more fitting, since he's going to strike out anyway." Cowboy snickered.

Sasha needed to get out of her own head and went for a distraction. "Remember that time Doc asked out the girl at the bowling alley and she turned him down?"

"Oh yeah. I remember that," Cowboy said. "He refused to go bowling for months after that."

"Didn't we miss a bowling birthday party because of him?" Dare asked.

The banter wasn't helping. She got up to refill her drink, hoping a little distance would make it easier for her to act normal. As she filled her glass, her father walked over to refill his.

"Hi, darlin'. You okay? You look like you've got something on your mind."

"Me? No. I'm good. I was thinking about something I forgot to order from the feed store."

"A'right. Doc mentioned a cat was chasing mice in the rehab barn. From the look on your face, I was worried they were causing trouble."

Her nerves flared, and her mother's voice trampled through her mind. *Your father might be a big man, but he's as stealthy and as clever as the day is long.* She felt like she was ten years old again, getting caught faking sick to stay home from school. Did he know about her and Ezra? Did Doc? *No way.* Doc would have called her out if he had. Wouldn't he? Yes. Of course he would. She was just being paranoid.

"Nope. No trouble. Everything is good."

"I'm glad to hear it." He put his hand on her back. "Any rascals give you grief, you tell your old man, and I'll take care of them. Enjoy the ribs, darlin'."

As he headed back to his table, she tried to pick her jaw up off the floor. She needed to pull herself together. There was no way anyone could know about her and Ezra.

Her phone chimed as she made her way back to her seat. She set her glass on the table and checked the text as she sat down.

Ezra: *I can still taste you.*

Her pulse spiked, and her cheeks burned. She stole a glance at him, unable to believe he'd send something like that when they were surrounded by her family and everyone else.

He had a wicked glint in his eyes as he licked barbecue sauce off his fingers.

She tore her gaze away for fear of spontaneously combusting and looked around the table again to see if anyone noticed her morphing to liquid heat. At this rate, she'd slip off the chair into a puddle before dinner was over. Luckily, her brothers were caught up in giving each other a hard time, and the girls were laughing at them.

Ezra pressed his leg against hers under the table, bringing her eyes back to his. He flashed a charming boyish grin, so different from the wickedness he'd radiated only seconds ago. Her heart pounded faster, trying to keep up.

How could something as middle school as their legs touching feel as taboo as the dirty text?

LATER THAT NIGHT, she was still trying to keep her mind off Ezra while folding laundry and talking to Bobbie on speakerphone. She'd hoped she might see him tonight, but she hadn't heard a peep from him since he'd taken off after dinner. Gus was supposed to be with his mother until Sunday afternoon, but she wondered if he'd been dropped off early.

"I can't believe you didn't take a spin on Flame's fire pole," Bobbie said.

"He's not a fireman. He's a smoke jumper, and I just wasn't feeling it."

"That's too bad. He'd be the perfect friend with benefits."

She hadn't told Bobbie what had happened with Ezra at the bar last night or anything that had happened since, but friends with benefits seemed to be the right label for her and Ezra, so she tiptoed carefully through the door her friend had opened. "Have you ever done the friends-with-benefits thing?"

"No, but Cindy is doing it right now. I told you about her and her neighbor." Cindy was another teacher Bobbie worked with.

"I forgot about that. I didn't know they were still seeing each other. Didn't they start hooking up last Christmas?"

"Yes, and she loves their arrangement. She said it's better than a regular relationship because there's no pressure."

This was a hundred times worse than a relationship for Sasha. It hadn't even been one day and she was already losing her mind. "It sounds more complicated to me. How does it work? Do they have set days or times when they get together, or is it spur of the moment? Does she wait for him to call or make the first move?"

"She said she calls him when she wants a booty call, and he calls her when he's in the mood."

Sasha couldn't imagine texting or calling Ezra and saying, *Hey, want to come over and fool around?* No matter how much she wanted to. But did she want to? She did at dinner, but now she was annoyed at him for leaving her hanging. Shouldn't there be some sort of follow-up after messing around for the first time? A text or a phone call?

"They also see other people," Bobbie said.

"Oh." Sasha's heart sank. She hadn't thought about that. Ezra had made it clear that he didn't want anyone else touching her, but what about *him*? Was he with someone else tonight?

Did he text her at dinner just to string her along? To make sure she remained one of his hookup girls? She was usually more confident with guys. Heck, she'd even been the one to teach Birdie all her tricks. Like when a guy asked for sexy pictures, she'd taught her to put a bra on her knees and take the picture from the perfect angle to make them look like her boobs. So why was she insecure with Ezra?

"Are you sure you don't want to come out with me tonight? You might meet someone new."

"I'm not in the mood. I already changed into comfy clothes and washed my face. I think I'm going to watch a movie and lie low." *And try to figure out what to do about Ezra.*

"Okay. If you change your mind, text me."

After they ended the call, Sasha put away her laundry and went into the kitchen to make popcorn. Maybe she could eat her worries away. Her gaze caught on Gus's drawings hanging on the refrigerator, and her chest constricted. She glanced at the arts-and-crafts area she'd set up for him in the corner of the kitchen. The cubbies were bursting with art supplies and toys. Swamped with emotions, she put a bag of popcorn in the microwave and scrounged through her pantry for M&M's. *Great.* She was out of them. If ever there was a time she needed junk food, it was tonight.

She dumped the popcorn into a bowl and headed into the living room.

Unlike Doc and Cowboy, who had built larger houses on the ranch, and Dare, who had taken over a rustic cabin that had been there forever, Sasha lived in a modest three-bedroom cabin with an open floor plan and cathedral ceilings. It had bleached hardwood floors, whitewashed walls with scalloped trim, and large picture windows overlooking a small grassy yard. Her couches were off-white, with pink, white, and mint-green pillows, which matched the distressed mint-green coffee and end tables and the white cabinets in the open kitchen.

She padded across the floral area rug in front of the fireplace and snagged the remote as she plunked down on the couch with the bowl of popcorn. Flipping through the movies she'd saved in her profile, she came to *He's Just Not That into You*. She definitely wasn't watching that, but it gave her an idea. She searched for *Friends with Benefits*, hoping the movie might teach her a thing or two.

She settled back against the cushions to watch the movie and was startled when her phone chimed with a text. Her pulse quickened at the sight of Ezra's name on the screen.

Ezra: *Hey. Are you home?*

Sasha: *Yes. Why?*

Ezra: *We should talk.*

She stared at the message, her stomach sinking. Had he taken time to think about what they'd done and decided it was a mistake? *Nonono.* She couldn't think like that. He'd said they needed to talk in the tack room, too, but they hadn't talked at all. Well, he did, but she'd been too stunned by his sudden jealousy, desire, and all that dirty talk to speak.

Sasha: *Talk with words or like we talked in the tack room?* Her thumb hovered over the screen for a few seconds before she got up the nerve to send it.

Ezra: *Do I have to choose?*

Relief and happiness bubbled up inside her, but she tried to act casual.

Sasha: *No. What's up?*

Ezra: *I have a problem.*

Sasha: *??*

She held her breath.

Ezra: *I can't stop thinking about all the dirty things I want to do to you.*

A thrill skittered through her. She started to respond but thought better of it. He'd left her hanging all day, not knowing where they stood. She wasn't going to let him off that easy. It was time for a little payback. She ate some popcorn and watched the movie for a good five minutes before responding.

Sasha: *Ezra, this is Wynnie. Sasha is in the bathroom. This is very inappropriate. I'd like to meet with you tomorrow morning.*

Three little dots danced on the screen like he was typing. They disappeared. Seconds passed like minutes. She was about to text and say she was kidding when the dots reappeared.

Ezra: *That's not funny.*

She sent a laughing emoji.

Ezra: *I'm going to have to punish you.*

Sasha: *Time-out?*

Ezra: *No, Bo Peep. When I get my hands on you, you're not getting ANY time-outs.*

Her body heated.

Sasha: *That's hardly a punishment. I might have to be naughty more often.*

A devil emoji popped up, and she couldn't stop grinning.

Ezra: *Can I see you?*

She turned off the movie and pushed to her feet, thumbing out, *Yes. When?* as she headed to her bedroom to change her clothes.

Ezra: *Open the door, Bo Peep. I'm here.*

She stood stock-still in the middle of the living room. She wasn't ready. She quickly pulled the clip from her hair and shook it out. A knock sounded at the door, sending her body into a flurry of anxious anticipation. *Shootshootshoot.* She looked down at her cotton shorts and faded pink sweatshirt as another knock rang out. This was *not* how she wanted to greet him for their first time alone since the tack room, but with no time to change and her thundering heart making it difficult for her to think, she forced a deep breath, reminding herself he'd seen her in worse, and went to answer the door.

Chapter Twelve

HOLY HOTNESS. EZRA stood before her, holding a paper bag and looking deliciously handsome in a gray T-shirt and jeans, his dark eyes taking a slow stroll down the length of her. Her nipples pebbled beneath his heated gaze. A devilish grin curved his lips, and she remembered she wasn't wearing a bra, making her even more nervous.

"Hey, Sash."

"Hi." She absently touched her hair, feeling a little awkward and embarrassed. "Sorry I didn't have time to change or do my hair or anything."

"You look as beautiful as ever."

The sincerity in his voice helped ease her discomfort.

"Are you going to invite me in?"

"Yes. *Sorry.* Come in." She stepped aside, and as he walked in, it felt like he'd sucked all the air from the foyer.

He reached over, putting his hand on hers on the doorknob, and closed the door. "Nervous?"

"A little," she admitted.

"I might have something to help with that." He reached

into the bag and lifted out a six-pack of Truly hard seltzer.

She smiled. "Thanks. That was really nice of you, but I think I'm too nervous to enjoy it."

"Then maybe these will help." He pulled out a big bag of peanut M&M's and cocked a brow.

She loved how well he knew her. "Now, *those* will do the trick, but I still need a minute before I can eat them."

"They're here when you're ready." He set the paper bag on the floor. "Listen, Sash. I'm sorry I was so aggressive this afternoon. I really did come by the barn just to talk, but I knew you hadn't come home last night, and when I saw you, I was consumed with jealousy, and I lost it. That wasn't fair to you, and I'm sorry. I don't even know how it happened. I've never felt this way before. It's like you unleash some sort of jealous beast in me."

She was touched by his apology. "You didn't hear me complaining, did you? I liked the way you were in the barn, and I like knowing I bring that out in you, but I owe you an apology, too. I haven't exactly been acting very mature. It wasn't fair of me to shut you out the way I did, but I was trying to move on, and it was too hard to see you and feel what I do."

"That drove me crazy."

"I'm sorry. I was trying to save my sanity, but it got us here, so maybe it's not a bad thing." She hooked her finger in the front pocket of his jeans. "But you should know that I didn't do anything with Flame."

His brows knitted. "But you didn't come home last night. Weren't you with him?"

She shook her head. "I slept at Birdie's. Flame's a great guy and a good friend to everyone here. I couldn't use him to try to get over you." She'd told Birdie what had happened with Ezra at the bar, but she'd sworn her to secrecy. Birdie had said she was proud of her for standing her ground. She hadn't spoken to her sister since, and although she was dying to share her secret, she'd already decided she wouldn't tell her anything more. If anyone found out, she didn't want Birdie to get in trouble, too.

He shook his head, smiling. "I'm a selfish bastard, because that makes me so fucking happy."

She laughed softly. "I guess that's good, but I have to be honest. I don't know how to do whatever this is we're doing. I've been a nervous wreck all day. I wasn't sure if you wanted to see me tonight or not, and all sorts of things have been going through my head. I don't want to assume anything, but not knowing is hard for me. I know you have experience with this, but—"

He silenced her with a soft press of his lips. "I don't have experience with this, either," he rasped against her lips. "I don't usually hook up with friends."

Friends. That's the clarification she needed, and it stung a little.

He tucked her hair behind her ear, his dark eyes peering deeply into hers as he caressed her cheek. "I wanted to text you and tell you I was thinking about you. Honestly, I wanted to go back to the barn and drag you into the tack room again and finish what we'd started. But we both have a lot at risk. I had to get my head on straight and think things through. I've been wrestling with that all day. I feel guilty because your mother is my boss and your father is the president of the club, and they trust me."

"They trust me, too," she pointed out. "But it's their stupid rule that's making us keep this a secret. I know it's bigger than that because of Gus, and he's the most important part of all of this, but unless you tell my parents about everyone you hook up with, I wouldn't bother feeling guilty. It's none of their business how we spend our free time. It's not like it's going to affect *how* we do our jobs."

"That's a fair point, and one I needed to hear. But the other thing I'm wrestling with is that you deserve more than a secret affair or a friend with benefits, or whatever you want to call us, Sasha, and I wish I could give that to you."

So did she, but she knew he was right in wanting to keep this a secret. No matter how intimate things felt, they did have a lot at risk, and this couldn't be more than what they'd agreed upon without upending all their lives. It wasn't ideal, but she'd rather have some of him than none of him. "What I deserve is to be with a man I truly *want* to be with, even if it's only in private, and I want to be with you."

"I want you more than you can imagine, but are you *sure* you're cool with this? I don't want you to resent me down the road."

"You're not making my decision for me, Ez. How could I resent you? I know it's not going to be easy, but I've enjoyed the benefits I've already reaped, and if this is all we can ever be, then I'm going to enjoy every second of whatever is yet to come."

"Not easy is an understatement." He shook his head. "You have no idea how hard it was for me to keep my hands off you at dinner. I couldn't resist sending you that text so you'd know you were on my mind, but after I did, the urge to drag you down the hall and into my office was so strong, I had to get away to clear my head."

I would have preferred the office. "I'm glad you texted, but when you disappeared, I thought maybe you had changed your mind or went to see someone else."

His brows slanted. "Why would I do that?"

She shrugged one shoulder. "You said you didn't want anyone else touching me, but we never talked about you."

"Sasha, I'm not a dick. I would never do that to you. If we're together, I'm not going to be with anyone else, and you can assume I want to see you whenever it's safe for us to do so. I went for a drive to fucking counsel myself and get my head on straight."

Now, *that* was very Ezra. "And what did Ezra the therapist say?"

He grabbed her hips, drawing her closer. "That he can't keep his hands off you, either."

"I like the way Ezra the therapist thinks."

He kissed her softly and trapped her lower lip between his teeth, giving it a tug. "Or his mouth."

She'd been taken by surprise in the barn. This time she was fully present, hyperaware of every little thing. The desire in his voice, the heat in his gaze, the way her body thrummed with anticipation. But mostly, she was thankful that he'd taken that time to think them through as much as she had, even if that silence had driven her nuts. While jealous and impetuous Ezra was exciting and sexy, rational Ezra was even more so, because she knew he'd not only given his heart time to weigh in, he'd also listened to it.

"Then *don't*," she said breathily.

He lowered his mouth to hers in a kiss that started slow and sweet, gaining momentum from both of them until it was deep and penetrating. Her body pulsed with need as he laced their hands together, growling against her lips. "I've been thinking about doing this all day." He drew her arms over her head, holding them against the wall as he took her in another mind-numbing kiss that had her entire body vibrating. "Once I get my hands on you, I'm not going to stop until I've touched and tasted every inch of your beautiful body and I'm buried deep inside you."

The desire in his voice emboldened her. "Good, because if what you did in the barn drove me wild, I can only imagine how good everything else will feel."

He recaptured her mouth, taking her in another passionate kiss. She bowed off the wall, rubbing against him. His hips pressed forward, his erection hard and tempting against her belly. He nudged her knees open wider without breaking their kiss or letting go of her hands, then lowered his hips, grinding his hard length against her. Heat spread like wildfire through her body. She moaned, trying to move with him, but he was grinding against her so perfectly, the friction had her going up on her toes, chasing the titillating sensations. A low, guttural sound climbed up his throat, and he intensified their kisses. His tongue delved deeper, forcing her mouth to open wider, like he wanted to possess *all* of it. All of *her*. Between the pain and pleasure of his demanding kisses and the feel of his erection pressing against her, she couldn't hold on to a single thought. He brought her wrists together, holding them with one hand above her head, and tore his mouth away, both of them breathing hard. His eyes bored into her as he pushed a hand beneath her shirt, teasing her breast. She closed her eyes, desire stacking up inside her. His breath left his lungs with a sound of relief that washed through her. He brushed his lips over hers, whispering gruffly, "I feel like I can finally fucking breathe again."

"Me too." She opened her eyes, struck by the emotions in his as he lifted her sweatshirt, and lowered his mouth to tease her nipple. She moaned at the feel of his hot, wet tongue sliding over the taut peak. When he sucked it to the roof of his mouth, pleasure radiated through her. *"Ohgod—"*

"Are you wet for me, Bo Peep?"

"As wet for you as you are hard for me." She could hardly believe she'd said it. But she wasn't going to be meek and miss out on a damn thing.

"Where has this little vixen been hiding?"

She grinned. "I guess you unleash the animal in me, too."

"You're so damn sexy." He brushed his scruff over her cheek, sending prickles of heat skating over her skin as he pushed down her shorts and panties with one hand, leaving them puddled at her feet. "Step out of them." She did as he asked, desperate for his touch. She didn't have to wait. His thick fingers slid through her wetness. "I want to do so many things to you right now, but I'm not going to rush." He rubbed his fingers over her clit, slid them through her wetness, and pushed two fingers inside her. She gasped at the pleasure gripping her. "You like that, baby?"

"Yes."

He held her gaze, making no move to kiss her as his fingers slid up to her clit again, then lower, pushing inside her, stroking over that hidden spot with deathly precision. He continued the mesmerizing pattern, moving excruciatingly slowly, hitting all the right spots, while holding her arms captive above her head. She felt laid bare, like he could see all the way into her soul, which turned her on even more. Every slide of his fingers sent rivers of heat slithering through her. Her eyes fluttered closed again. "Look at me, baby," he said coaxingly, and she opened her eyes. "That's my girl."

My girl. She told herself not to take those special words to heart, but her brain wasn't listening, and she tucked them away for safekeeping.

He brushed his lips over hers, but he didn't kiss her, didn't speak as his fingers drove her to the edge of madness. He just gazed deeply into her eyes. She sensed that he could feel every scintillating sensation he caused. Every time the tips of his fingers brushed her clit, sparks seared through her core, causing a sharp inhalation, and he lingered there a little longer. His every stroke earned more unstoppable, needy sounds from her and greedy, hungry sounds from him that caused her entire body to ignite. There was something erotic about letting him touch her while he watched. While he learned what she liked, teasing her until her pussy throbbed and her nipples burned. She should probably be embarrassed, but he was so focused on her pleasure, those dark eyes studying her, reacting to her body, *her* desires, she felt empowered and beautiful.

"That's it, baby. Feel the need building inside you? Feel your pussy aching for me?"

"*Yes*," she panted out.

"I want you to think about how good I make you feel every time you walk through your door."

She realized with a start that they were still in her foyer, and she knew she would think of him every single time she walked through it. She hadn't been able to even go into the barn that afternoon without thinking about what they'd done.

He quickened his efforts, rubbing and stroking until her eyes slammed shut, her hips shot off the wall, and his name flew from her lips. "That's it," he said gruffly, his voice full of restraint. "You're so fucking beautiful when you come for me." He continued touching, taunting, and praising her as her orgasm ravaged her. When she went limp, he released her wrists, pulling her into his strong arms, and slanted his mouth over hers. He breathed air into her depleted lungs, kissing her so thoroughly, she came away dizzy. "Still with me, baby?"

"Barely," she whispered.

He kissed her tenderly. "Maybe this will give you a second wind."

He dropped to his knees, splayed his hands over her inner thighs, and buried his mouth between them. *Ohmy…* She clung to his shoulders as he feasted on her, his scruff abrading her skin, heightening her arousal and sending overwhelming pleasure coursing through her.

"So fucking sweet," he gritted out.

Every slick of his tongue, every suck and nip, sent pinpricks chasing over her skin. When he brought his fingers into play, she dug her fingernails into his shoulders, rocking against his mouth. *"Yes. Don't stop. So good."* He intensified his efforts, licking, sucking, and teasing as his fingers invaded her, pumping and stroking her most sensitive nerves. When he sealed his mouth over her clit, it sent her careening into ecstasy. She cried out, consumed with pleasure so intense, she could barely breathe. She bucked and writhed, and he stayed with her, keeping her at the peak for so long she was sure she'd pass out. As she started to catch her breath, he did something incredible with his tongue, sending another hailstorm of sensations raining down on her. She clung to him, trying to steady herself as the world spun away, and she had no choice but to give herself over to the blissful pleasures engulfing her.

This time when she floated down from the high, he rose to his full height and took her face between his strong hands. "You taste so fucking good, I'm going to taste you in my sleep." He kissed her slowly and deeply, her arousal mixing with the unique taste of him. "Guess who's just become obsessed with pleasuring you."

God, the things he said…

He took her in another sensual kiss, making love to her mouth, his tongue sweeping and dipping, making her want and need and *crave* so much more. When he drew back, brushing his thumb over her lower lip, he said, "I'm going to do very dirty things to this sweet mouth one day." He pressed his warm lips beside her ear. "Is that too much for you, Bo Peep?"

"No. I want that." She didn't know who this brazen woman was speaking for her. She'd never enjoyed giving oral sex, but she had a feeling she'd enjoy everything with Ezra, and now she was hungry for him.

He kissed her again, slow and sweet and just as passionately. "I think we're in trouble, Sash," he said huskily.

"Why?"

"I have a feeling I'm going to be obsessed with a lot of things about you."

She'd waited her whole life to be wanted by him, and this was so much bigger. "I hope so," she said as he lifted her into his arms and carried her into the bedroom. "I'd tell you I can walk, but I'm not sure my legs would work."

"I'll take that as a compliment." He set her down beside the bed and kissed her again, slowly and sweetly. He gently took off her sweatshirt, tossing it to the floor, and took a long, lascivious look at her naked body. "You are absolutely stunning."

Her cheeks burned.

"That blush makes you even sexier." He lowered his lips to hers in a sweet kiss before reaching over his back and pulling off his shirt.

"My turn." She went for the button on his jeans.

A Taste of Whiskey

He covered her hand with his and brought it to his mouth, kissing her palm. "I've got it, sweetheart." He pulled a string of condoms from his back pocket and tossed them on the bed.

"Wow. I guess you knew I was a sure thing." She was on birth control, but she was glad he'd thought to protect them both.

"*No.* I was hoping we'd end up here, and I didn't want to show up unprepared, but I wasn't expecting it." He brushed his lips over hers, speaking huskily. "It's been a while for me, so I had to buy a box of condoms, and I knew if we ended up here, one or two wouldn't be enough."

"But *six* was the right number?" she teased.

"Don't worry, baby. I won't shortchange you. The rest of the box is in the bag with the drinks."

They both laughed. He pulled her in for another kiss, turning their laughter into greedy moans. He made quick work of ridding himself of his boots and stripping down to his black boxer briefs. His erection strained against the dark cotton, the broad head trapped beneath the waistband. Aching to touch him, to taste him, and feel him lose control for *her*, she reached over and tugged them down, freeing his erection. He was even more beautiful than she'd imagined. Her heart hammered as he stepped out of them and drew her into his arms, kissing her so deeply, her entire being vibrated with desire. The feel of his nakedness against her brought a whole new level of arousal and unexpected urgency.

"I want to taste you," she said feverishly, and palmed his thick cock, earning a rough moan. His skin was hot and smooth, but it was the salacious look in his eyes that had her salivating as she dropped to her knees before him. She licked his length, and he groaned hungrily. She wrapped her fingers

141

around his thickness, swirling her tongue over the broad crown, teasing the slit. His jaw clenched, his eyes boring into her. She continued teasing him, licking and stroking.

He buried his hands in her hair. "That feels good, baby."

His praise spurred her on, and she lowered her mouth over him, earning a gruff "*Fuuck.*" She sucked and stroked, chasing her mouth with her fist as she took him deeper. "That's it. Take what you want." She quickened her efforts. His eyes blazed into hers as his hands tightened in her hair, causing a pinch of pain that quickly morphed into erotic pleasure. She moaned around his shaft, and he uttered a curse. It was so damn hot, so empowering, she did it again, craving the greedy sound. His hips shot forward, and she continued stroking him faster and tighter as she sucked and licked. "*Baby...fuck...Sasha.*"

Loving the feral look in his eyes, the restraint cording his muscles, she didn't relent. He grabbed the base of his cock, stilling her head with his other hand. "Your mouth is fucking heaven, but I want to finish inside you." The greed in his voice amped up her desire as he lifted her to her feet and took her in another toe-curling kiss.

He reached for the condoms, tearing off one packet and tossing the rest to the nightstand.

"Let me," she said.

Their gazes locked as she sheathed his length. She hadn't expected the rush of emotions swamping her, and once again it took everything she had not to allow herself to get carried away by the intimate moment.

"I want to watch you ride me." He took her hand, leading her to the bed, and sat down with his back against the headboard. He helped her straddle him, but as she tried to lower herself onto his cock, he clutched her hips tighter, stopping her.

He looked like he was going to say something, but he didn't.

"What's wrong?" she asked.

"Absolutely nothing. You're perfect. I've waited a long time for this. I want to remember everything about this moment." His gaze moved slowly over her face and down her body. When his eyes found hers again, they brimmed with emotions so deep, they mirrored her own.

Not getting carried away was becoming harder by the second.

He loosened his grip, holding her gaze as he guided her onto his hard length. Her breath left her lungs as she felt every blessed inch of him stretching her, filling her completely. Nothing had ever felt so good or so right.

"*Sasha,*" he said heatedly as his arms circled her and their mouths came together. He drove into her from beneath, harder with each thrust, his strength rippling through her core. She rode him faster, her fingernails digging into his flesh. His muscles bunched against her palms as his hands traveled over her ass, up her back, and into her hair. Guttural noises climbed up his throat, and he tore his mouth away, kissing her lips, her cheek, her jaw. "You feel so good," he gritted out.

"Don't stop."

"There's not a chance in hell I'll stop." He grabbed her hair with one hand, tugging her head back, and sealed his mouth over the base of her neck, sucking so hard, heat seared between her legs, and she cried out. "That's it, baby. Show me what you like." His other hand clutched her hip, holding her tight against him as he thrust harder, sending lightning bolts racing through her. She'd never felt anything so intense, so addicting, so *real*. All sense of time and space fell away, and she was consumed with the feel of their bodies pumping and grinding, their illicit sounds filling the air, and the feel of his teeth and hands on her as they chased their highs. He moved his hand from her hip to her clit, working her so perfectly, pleasure raced through her chest and limbs, and she exploded into a million quivering pieces, desperate pleas flying from her lips as they rode out her pleasure.

As she came down from the high, he lowered her to her back and came down over her. "I could make you come all night."

"I want you to come with me," she panted out. "And *then* you can make me come all night."

A devilish glimmer sparked in his eyes. "As you wish, Bo Peep."

His smiling lips covered hers in a long, luscious kiss that sang through her, making her greedy for more. She'd thought he felt good when she was riding him, but nothing compared to feeling the weight of his big body, the flexing of his muscles, or his fervent kisses as he drove into her. They found their rhythm, and their kisses turned frenzied, his thrusts fast and powerful. She met each pump of his hips with a lift of her own, clawing at his back for purchase. He grabbed her legs beneath her knees, hiking them up to his waist, taking her impossibly deeper. "You feel so good," he rasped against her mouth. "I should've bought two boxes of condoms."

She laughed, and he smothered that sound with more heated kisses. When she grabbed his ass, his hips shot forward, making her giggle. She couldn't remember ever feeling this good or having this much fun in bed.

He grinned down at her with fire in his eyes. "I like your hands on me almost as much as I like your mouth on me."

"*Mm.* I'll have to remember that for next time."

"Next time," he rasped. "I like the sound of that."

He reclaimed her mouth as if he hadn't left her heart reeling and quickened his efforts. Blood pounded through her veins as they devoured each other, clawing and groping, moaning and pleading for more. Their bodies grew slick from their efforts, their breathing ragged. He guided her legs around him and pushed his hands beneath her ass, lifting and angling, his every thrust taking her higher, until she was hanging on to her sanity by a thread. She tried to hold back, to make it last, but he felt too good. "*Ez...I'm gonna...*"

"Me too." His eyes drilled into her, and she couldn't look away. She didn't want to miss a second of the glorious sight that was Ezra Moore on the verge of losing control for *her*. "Come for me, baby. Give me everything you have."

That was all it took for her to surrender to the whirlwind of sensations they caused. Electricity torched through her as he roared out her name, giving in to his own powerful release. They clung to each other, their bodies ravaged with pleasure as they rode the waves of their passion. When they finally collapsed, breathless and sated, to the mattress, he gathered her in his arms, kissing her so tenderly, emotions billowed inside her. It was all too much, feeling the man she'd wanted for so long buried deep inside her, consumed by the emotions in his touch, the way he was looking at her like she was some sort of goddess, and knowing this was all it could ever be. She wanted to memorize every little thing about them, but she buried her face in his neck, afraid her eyes would give her heart away.

Ezra moved her hair off her face and kissed her shoulder. "That was incredible."

"Mm-hm," she murmured against his skin. As she lay in his arms, surrounded by the scent of their intimacy, anxiety about what would happen next crept in. She wasn't ready for their night to end. She wanted more, but what if he didn't? What if he just said *thanks* and got up to leave? Her heart hurt at the thought. She had to get ahold of her runaway emotions, or she was going to be a mess when he left. "I'll be right back."

As she rolled away to get out of bed, he pulled her back to him and kissed her. "New rule. No leaving the bed without a kiss."

Happiness pushed her earlier worries away. "I didn't know we had rules."

"Neither did I, until you tried to escape."

"I see how you are," she teased. "Mild-mannered therapist by day, demanding rule maker by night?"

"With you, I guess I am."

He kissed her again, and she headed into the bathroom feeling high.

She looked at herself in the mirror. Her hair was a tangled mess, her cheeks were flushed, and there was a new, happier light in her eyes. How could there not be? She'd waited a lifetime to be with him, and her dreams were finally coming true. Even if only in secret.

After she freshened up, she went to join him and found him climbing out of bed, tall and broad and gloriously naked. He leaned in for a kiss on his way into the bathroom. How could it feel so natural? And why, after he closed the door, did she get nervous again?

Should she get dressed? Get back into bed?

She saw his shirt on the floor and desperately wanted to put it on, but if he chose to leave, he'd need it. She was still trying to decide what to do when he came out of the bathroom with a sexy smile and a wanting look in his eyes. His half-hard cock dangled temptingly between his thick thighs as he drew her into his arms and nuzzled against her neck. "Trying to figure out how to get rid of me?"

"Quite the opposite, but I wasn't sure if you'd want to leave."

"Leaving is the last thing I want to do." He nipped at her jaw, making all her no-longer-lonely parts tingle with anticipation. "Are you up for round two?"

"Rounds two, three, four…" She went up on her toes, meeting him in a deep, sensual kiss. They tumbled onto the bed in a tangle of gropes and kisses, their laughter filling the room—and her heart.

Chapter Thirteen

EZRA AWOKE TO the feel of Sasha's soft body intertwined with his hard frame, her warm breath whispering over his chest. They'd fallen asleep lying on their sides embracing, her knee tucked between his legs and her cheek resting on his chest. They were still in the same position, holding each other just as tightly, as if neither wanted the other to get away. He smiled to himself. He'd been fantasizing about being close to Sasha for years, but nothing he'd conjured had come close to how incredible it was to hold her in his arms, taste her on his lips, and make love to her all night long.

His gaze moved over the half-empty bag of M&M's they'd snacked on in the middle of the night and the empty condom packages on the nightstand, bringing an onslaught of memories and a rush of emotions. Afraid of what those emotions would do to him, he struggled to lock them down and shifted his gaze, looking for something else to focus on. Sunlight streamed in through the curtains, reminding him of the way Sasha had snuck into his life all those years ago. When he'd seen her climb out of his buddy's car at that party, looking as shell-shocked as she had intrigued, without an introduction or even a glance in his direction, she'd outshone everyone around her.

Sasha snuggled closer, making a sleepy sound. "You're still here."

He ran his hand down her back, caressing her gorgeous ass. "Did you think I'd take off without telling you?"

"Maybe." She tipped her smiling face up.

She looked so damn beautiful, she took his breath away, and a little bashful, which made his chest feel squirrely. He wanted to protect her, to take away the nervousness he knew she felt about what they'd done and what he hoped they would continue to do, but if he had any hope of not being found out, he also had to keep his own emotions in check.

He kissed her softly. "That would be breaking our number-one rule."

"Speaking of rules, how does this morning-after stuff work? Are there rules about leaving? Am I supposed to make an excuse and kick you out?"

"You've got this friends-with-benefits thing all wrong." He moved over her and laced their hands together, pinning hers to the mattress on either side of her head. "There is no kicking out. *Ever.*"

"Ever?" Her eyes danced with mischief. "What if I get tired of you?"

"That won't happen," he said arrogantly.

"What if my father knocks on the door? I can't tell you to leave through the window?"

He didn't even want to think about that. "Does he come over in the morning often?"

She shook her head, grinning like a Cheshire cat. "Never."

"You wicked thing." He nipped at her neck, earning another giggle. "Now you're in for it." He bit her earlobe just hard enough to make her gasp and giggle. "Don't fuck with me, Bo Peep." He ran his tongue along the shell of her ear and sucked the lobe into his mouth, earning a sexy moan.

"If this is what I get for fucking with you, I think I'm going to have to continue."

"You *are* a troublemaker." He released her hands, kissing a path down her chest and across the swell of her breast. "Just be honest with me. If you want me to leave, tell me." He lowered his mouth over her nipple, teasing it with his tongue.

She bowed off the bed beneath him, clutching his arms. "What if I want you to *stay?*"

He trailed open-mouthed kisses along her ribs. "Then you'll have to feed me." He met her lustful gaze. "And fair warning. I'm ravenous this morning."

"Oh *darn*. A hot, hungry man in my bed? What ever will I do?"

"Hopefully scream the right name when I make you come." He nipped at her ribs.

She giggled again, and he turned those sweet sounds into moans of pleasure as he kissed, licked, nipped, and sucked his way down her body, cherishing every inch of her. She clawed at the sheets as he teased her most sensitive nerves, and she pleaded for more when he devoured her slick heat. He pushed two fingers inside her, using his mouth where she needed it most, and she dug her heels into the mattress as his name flew loud and unabashedly from her lungs. *Music to my fucking ears.* Desire pounded through him, but bringing her pleasure was the highest of highs, and he wanted more of it. As she came down from the peak, eyes closed, her body shuddering, he sent her right back up to the edge. He teased and taunted, holding her on the verge of release, loving the sinful sounds of her begging for more as she trembled and writhed.

"Open your eyes, beautiful."

She shot him a desperate look, her hazel eyes brimming with need. Using his hands and mouth, he sent her soaring again. This time when she collapsed to the mattress, he loved his way up her body, earning more gasps and giggles.

"Your scruff tickles."

"Good."

He snagged the last of the string of condom packages from the nightstand and went up on his knees to roll it on. She watched him with hungry eyes and reached for him as he came down over her. He had every intention of going slow, but as he gathered her in his arms and their bodies came together, she felt too fucking good. "*Damn*, baby. I've never felt anything so perfect as being inside you."

"I thought I'd dreamed up how good we felt," she whispered incredulously.

She couldn't know what hearing that did to him. He captured her mouth, pouring all of his pent-up emotions into their connection, and there was no holding back. They lost themselves in a frenzy of greedy gropes, lustful thrusts, and breathless kisses as they were transported into ecstasy.

When they finally fell sated and spent to the mattress, he gathered her in his arms, kissing her forehead, trying again to shut down the emotions swamping him, but it was a losing battle. He should know better than to try to fool himself into thinking they were only fucking or scratching an itch. This was Sasha Whiskey, the woman he'd wanted for so long, he could barely remember a time when he didn't. But he had to find a way to keep his feelings in perspective for both their sakes, and that meant keeping them to himself.

"I wish we could stay right here all day," she said, snuggling closer.

He wasn't anywhere near ready for their first morning together to end, either. Especially since he had no idea when they'd get another one. But she had the horses to look after, and the guys were expecting him to ride with them before he picked up Gus. He kissed her forehead. "What time do you have to be at the barn?"

She glanced at the clock on the nightstand. "In about forty-five minutes."

"Let's have breakfast together. I make a mean chocolate chip waffle."

"That would require the right ingredients, which I don't have. I eat at the big house, remember?"

"What about on the days you don't?"

"You mean when I was hiding from you?"

He went up on his elbow, gazing down at her. "I knew you were hiding from me. Don't do that shit again."

"Don't piss me off, and I won't."

"I'll try not to." He brushed his lips over hers. "We can head over to my place for breakfast."

"What if we run into someone? How would we explain why we're together this early and coming from my place?"

Fuck. Where was his head? "We'll tell them I was sleepwalking and ended up in your bed."

She laughed. "Oh yeah, *that'll* go over well."

"Then I guess we can skip the waffles and use the extra time to get naughty in the shower."

She wound her arms around him. "Just when I didn't think

A TASTE OF WHISKEY

the morning could get any better, you go and offer the icing on the cake."

FORTY MINUTES LATER they were standing at her door saying goodbye, but leaving was the last thing Ezra wanted to do.

"I wish we could shower together every morning." Sasha went up on her toes to kiss him.

"That makes two of us." The image of Sasha on her knees in the shower as she sucked him off was going to wreak havoc with him all day. Then again, so were dozens of other images that were etched into his mind from their time together.

"I should probably warn you that you used the bodywash Birdie buys from that woman in Upstate New York who claims to put love potions in everything she makes."

He'd seen the label, and Dare and Cowboy had told him all about Birdie's claims that Roxie Dalton's love potions had helped seal their love. "Nothing could be more powerful than the spell you cast on me ages ago." So much for keeping his emotions in perspective. Her hopeful smile had him feeling like a heel, and he tried to rein in his emotions.

"This may sound cheesy, but I had a great time last night."

"So did I."

"Can I see you Tuesday night after church?"

"I was hoping you'd want to."

"Tuesday feels a lifetime away." He kissed her again. "What do you have going on after you're done with the horses?"

"I don't know yet. Maybe I'll go for a trail ride or head into town."

He'd like to go on that trail ride with her. "Will we see you at dinner?"

"Definitely. I miss Gus. It wasn't fair of me to disappear the way I did."

"It's okay, but I know he misses you, too." He drew her into his arms, wanting to tell her how much he hated leaving her and how he wished she could go with him on the motorcycle ride. He'd love to have her warming his back, showing everyone she was his. But sharing those pipe dreams would only make their reality harder, so he silenced them with another kiss.

His phone chimed, and he pulled it from his pocket to read the text.

Tina: *Something came up. I need you to come get Gus.*

Fucking Tina. He thought about the extra effort it had taken to get Gus excited to see his mother for the weekend on Friday morning when he'd taken him to camp and made a mental note to talk with Tina again about her unreliability.

"Looks like the ride is out. Tina needs me to pick up Gus."

Sasha's mouth pinched. "I swear that woman has no shame. Isn't she supposed to have him until four? What's her excuse this time? A yoga class? Drinks with a friend?"

"She didn't say, but it doesn't matter. I get time with my boy, and that's a win for me."

"It's definitely *her* loss. I'd ask if you want me to watch him while you go riding with the guys, but I know you won't go."

"You know me well, Bo Peep." When Tina pulled this shit on her weekends, Ezra tried to give Gus extra attention to make up for it.

"It's supposed to be a beautiful day. Why don't you do something special with him? You could take him to the water park or the climbing park."

"The water park is a great idea. Why don't you come with us?"

"I would love to, but you should probably ask Gus first, in case he wants time alone with you."

"As if he ever chooses me over seeing his *Sugar*." He leaned in and kissed her. "I'll text you after I pick him up."

"Wait." She opened the door a few inches and peered out. "Okay, the coast is clear. *Go*."

"Way to make me feel like your dirty little secret." He pulled her behind the door and kissed her breathless.

Half an hour later he pulled up in front of the two-bedroom rambler Tina rented and parked next to her boyfriend's car. He gritted his teeth against the anger eating away at him. She was too fucking busy for their son but not for her boyfriend? Tina had a thing for clean-cut guys with money, and she usually had a new boyfriend every few months, although her latest had lasted seven or eight months. Ezra made it his business to have those men checked out by Maya's older brother, Hector "Hazard" Martinez, a local cop and fellow Dark Knight. Tina's latest boyfriend, Collin Frye, was a well-to-do real estate agent. Ezra had wrongly hoped the guy might help her settle down and become more responsible where Gus was concerned.

He headed up the walk, tension rising in his shoulders as he knocked on the front door.

Tina answered wearing a black sleeveless dress and heels. At twenty-nine, she was classically beautiful and turned heads everywhere she went with her slim figure, flawless olive skin, perfectly applied makeup, and long, glossy dark hair that fell to the middle of her back in carefully coiffed waves. But to Ezra, the way she treated Gus irreparably marred that beauty.

"Hi," she said with fake cheeriness. "Thanks for coming to get him. Collin's parents invited us to brunch at their country club."

"Dad!" Gus bolted out the front door and threw his arms around Ezra's legs. "I missed you."

"I missed you, too, buddy. Why don't you wait for me in the truck so I can talk to Mommy for a minute."

"Okay!"

As Gus ran to the vehicle, Tina called out, "See you Tuesday!"

"Okay!" Gus hollered as he scrambled into the truck.

Ezra turned back to Tina, taking Gus's backpack from her. "You couldn't take Gus to brunch?"

"You know how rambunctious he is. I don't want to make a bad impression."

"I thought you spent Thanksgiving with his parents and that was why you didn't take Gus for the holiday."

"I did, but I just told you we're meeting them at their *country club*." She said it like it should answer any and all of his questions.

"Right, and people who are members of country clubs don't have kids?" He was being a sarcastic dick, but he couldn't help it. He hated when she pulled this shit.

"Of course they have kids." She crossed her arms with an irritated expression. "I thought you'd be happy to take him. Would you rather I called a sitter?"

"No. I'd rather you'd stop putting our son second and start making him a priority. This kind of thing can affect every relationship he has as he grows up."

She rolled her eyes. "Stop being so melodramatic. He's fine, and I'm not your mother. I'm not abandoning him."

He gritted his teeth. "No, you're just making him feel second best." He headed back to his vehicle, made sure Gus was strapped in, and drove away. "Sorry your visit with your mom was cut short."

"It's okay. I'm hungry. Mom didn't have time to make breakfast. Will you make me pancakes?"

When Gus was chatty and excited, it was easy to write off his *It's okay* as a glib comment, but Ezra took note of the way his son casually disregarded his time with his mother. "With chocolate chips?"

"Yeah!" Gus cheered.

"How about we make them together?"

"Okay. I'm gonna put in lots of chocolate chips. Can we bring some to Sasha? She's missed a lot of breakfasts."

He thanked his lucky stars that Gus was still at the age where he didn't read into things like adults avoiding each other. "I think she'd like that. How would you like to go to the water park today?"

"The *water park*? I *love* the water park! Can Sasha come with us? She likes the water park. Remember that time she went down the slide with me and you raced us? I bet we can beat you this time. I'm bigger now…"

LATER THAT AFTERNOON, the scents of chlorine, sunscreen, and fried food and the sounds of people shouting, water splashing, laughter, and conversations hung in the air at the Splash 'N Slide water park. They had something for everyone, from an enormous kiddie area with massive kiddie pools and slides, climbing equipment, and elephants that sprayed water from their trunks to adult-level obstacle courses, waterfalls, long and winding tube slides, and inner-tube rivers.

"Hurry up, Dad!" Gus was a bundle of excited energy in his goggles and swimsuit, with his wet curls sticking to his forehead, as Ezra helped him into the middle seat of a three-person raft, preparing to go down the Wet and Wild slide.

"Yeah, hurry up, slowpoke," Sasha teased.

She'd been teasing him all day, sauntering around in that pale pink bikini, with her flirtatious looks and furtive touches. He was just as guilty, eating up the time with her, loving her competitive nature, and getting off on every stolen glance and brush of their bodies. He couldn't resist teasing her right back.

"I thought you liked it when I went slow." He winked and climbed into the back of the raft, enjoying the blush spreading over her cheeks.

"No, she doesn't!" Gus exclaimed. "She likes to win! Come *on*, Dad!"

"I'm ready, buddy."

"Hold on to the handles," the teenage attendant said. "And remember to stay in the raft."

"We will," Gus reassured him.

They all gripped the handles as the raft moved along the straightaway and climbed to the top of the slide, shooting them into a downhill tunnel. Gus cheered, Sasha screamed, and Ezra laughed as they zipped around curves and sped down open slides and through more tunnels. They were all cracking up as they flew off the last slide, crashing into the pool. They climbed out of the raft, and as Ezra scooped up Gus in one arm, he stole a grope of Sasha's ass under the water with the other, earning another pink-cheeked grin.

"That was so fun!" Gus exclaimed, wriggling out of Ezra's arms as they climbed out of the pool. "Can we go to the buckets that dump water on us?"

"We sure can."

Gus took off running for the buckets.

"Slow down," he hollered to Gus, and reached for Sasha's hand. "Let's go, beautiful." They hurried after him. "Are you having a good time?"

"The best time. Gus is having so much fun, and it's been forever since I've laughed so much."

"Me too." He leaned in to kiss her, and her wide eyes stopped him short. "Shit." He glanced at Gus, walking a few feet in front of them, and reluctantly released Sasha's hand. Gus didn't see him almost kiss her, but his own fucking heart did. Apparently he could no longer hold her hand without wanting more. "Sorry."

"He didn't see you," she said.

"The apology was meant for you. I'm sorry we're stuck hiding like a dirty fucking secret."

"Well, I happen to like the dirty and I like the fucking, so don't reveal our secret, and keep your hands to yourself when we're in public."

He chuckled. "Maybe if you didn't tempt me in that sexy bikini, it wouldn't be so hard."

"Oh, you like this old thing?" She feigned innocence and looked down at her body, wiggling her chest.

"You know I do."

"Sorry it makes it so *hard* for you." She strutted off with an extra sway in her hips and took Gus's hand, tossing a taunting glance over her shoulder.

She was going to be the death of him.

"Come on, Gusto. After the buckets, let's beat Daddy on the obstacle course!"

They got doused by buckets, sprayed by elephants, and they rode the lazy river and a handful of other rides. By late afternoon, Gus was slowing down. As they came off the obstacle course, he pointed to a boy eating ice cream and said, "Can we get ice cream?"

"I think we can do that." Ezra ruffled Gus's hair. "Then we should think about heading home."

"I don't *wanna* go home," he whined.

"I know, buddy, but it's getting late."

"I've had a lot of fun today, but I have to get back to take care of the horses," Sasha said.

"O*kay*." Gus leaned against Ezra's leg.

He ran his hand through his sleepy boy's hair. "Getting tired, buddy?"

"No." Gus shook his head.

Ezra exchanged a knowing glance with Sasha, and her sweet smile cut straight to his heart.

They got ice cream and headed for a table with an umbrella.

"I forgot napkins. I'll be right there." Sasha hurried back toward the ice cream stand.

A little girl yelled, "Mom! It's Gus!"

Ezra looked around.

"Dad, Annie's here." Gus pointed to a little blond girl tugging her mother in their direction.

Ezra recognized them from preschool. Annie's mother, a tall blonde wearing a short white cover-up, had tried to lure him into conversations a few times, but he had no idea what her name was.

"Gus!" Annie ran over, and the kids squealed with delight,

gabbing about the rides they went on.

"Hi, Ezra." Annie's mother flashed a flirtatious smile. "Imagine running into you here."

"Hi." *Fuck.* What was her name? He saw Sasha closing in on them, looking curiously at the girl's mother, who was looking at Ezra like he was a steak and she was starving.

"Here you go, Gusto." She wiped ice cream from Gus's cheek and handed him a napkin.

"Is that your mom?" Annie asked.

"No. That's Sugar." Gus beamed at Sasha.

"The one who takes you horseback riding?" Annie asked.

"Ah, *you're* the infamous Sugar," Annie's mother said.

"Actually, my name is Sasha. Only Gus calls me Sugar."

"Well, *Sasha*, I'm Layla. I volunteered in their preschool class two days a week, and Gus talked about you a lot." She said it like she was tired of hearing about her.

"Really?" Sasha asked.

"Yes. I've heard *all* about the cookies you bake, horseback rides, and a dozen other things. Are you his nanny, or...?"

"Oh, *no*," Sasha said, looking uncomfortable at Layla's prodding. "I'm..." She glanced at Ezra. "Just a family friend."

Just a family friend, my ass. She wasn't *just* anything, but he couldn't tell this woman that. He had no idea who she'd blab it to.

"Really?" Layla's eyes lit up, and she zeroed in on Ezra again. "In that case, we should get the kids together for a playdate. Maybe we can do pizza and a movie one night."

Fucking secret. "Our schedule is super busy, but I'll see what we can do."

"Great. You can get my number off the family roster," Layla suggested, her eyes remaining trained on Ezra, as if Sasha didn't exist.

Grinding his back teeth, he put his hand on Sasha's back. "We should get going."

"It was nice to meet you," Sasha said.

"Yes," Layla said coolly, turning a warmer tone to Ezra. "I look forward to hearing from you." She called out, "Annie, honey, let's go."

"Bye, Gus!" Annie skipped over to her mother.

"Bye!" Gus hollered.

As they walked away, Sasha said, "Someone wants to have an adult playdate with you."

"That's *not* happening."

GUS FELL ASLEEP on the drive back to the ranch, and Sasha was glad Ezra had taken advantage of that time to hold her hand. He must have brought her hand to his lips and kissed it half a dozen times as they'd talked quietly. When they got home, Gus asked him to make hot dogs over the fire for dinner and begged Sasha to join them and to bring her guitar so they could play together.

Sasha took care of the horses and went to shower. Ezra's scent lingered in her bedroom, and when she showered, she felt him there, too, bathing her with his caring hands, kissing her beneath the warm spray, and loving her body like it had never been loved before. She wanted to bottle up those feelings and scents so they never disappeared.

They ate by the fire and played I Spy with Gus. Ezra was being playful and silly, saying he spied an ant and a hot dog in

Gus's belly and other ridiculous things that he insisted he saw, which made Gus crack up. When it was time for Gus to go to bed, he turned those big brown eyes on Sasha, asking if she would read him a bedtime story with his daddy.

One story turned into three, but Sasha didn't mind. She loved listening to Ezra's deep, soothing voice as he read the last pages of *If I Was a Horse*, Gus's final bedtime story. Gus was lying between them in his twin bed. His cheeks were sun-kissed, his eyelids heavy, and in his pudgy little hand, he clutched Moxie, the stuffed horse Sasha had given him when he was three. He'd named it after her horse. Its ear was threadbare from Gus rubbing it between his tiny fingers and thumb. He'd done it since the day she'd given it to him, and she'd already had to sew the ear back on once.

She let her mind wander to places she shouldn't, imagining a future with them. One in which they wouldn't have to hide that included Sunday afternoons like today and nights like this. She thought about Layla and knew she was probably one of many women who vied for Ezra's attention. Sasha had wanted to tell her that they were more than friends, but she could never risk everything Ezra had worked so hard for just to stake her claim on him. The funny thing was, while she was jealous of Layla flirting with him, she wasn't insecure about her arrangement with Ezra. She trusted him and knew in her heart that when he said he'd only be with her, she could take him at his word.

Ezra quietly closed the book, drawing her from her thoughts, and she realized Gus was asleep. He looked peaceful and happy, and so did his daddy, gazing at her like she belonged there. She knew that was her heart running away with her thoughts again, and she needed to get a grip on that. But it felt good, so why not tiptoe in that field while she could?

She started to get off the bed, and Gus's eyes opened.

"G'night kiss," Gus said sleepily, reaching for her.

She hugged him and kissed his forehead. "I love you, Gus-to."

"Love you, too." He kissed her cheek, skinny arms still around her neck. "Can we have a sleepover?"

Yes, please. She looked at Ezra and saw the same desire in his eyes.

"Tomorrow's a work and camp day, buddy," Ezra said.

"Another day?" he pleaded.

Ezra's lips twitched, like he wanted to agree. "We'll see."

"Okay." Gus kissed Sasha's cheek again. "Another kiss?"

She laughed softly and kissed him again before climbing off the bed. "Good night, sweet boy."

"G'night, Sugar."

Gus turned and snuggled into Ezra. He brushed Gus's hair off his forehead, whispering, "I had a great day with you, buddy."

"Me too," Gus said sleepily.

"You're getting so big, riding all the big-kid rides. Daddy's proud of you for following the rules while we were there and being nice to the other kids."

Sasha's heart squeezed, and she walked out of the bedroom, giving them privacy. She remembered Ezra standing over Gus's crib when they'd first moved to the ranch, rubbing his little boy's back and telling him how much he loved him. She'd seen him softly and determinedly drilling that love into Gus's little heart many times over the years, but after being in Ezra's arms, everything hit differently.

She stood in the living room, getting nervous. Normally, if

they'd hung out with Gus in the evening, after he went to bed, they'd watch a movie or sit outside together. But after spending the whole day together, and with their new arrangement, she wasn't sure what to do. Her phone chimed with a text, and she pulled it from her pocket.

Birdie: *What are you doing?*

Sasha: *I'm at Ezra's.*

An eyeroll emoji popped up.

Birdie: *Are you pining again? Do I need to come over there and beat your ass? I swear all those Moore boys need to do is bat their eyelashes and you turn into a pile of mush.*

Sasha considered telling her what had happened between them, but she heard Ezra moving around in Gus's room and knew she wouldn't have time to explain.

Sasha: *It's not like that. I can't text right now.*

Another eyeroll emoji popped up as Ezra came out of the bedroom leaving the door ajar. Sasha pocketed her phone and put on a smile. "I don't know how you stand that cuteness every night."

He came to her side. "My boy is a Casanova."

She almost said, *Like his daddy,* but that wasn't how she felt, and she didn't want to minimize the truth. "He's just full of love and not ashamed to show it."

"Like I said, he's a Casanova."

"Maybe a little, but I think it's bigger than that. I know you worry about how his relationship with Tina will affect him, and I see how hard you try not to be closed off like your dad." She touched his arm. "I hope you can see how incredible a father you are and that all your efforts are paying off. That little boy in there knows how to give and receive love because of you."

His jaw tightened, and she felt his muscles tense up.

Fearing she'd overstepped, her nerves flared again. "Thanks for letting me hang out with you guys today. It was a lot of fun. I guess I'll see you at breakfast tomorrow."

"You're leaving?"

"We spent last night and all day together. I figured you'd want some time to chill, and I obviously overstepped with what I said. It's true, so I'm not taking it back, whether it bothers you or not to hear it, but I don't have to be in your face after saying it."

"First of all, I do want to relax, but I'd like to do that with you."

Relief trickled in. "You would?"

"Yes. I like *you*, Sash, and I enjoy spending time with you whether or not we hook up. Our friendship is the foundation of everything, and it's a big part of why we're so good together. I don't want to lose the fun and comfort of hanging out just because we're sleeping together."

She exhaled with relief. "Neither do I."

"Good, and as far as what you said about Gus giving and receiving love, you didn't overstep. I'm sorry if I reacted strangely, but it hit me pretty hard. You and your mother are the only ones who know how much I worry about those things, and I haven't talked with your mom about it in years. It means a lot to me that you noticed and that you think I'm doing a good job as a father."

I notice everything. "You're an amazing father. I would tell you if I thought you were doing something that was bad for Gus. Not that I know much about parenting, but you know me. I'm not one to keep my opinions to myself."

He laughed softly. "That's one of the things I like most about you. You always tell me the truth." He drew her into his arms. "I don't want things to be weird between us."

"Neither do I, but after last night...sometimes it's going to be a little awkward."

"I know. We're navigating new territory, and that's going to take some figuring out. But if we talk to each other when we feel that way, like we are right now, hopefully it won't negatively affect our friendship."

"That sounds good to me."

"Good, because it's still early, and I'd really like you to stick around and watch a movie with me like you usually would."

She narrowed her eyes. "Do you still have that Truly?"

"Yes, and popcorn *and* peanut M&M's."

"Then you've got yourself a movie date."

Chapter Fourteen

LATE TUESDAY AFTERNOON, Sasha was coming out of the barn when her phone rang, and her father's name flashed on the screen. Anxiety prickled her nerves. Ezra had come to see her at the barn this morning when he was between clients, and her father had been there talking to her about one of the horses. Poor Ezra had looked guilty as sin, but he'd thought fast and said he was on his way to pick something up at his cabin and wanted to come by and tell her that he didn't need her to watch Gus after all during church tonight, because Tina was going to take him. Sasha had worried her father hadn't bought it, especially since she felt like she was walking around with a neon sign on her forehead that read CURRENTLY HOOKING UP WITH EZRA MOORE.

She thought about when they'd watched the movie together Sunday night and had been unable to keep their hands to themselves. They'd ended up tangled together in his bedroom. When he'd kissed her goodbye, he'd pulled her back for more about a dozen times. She'd felt like a giddy girl when she'd left at two in the morning, and he'd insisted on talking to her on the phone the whole way back to her cabin to make sure she got there okay since he couldn't leave Gus. She loved that protective side of him. She also loved that he'd sought her out between clients yesterday, smooching her in the tack room again. But now she wondered, what if someone saw them go in there? Or what if her father could tell there was something going on? Keeping her emotions hidden felt impossible, and she swore that neon sign was flashing at mealtimes when they sat so close and fought the urge to touch.

Her phone rang again, startling her from her thoughts. She took a deep breath and answered it, trying not to sound anxious. "Hi, Dad."

"Hi, darlin'. Can you meet me in your mother's office in ten minutes? We'd like to speak with you."

Shitshitshit. "Sure. What's up?"

"We'll talk when you get here."

The line went dead. Her father was a man of few words, and he wasn't one to linger on the phone, but as she looked up at the darkening clouds, she wondered if she was walking into a storm of a different kind.

"Looks like the rain is coming sooner rather than later," Sully said as she came out of the barn. "Are you okay? You look like you've seen a ghost."

"Hm? Yeah, I'm fine. I need to run up to the big house to talk to my parents. Do you have time to bring the last three horses in?"

"Sure."

"Thanks. I'll see you later."

On her way to the big house, Sasha thought about texting Ezra to see if her father had said anything to him, but if he hadn't, she didn't want to worry him. She tried to calm herself down on the way up the hill, but by the time she got to the main house to meet with her parents, she was even more nervous.

She headed down the hall toward her mother's office and nearly ran into Maya Martinez, a curvy brunette with a sassy attitude, as she was coming out of the break room. "*Oops.* Sorry, Maya."

"No worries. Where are you going in such a hurry?"

"My mom's office. Dad called and said they wanted to talk to me. Do you know what it's about?"

"No." She leaned closer, speaking conspiratorially, dark eyes lit with mischief. "Why? What did you do?"

"Nothing," Sasha said with what she hoped was a casual laugh.

"Darn it. I was hoping for some juicy gossip. You know what? Your dad might want to talk to you about the horse that's coming in tonight. She's blind."

"A rescue?" Sasha had learned to work with visually impaired horses when she'd interned at a rescue in Montana that specialized in disabled horses. She'd worked with visually impaired horses at the ranch, but she hadn't worked with horses that were completely blind since the internship.

"Yes. Her owner can't afford to take care of her anymore. I was just getting ready to send you all of the paperwork she filled out. The poor horse has not had an easy life, but her owner said she's healthy. She's bringing her tonight between seven and eight, while the guys are at church."

"That's okay. I can handle the intake," she said, hoping that was what her father wanted to speak with her about. But that wouldn't explain why *both* her parents wanted to speak with her. "I'll review the paperwork after our meeting."

Ezra's office door opened, and he and Mike walked out. "I'll see you Thursday, and we can discuss a family session."

"Great. Thanks again." Mike nodded at Maya and Sasha. "Have a good afternoon, ladies."

"You too," Sasha said at the same time Maya said, "Thanks," and Mike headed down the hall to leave.

Ezra's gaze found Sasha, and her pulse quickened. She tried to suppress the smile tugging at her lips, for fear of that neon sign blinking again.

"Why do you two look like you're up to no good?" Ezra asked.

Maya looked between them, arching a brow at Sasha. "Good question."

As she headed back to her desk, Ezra whispered, "It should be against the law for you to look as gorgeous as you do after working all day. Think anyone will notice if I drag you into my office and have my way with you?"

"As much as I'd like to say no and let you do just that, has my dad said anything to you since he saw you at the barn?"

His brows knitted. "No, but your mother asked to speak with me when I was done with my client. That's where I was heading."

"*Shit.* I'm supposed to meet with them, too."

Worry tightened his jaw.

Her mother's office door opened, and her mother walked out. "Oh good, you're both here." She turned to Maya. "Maya, honey, can you please hold our calls for twenty minutes?"

"Sure can."

Sasha and Ezra exchanged a worried glance as they followed her mother into her office. Her father was leaning against the windowsill, arms crossed. "Tiny," Ezra said with a nod.

Her father nodded.

"Why don't you make yourselves comfortable." Wynnie waved to the couch and armchairs.

Sasha was sure everyone could hear her heart thundering as she and Ezra sat on the couch. Ezra cast an *oh shit* glance in her direction. She had the urge to reach for his hand, which made no sense because it would only make things worse. He pressed his hands flat against his thighs, as if he were fighting the urge to reach for her, too.

"Thanks for making time to come in," her mother said as she sat in an armchair.

"Of course," Ezra said.

Sasha was too nervous to respond.

Her father pushed from the windowsill and walked over. "We wanted to talk with you about the networking dinner."

"You do?" It came out so enthusiastically, Sasha might as well have said, *Yay! That's great!* "I mean, I'm glad you're bringing it up. I've been so busy, it wasn't at the forefront of my mind." She turned to Ezra, seeing the relief in his eyes. "Did you know about it?"

"Yes. Wynnie mentioned it to me. I was going to talk to you about driving over together, but I was a little sidetracked this weekend. I meant to mention it last night, but it slipped my mind." His eyes glimmered knowingly.

After Gus went to bed, they'd been busy exchanging flirty texts. Sasha tried to tamp down her grin.

"Sasha," her mother said imploringly. "This dinner is important. We're counting on you to do a good job representing the ranch. Please don't forget to prepare your talk."

"I won't. Don't worry. I have it on my calendar. I'm going to start working on the talk next week. I was just busy with other things the last couple of days."

"So we've heard," her father said.

Sasha's heart nearly stopped. "You *have?*"

"I spy with my little eye…" Her father arched a brow.

Sasha's chest constricted. She didn't dare look at Ezra, but she could feel tension billowing off him. She scrambled for something to say, but before she came up with anything, her mother spoke.

"There are no secrets on this ranch with a little one running around," her mother said.

Sasha held her breath.

"While you kids were gabbing with the others yesterday morning about the paintball party, Gus told us all about the fun day you had at the water park and the cookout that followed," her father explained.

A relieved laugh tumbled out. "He did?"

"Yes indeed," her father said. "I gotta tell you, Ezra. I was a little worried about you raising that boy here at first, since there are no other children around. But he seems to be thriving. I think he's been good for all of us." He nodded to Sasha. "Especially this one, who's been working so hard, she's been missing meals."

"I'm glad to hear that," Ezra said. "I'm thankful every day for the home we have here and for the family we've found."

Sasha was thrown back to years earlier, when they were celebrating Ezra's graduation from his master's program. She could still see him lifting his glass, still hear him thanking everyone for their support. *I was lost when I first came to the ranch. I felt alone and had no direction and no interest in finding one. Then Wynnie got me out of my own head, and you all showed me what a family should be like. You helped me find my purpose, and I'm honored to be given the chance to help others do the same. I won't let you down.* Guilt swamped her. She had been so caught up in the chance to finally be with Ezra, she hadn't given enough weight to what he had on the line.

"We're thankful for you, too, honey," her mother said. "Now, to get back to the point of the meeting, Tiny and I were talking about how to make the best use of the audience you'll have at the networking dinner…"

As her parents went over topics they'd like her and Ezra to focus on during their talks, Sasha wrestled with what she and Ezra were doing. She might be risking her parents' trust and respect, but Ezra was risking everything. And for what? For something that as long as they both worked there could never be more.

By the time the meeting was over, Sasha's mind, and her heart, were in turmoil.

"Hold on, darlin'," her father said.

She tried to mask her emotions as Ezra walked out, and she turned to face her father. "Yeah?"

"We've got a rescue coming in tonight between seven and eight. A blind mare."

"Maya told me. I'll be ready for her, and I'll text Cowboy and Doc once she's settled."

"Thanks, darlin'." He put his arm around her, hugging her against his side. "Thanks for attending the networking dinner. You know how I hate those things."

"No problem. I'm going to check with Ezra to see if we can combine parts of our talks so we don't duplicate information."

"Good idea, honey," her mother said.

Sasha headed down to Ezra's office with her heart in her throat, and peered in at him. "Hey. Do you have a sec?"

"For you? Always."

She walked in and closed the door behind her. "In case they ask, I told my parents I wanted to talk with you about combining parts of our talks."

"Good cover, Bo Peep. Are you as relieved as I am?" He drew her into his arms and kissed her. "I've been dying to do that all day."

She smiled, but worry stole it away, and she forced herself to step out of his arms. "Ez, while we were in there, the impact of what you're risking for whatever this is between us hit me like a brick in the face, and it scares me."

"It scares me, too, but we talked about the risks."

"I know we did. But now that we're in it, and after sitting with my parents thinking they were going to fire you..." Too nervous to stand still, she paced. "You worked so hard to get this job and to build a life here with Gus." Her throat thickened, but she forced the words to come. "I just don't know if we should continue to risk it."

His brows slanted. "Sasha—"

The intercom on the desk buzzed, and his jaw tightened as Maya's voice came through. "Excuse me, Ezra?"

His jaw tensed. "Yes, Maya?"

"Your next client is here."

"Thank you. I'll be right out." He gritted his teeth, both of them watching for the light on the intercom to go off.

When it did, Sasha reached for the door. "I'd better go."

"Sash." He touched her arm, drawing her eyes to his, which were as serious as they were distraught. "We need to talk about this."

Too emotional to speak and knowing it wasn't the time or place to discuss it anyway, she nodded and headed out the door.

Chapter Fifteen

IT WAS DRIZZLING rain when Kathy Lethango, a short, stout woman, arrived with Posey, the roughly sixteen-year-old Appaloosa she was relinquishing. Posey was blind in her right eye, and her left eye had been removed because she'd suffered from uveitis, an inflammation of the eye's uveal tract, a painful condition that had gone untreated for too long by her current owner.

Sasha peered into the horse trailer.

Posey was cowering against the back wall, wearing a rope halter, which was dangerous and could be painful. Sasha's chest constricted. It had taken a monumental effort for Sasha to push aside her personal heartache to get through the evening, and seeing Posey's anxious state brought it back to the surface. She ached for the horse, but she knew better than to show it. No matter what a horse had been through, she always led with admiration and not pity, because that's what horses needed to gain confidence.

"The poor thing doesn't do well with people," Kathy said. "Right, Posey? You don't like the way we move or the noises we make, do you? She just doesn't understand what's going on around her."

Kathy had that backward. The problem wasn't that the horse didn't understand people. It was her caretaker who didn't understand what the horse needed. A horse who was treated as if it were fragile would act fragile. And a horse who had lost her eye because of its owner's negligence had good reason to fret.

Sasha pushed the ugly feelings she felt toward Kathy down deep and focused on getting Posey settled. "How much time did you spend with her?"

"Not much. I thought I'd have more time for her, but the only barn where I could afford to board her was almost an hour away, and I work full time, so I couldn't get there more than two or three days a week. I'd stay for a little while in the evenings. But she had a nice stall. She was happy there."

Would you like to be kept in a stall for days on end? "On the intake documents, you indicated that you don't know what she'd been through before you took her on or how she lost her sight in her right eye. Is that correct?"

"Yes. She was already blind in her right eye when I got her. A few months later she got an infection in her other eye, and I couldn't afford to get it fixed."

"Right." Sasha would go without whatever it took before she'd make a horse suffer, but unfortunately, she knew it wasn't always that way for others. "You can lead her into the empty paddock and say goodbye to her there. I've put Dream, one of our gentlest mares, on the other side so they can bond." She motioned to the side-by-side paddocks, which were partially covered.

"But it's raining. Shouldn't you put her in a stall?"

It was only drizzling, but she didn't bother pointing that

out. "Horses can be overwhelmed by too many unfamiliar smells, like in the barn, and it's worse for a horse that's blind. I'm going to give her some time to adjust with a friend first, and assuming she and Dream do okay together, they'll be put in neighboring stalls so she can still smell her nearby. Would you rather I walked her out?"

"No," she said quickly. "I want to say goodbye."

Kathy lured a very tentative Posey out of the trailer with a treat. While Kathy led her into the pen, Sasha hurried into the barn to grab her rain jacket and a breakaway halter for Posey. When she came back out, Kathy was already heading back to her truck.

"That was quick." *So much for a heartfelt goodbye.*

"I've got a long drive home," Kathy said. "Good luck getting that halter on her. It took me forever to get this one on her." She held up the rope halter.

Great. You could have left it on while I got mine on her. "We'll be fine. Thanks for bringing her in. I'll take good care of her." She headed over to the paddock.

Dream stood by the partition between the pens, gazing curiously at her frightened new friend. Posey was a beautiful horse, with a chestnut coat and a white splash with chestnut spots along her hips and loin. She didn't look malnourished or injured, but she was cowering. Her ears were back, her muzzle pursed, and her nostrils flared. Sasha's heart went out to her. Not only was every smell new to her, but she'd also gone on a long trailer ride, which could be unsettling for even the most confident horses.

"You're okay, my sweet, strong girl. I'm Sasha, and we're going to be good friends." She needed to earn Posey's trust and help her be less anxious. But she also needed to get a halter on her so she'd be able to safely lead her into the barn later. "We'll take things slow. I'm going to come into the paddock with you."

She opened the gate, and Posey backed away from the sound.

"You're okay, Posey," she reassured her as she walked slowly toward her, but Posey shrank back. "You're safe here, sweetie." Every time Sasha moved, Posey scrambled away. She didn't want to chase her, because it would only make her more anxious. She needed Posey to come to her, and she had an idea of what might work, a trick she'd learned during her internship in Montana.

"I'll be right back. Don't worry. We'll figure this out together."

She went out of the paddock and retrieved a bucket of senior feed, which horses were drawn to because it smelled like molasses. She put the halter in the bucket, with the nose piece on top of the feed. If she could get Posey to trust her enough to eat from the bucket, she could put the halter on her while she was eating.

Knowing it was going to take a while, she sent a group text to Doc and Cowboy.

Sasha: *Posey is safe and sound. She looks healthy, but she's not halter trained, and she's terrified. I've got her in the side-by-side with Dream. It's going to take some time to get a halter on her, and you won't be able to get near her tonight, so please don't come by. I don't want to make her more anxious. I'll text you when she's in her stall. On the plus side, Dream is curious and is being a very good girl. I think she's the perfect friend for Posey.*

Cowboy: *Good job. Text me if you need a hand.*

Doc: *Sounds good. I'll check with you in the morning.*

She considered texting Ezra and felt a pang of sadness. She'd hated questioning what they were doing, but she'd never forgive herself if she didn't put Gus first. She didn't want to get upset while working with Posey, so she pushed those thoughts away and pocketed her phone without reaching out to him.

It was raining harder now. She zipped her rain jacket, put on her hood, and carried the bucket into the paddock. "I apologize ahead of time for my singing, Posey, but it's going to be the easiest way for you to know where I am. I know you're nervous, but we'll get through this together. Even if it takes all night."

Sasha stood in the middle of the paddock holding the bucket of feed. She grabbed a handful of it and held it out for Posey as she tried to figure out what song to sing. Thinking of Posey and Ezra, the answer came to her, and she began singing "Lean on Me," so Posey would know that she'd never be alone—and maybe also to soothe her own confused heart.

EZRA SKIPPED HAVING a drink with the guys at the Roadhouse after church and headed back to the ranch. He was losing his mind. He'd texted Sasha after the meeting, but she hadn't responded, and there was no way he could leave things up in the air overnight. He drove to her cabin and was relieved to see the lights on and her truck parked out front. He climbed out of his SUV, jogged through the pouring rain up to her porch, and knocked on the door.

When she didn't answer, he knocked again. He didn't think she was avoiding him again. She wasn't that type of person. He headed back to his SUV, and as he drove away, he glanced down the hill at the rehab barns and saw a light on outside one of them.

He drove down and spotted Sasha standing in one of the paddocks with a horse. He parked by the barn and forced himself not to jog over for fear of startling the horse. He moved slowly, watching her. She stood in the middle of a paddock, holding a bucket as a horse ate out of it. As he neared, he heard her singing "Lean on Me" and was hit with memories of her singing that very song to Gus when he was a baby and Ezra had been newly separated and sleep deprived and had needed a helping hand with him. Like Ezra, Gus had always been drawn to, and comforted by, her voice.

When he reached the paddock, he realized Sasha wasn't wearing a jacket, and her clothes and hair were drenched. He wanted to wrap her in his arms, but he didn't dare move, for fear of jeopardizing whatever she was doing with the horse.

She continued singing but glanced over at him, and he realized she was singing with the same cadence, but her words were meant for him. "I'm going to be a little while longer. She's just getting settled."

He heard a tremble in her voice. How long had she been out there?

"Can I help? Do you want my jacket?" he asked as quietly as he could over the rain.

She sang, "No, thank you. I know we need to talk, but you should go."

"I'd rather stay in case you need anything."

"You'll make her nervous," she sang, smiling. "I'll text you when I'm done."

With a nod, he reluctantly headed back to his truck. As he

drove away, instead of heading home, he drove into town. He may not be able to help with the horse, but he sure as hell could take care of her afterward.

SASHA TEXTED HIM an hour and a half later.

Sasha: *Hi. I just finished. I'm heading home.*

Ezra gathered the things he'd bought and an umbrella and climbed into his truck, heading toward the barn. Sasha was trudging up the hill, her arms crossed over her chest, like she was hugging herself. He pulled over, grabbed the umbrella, and jogged across the grass to meet her. She looked at him a little warily. After the way they'd left things that afternoon, it was no wonder. She probably thought he was going to try to force the subject. But that could wait.

"You didn't have to come get me," she said as he fell into step with her, holding the umbrella over both of them.

"And here I thought I might get bonus points for being chivalrous. Let me warm you up." He handed her the umbrella and put his arm around her, pulling her against his side as they headed for the truck.

"You definitely get bonus points."

"What were you doing with that horse, and why weren't you wearing a rain jacket or at least a hat?"

"I was wearing a jacket, but she's a rescue named Posey. She's blind and super anxious. She was dropped off a few hours ago, and she's not halter trained. I needed to get her to trust me enough to let me put a halter on her, and she was afraid of the noise my rain jacket made, so I took it off."

"Were you out there singing to her the whole time?" He opened the passenger door and helped her in.

"Yeah. I was trying to get her to eat out of the bucket. Singing is soothing, and it gave her an auditory clue as to where I was." She told him how she'd put the halter in the bucket and had eventually gotten it on the horse.

"That was smart thinking. I'm glad it worked." He went around the driver's side and climbed in. "You probably don't remember, but you sang that song to Gus when he was a baby."

She turned those gorgeous, tired hazel eyes on him. "Actually, I sang it to both of you, because you kept apologizing for asking me to help, and everyone needs someone to lean on now and again."

"You pulled us through some rough times."

She shook her head. "I did what any friend would."

"Well, we were lucky you were there to help." He drove to her cabin and parked out front. "Now it's my turn to repay the favor. I brought a few things to help you warm up." He reached behind the seat for the bag of goodies he'd bought and handed it to her.

She peeked into the bag. "Hot chocolate, whipped cream, mini M&M's." Her gaze flicked briefly to his. "Soup? Bubble bath, and…What are *these*?" She reached into the bag and pulled out the pink fuzzy socks he'd bought her. She touched the material to her cheek. "They're so soft."

"Those are for your cold feet."

"How did you know my feet were cold?"

"Because you said you weren't sure we should keep seeing each other." He cocked a brow. "If that's not cold feet, then I don't know what is."

"*Ez*," she said softly, her brow arched. "As much as I hated bringing it up, I was serious. I'm worried."

"I know, and I want to talk about it, but you've had an exhausting night. Why don't you let me draw you a hot bath, and while you're warming up, I'll make you some soup or hot chocolate, or both. Then I'll take off, and we can talk another time."

"You want to *take care* of me?" she asked with a hint of incredulity and a little sass.

"I do. I care about you, Sash, whether or not you want to keep seeing me."

"I *want* to keep seeing you more than anything, but that's just me being selfish. I was so caught up in being with you, I didn't slow down enough to *really* understand what you had at risk. But today it hit me. This is the only place I *ever* wanted to work. It's my heart and soul, and I realized today that it's yours, too. I was there when you were interning and studying and preparing to become the incredible therapist that you are. But, Ezra, you're risking everything for an arrangement that can never be more than temporary."

"Maybe right now we seem temporary, but I don't think of us that way." *I think of us as…Finally.* He had to be careful not to promise more than he could give, but he didn't want her to give up on them. "Who knows what the future will hold? You could hate me next week."

"Not likely, since I've known you forever and never once hated you."

"Yeah, I'm not very hateable," he teased, earning a smile that made him want more. "Seriously, Sash. We don't know what'll happen, and we both want to be together. Can't we hope for the best? Maybe one day things will change."

"You mean, like when Gus goes away to college, and we

won't have to worry about messing up his life?" she asked with pained amusement.

He sure as hell hoped he'd figure something out before then, but for now he tried to lighten the air. "That doesn't sound so bad, does it?" He reached across the seat and took her hand. "I don't have the answers yet, but you have to know that I went into this with my eyes open. I know the risks, and I *want* to be selfish with you, Bo Peep. But if you're not comfortable with it and don't want to continue—"

"I *want* to. I just don't want to mess up your lives. I don't think I could handle that."

"I love where your heart is, but you could never mess up our lives." They were parked by her cabin, shrouded in darkness. He leaned in, sliding his hand to the nape of her neck and drawing her closer. "You make our lives better in every way. If things go south and trouble hits, that's on *me*, baby, not you. Do you understand?"

She wrinkled her nose. "It's kind of on both of us."

"No. You're not responsible for me and Gus. I'm the only one who holds that responsibility. Got it?"

She nodded. "You and Gus make my life better, too."

"I'm glad." He kissed her softly. "Is there anything else on that beautiful mind of yours?"

She bit her lower lip, trapping a smile. "Just one thing."

"Then let's talk about it."

"It's more of a *touching* thing," she said sweetly.

"Even better." He kissed her again. "What did you have in mind?"

"A bubble bath for two."

"Now, there's an idea I can get on board with."

Chapter Sixteen

SASHA SETTLED BACK against Ezra's chest in the warm bath and closed her eyes, reveling in the feel of his thick thighs nestling her body, the vanilla scent of the bubbles, and the soothing touch of the man who was gently bathing her. He kissed her shoulder as his capable, caring hands moved slowly over her skin, pampering her in a way no man ever had.

"I haven't taken a bubble bath in years, and I've never taken a bath with a man."

"Neither have I."

She tipped her face up, taking in his playful expression over her shoulder. "How about with a woman?"

"You're the first." He pressed his lips to hers.

"Really? I like that."

"So do I." He ran his hands along her thighs. "Warming up?"

"*Mm-hm.* No one has ever taken care of me like this before."

"You were obviously going out with the wrong guys."

Throwing caution to the wind, she said, "I always knew I was. But the one I really wanted either wasn't into me, or he was married or off-limits."

"Hyde's never been married," he said all too seriously.

"Not Hyde, you fool." She slapped his leg, sending bubbles sloshing over the side of the tub.

He laughed and wrapped his arms around her, hugging her, and brushed his scruff against her cheek. "Oh, you mean *me?*" he said with feigned innocence.

"I'm starting to question my choice."

"You should be rethinking all those wrong guys you went out with." His hands skimmed over her thighs, resting so close to her sex, desire bloomed hot and needy inside her. "But as far as I'm concerned, I don't think there's ever been a time I didn't want you."

"I mean after you were a teenager."

"Hey, don't negate those teenage years. That's when it all started. I used to ask to work late just so I could see you more. I'd watch you following that woman around who used to work with the horses and doing homework in the rehab barn, sitting with the injured animals." One hand slid up her belly, brushing the underside of her breast, making her even greedier for him. "You were so dedicated. It was impressive. You were a big part of the reason I cleaned up my act."

"I was *not*," she said with a laugh.

He teased her nipple, speaking into her ear. "Yes, you were, Bo Peep. I wanted to be good enough to be with a girl like you."

Goose bumps chased up her limbs, and she felt him tense up.

"Fuck it. That's not true," he gritted out. He wrapped his

arms around her. "My goal was to be good enough for *you*."

Her heart stumbled, and she looked at him over her shoulder. "Is that true?"

"One hundred percent."

As she tried to process that, she remembered the painful truth. "And I treated you like you weren't good enough."

"Only when I was in the program, and at first I didn't deserve to be treated any other way. You were too smart to take a chance on a kid like me. It was a good thing you held me at arm's length. Your self-respect taught me to respect myself."

She tried to calm her racing heart, but the truth did it for her. "And then you went off to college and forgot about me."

"Bullshit. You were unforgettable as a teenager and even more so as we got older. I still wanted to be with you, but our timing was always off. We were away at school, seeing other people, living our lives."

Knowing he'd wanted her the whole time filled all those lonely places inside her that had longed for him over those years. "Why didn't you tell me?"

"Because when we were at the ranch, your brothers were threatening any of the guys who so much as looked at you or Birdie."

"They probably would have broken your legs back then."

He laughed. "I don't doubt it."

"But you became a Dark Knight, and they trusted you, or you never would have become a patched member."

"That's true, but what you probably don't realize is that I had prospected the club at eighteen. I had to work hard to prove myself to your father and Manny and all the other members. Most guys prospect the club for a year. It took me two, and by then your family had become my family."

How could family be a double-edged sword? "I know how important they are to you."

"I had too much respect for all of you to topple that apple cart." He held her tighter, his voice thick with emotion. "Once I started interning with your mom, you became officially off-limits."

"I still am," she said softly, her own emotions whirling. She needed to be closer to him and tried turning around, but she couldn't figure out where to put her legs, sending water sloshing over the side of the tub. They both laughed as he scooched forward and guided her legs around him.

"You need a bigger tub."

"Or you need a more adept girlfriend." She hadn't realized what she'd said until that G word was hanging between them like a ticking bomb. "I mean friend with benefits."

He put his arms around her and ran the tip of his nose along her cheek. "Like I said, our timing is always off." He drew back and cradled her face in his hands. "Don't ever take our bad timing as a lack of desire, because *that* has never wavered."

His eyes held pools of emotions too deep for her to even try to dissect, but she ached to feel all of them. The lust and passion, the uncertainty and pain over the lost years they could have had, and the visceral need to hold it all in. She opened her mouth to say, *Show me*, but couldn't wait and pressed her lips to his. He was right there with her, one hand pushing into her hair, cradling her head as he took the kiss deeper, possessing more of her, his other hand cupping her bottom, pulling her closer. As his tongue swept and delved, her hands traveled over his arms and shoulders, into his hair, grasping for purchase. He groped her breast, teasing her nipple until she was out of her mind with need, moaning and arching into him. She couldn't take it anymore. As his hand moved between her legs, she reached between them, fisting his hard length. Water splashed around them as she stroked his long, thick cock. He growled into their kisses, the sound turning her on even more as his fingers expertly worked their magic on her clit, sending pleasure spiking through her. *"Yes. Ohgod. Yes—"* She arched and moaned, releasing his cock to hold on to his arms as pleasure ravaged her. He stayed with her, teasing and pleasuring her, until she came down from the high.

"You're so sexy, baby. *Again.*" The demand was accompanied by his quickening fingers, sending her thoughts reeling. He reclaimed her mouth, fierce and devouring, and rolled her nipple between his finger and thumb, driving her out of her mind with his other hand. Scintillating sensations prickled her limbs like a thousand needles, taking her right up to the precipice of madness. She grabbed his cock again but couldn't concentrate enough to stroke it, so she clung to it like a trophy. He tore his mouth away, sealing it over the curve of her neck. His teeth grated against her skin, sending erotic pleasures bolting through her. It was all she could do to release his shaft and grab hold of his arms as her orgasm crashed over her. Her vision went black, her body clenching and rocking, a stream of libidinous noises sailing from her lungs like a girl possessed.

When she started to come down from the peak, he took her in a slow, deep kiss. "I fucking love making you come."

"Yeah? I couldn't tell," she panted out. He laughed, and his delicious mouth found hers again, both of them smiling as they kissed. "I want you inside me. I'm on birth control."

His eyes flamed. "You shouldn't've told me that, Bo Peep. Now I know I can make love to you anywhere the urge hits."

"Maybe I should have told you a week ago."

He took her by the hips, guiding her onto his erection. She gasped at the pleasure flaring in her chest and loins as she sank down, burying him to the hilt, and he gritted out, "*Fuuck.*" He held her still. "Christ, baby. Nothing in my life has ever felt as good as you do right now." She gyrated her hips, and he groaned deep in his throat. "You make me feel like a fucking teenager ready to blow."

She laughed. "Don't let that happen, or the guys are going to wonder why I call you One-Minute Moore."

"The fuck you will." He thrust into her impossibly deeper, stealing her breath. "I said you make me feel like it, *not* that it was going to happen."

"Let's hope not," she teased, gyrating again.

"Careful what you wish for, Bo Peep. This wolf can go all night long and leave you unable to walk tomorrow."

"Prove it."

Their mouths came together in feverish kisses, but he slowed her down, his tongue sliding sensually over hers as he guided her along his shaft. Every upward thrust stroked over that secret spot inside her, sending electric shocks shooting through her. She tried to ride him faster, to chase the sensations, but he wouldn't allow it. "You feel too good to rush through this."

"*Ezra, please.*"

"Don't worry, baby. You're going to come for me so many times, your legs will turn to rubber." He dragged his tongue along her lower lip, continuing to control their speed. "These lips are so perfect. They fucking taunt me every time I see you." He nipped at her lower lip. "I love your mouth." He crushed his lips to hers, kissing her ravenously but still loving her slowly. The clashing sensations caused an inferno inside her. "I especially love when you suck my cock."

His dirty talk made her as needy as the way he touched her did.

"And your gorgeous breasts bring out the animal in me." He slicked his tongue over and around one nipple and then the other, until every inch of her burned for more. "I want to come on them one day."

"Yes." She dug her fingernails into his shoulders with the erotic thought.

"*Mm.* My girl likes that idea."

"I want to do everything with you," she said breathlessly. "Fuck me faster."

He increased his speed a smidgen, making her practically salivate for the orgasm that was hovering just out of reach. The man knew how to draw out her pleasure, and she was loving every excruciating second of it. "Is my girl ready to come on my cock?"

"So ready."

He sucked her nipple to the roof of his mouth, sending her orgasm barreling into her. He stayed with her as her body bucked and writhed. As she floated down from the peak, he intensified his thrusts and sucks, sending her spiraling into oblivion again. He released her hips, belting one arm around her, holding her tight against him as she rode out the last of her climax. The feel of his muscles flexing was as arousing as his touch as he lowered his mouth to her breast again. He sucked her nipple harder, sending an intoxicating mix of pain and pleasure careening through her. "*Do it again*," she pleaded. He sucked harder, thrusting faster, until she lost control and cried out his name. She was vaguely aware of water splashing as he pulled her mouth to his, taking her in a possessive, penetrating kiss that magnified the sensations engulfing her.

Their kisses turned wild and passionate, their thrusts fast and frantic, causing a torrent of sensations that took her right up to another peak. She was dizzy with desire, craving more of him like an addict to their favorite drug. He grabbed her ass with one hand, her hip with the other, moving her faster and harder along his cock. Prickles of pain morphed into all-consuming pleasure, and she couldn't get enough of it. She met his every effort with a rock of her hips, their bodies moving in perfect sync. She was engulfed in pleasure so intense, every touch sent lightning searing through her. She clawed at his arms and shoulders, the gratified sounds he made carrying her into another magnificent orgasm. He was right behind her, growling out her name, pumping and thrusting through his own powerful release.

When she collapsed against him, resting her cheek on his shoulder, he dusted kisses over her cheek and shoulder as the world came back into focus.

"God, baby. That was unbelievable."

"Uh-huh," she managed.

He ran his hand up her back. "It looks like there was a tsunami in here."

She peered over the side of the tub at the water on the floor. "Want to go for another?"

He pushed his fingers into her hair, taking her in a toe-curling kiss that went on and on. She felt his cock swell. He drew back with a wolfish grin. "What do you think?"

AFTER ANOTHER TSUNAMI, a warm shower, and cleaning up the mess they'd made, Ezra made a fire in her fireplace. He was heading into the kitchen when Sasha padded into the living room in her new fuzzy socks, her old cotton shorts, and *his* T-shirt. What a sight she was, adorably comfortable with that sated look in her eyes. He loved being alone like this with her, in her home where his son's drawings decorated her refrigerator and Gus's craft area was stuffed to the gills. It was like they were always meant to be.

"You made a fire," she said sweetly. "Did I take that long getting dressed?"

"No. I've got fire making down to a science."

She eyed his bare chest. "I could get used to seeing you barefoot and shirtless in my kitchen."

He tugged her into his arms. "Careful or *you'll* end up naked again." He kissed her softly. "What would you like? Soup? Hot chocolate?"

"Hot chocolate, but I can make it."

"Relax. I've got it. You had a long, hard night with the horse and then a greedy guy in your bathtub."

"I'm sorry, but did you hear me complaining? Because I sure didn't." She went up on her toes and kissed him, then reached into a cabinet for a mug.

He made her hot chocolate, and she snagged the can of whipped cream and shot some into her mouth. He laughed and shook his head. "You're as bad as Gus." He reached for the whipped cream.

She pulled it away, shooting more into her mouth, eyes dancing with delight.

"I've got something you can put in your mouth." He cocked a brow.

Her eye sparked with heat. "Maybe we'll have to take this can into the bedroom later."

She turned to put whipped cream on her hot chocolate, and he wrapped his arms around her from behind, kissing her neck. Feeling her soft curves made him want her all over again. But as much as he wanted to carry her into the bedroom and make love to her until morning, he'd already strayed from pampering to devouring. He might not be able to publicly be the man he wanted to be for her, but in private, he sure as hell would treat her the way she deserved.

"*Sasha à la whipped cream* sounds perfect to me." He sprinkled M&M's on the whipped cream. "But that's going to have to wait, because you need to rest those tired bones." He picked up the mug, and with a hand on her back, he guided her into the living room.

"I'm fine. Aren't you going to have some hot chocolate?"

"I have all the sweetness I need right here." He kissed her temple.

She sank down to the couch with a sigh, and he handed her the mug. She took a sip. "*Mm.* Thank you."

"Where do you want me? Rubbing your feet or your shoulders?"

"Ez, you don't have to do either."

"I need to keep my hands busy around you, or they might wander. How about I start with your feet?" He lowered himself to the other side of the couch and lifted her feet onto his lap.

"Ezra, you really don't—"

He started massaging her foot.

"*Holy cow*, that feels *so* good. Forget what I said. Just keep doing what you're doing."

He laughed and continued massaging her foot, working his

way up her calf.

"Oh, wow. That feels amazing. Are you sure you went to talk therapy school and not massage therapy school?"

"I've been faking it all these years. Don't tell anyone." He squeezed her foot. "Now tell me about Posey. What will happen to her tomorrow?"

"Do you really want to know about her?" She took another sip and licked the whipped cream off her upper lip.

So damn sexy. "The horses are your life, and I like hearing about the things that are important to you."

"Well, Doc will check her out tomorrow, and I'll keep working with her to gain her trust. Hopefully she and Dream— the horse that was out there with us—will continue bonding, so she can settle in."

"How do you facilitate that?"

"The same way you do with people. You give them access to each other and make sure there's no aggressive behavior. Dream was a doll with her tonight. After you left, I put them in special adjoining stalls that have welded wire between them instead of a wooden panel. There are no sharp edges, so Posey can't hurt herself, but she can put her nose against it to feel closer to Dream. Horses are herd animals, and I'm hoping that'll help her feel safe."

"That makes sense. But then what? Will she be able to go out in the pasture with other horses?"

"There's no reason she can't have a full, happy life. As far as being pastured with the herd goes, we'll probably keep her closer to home with Dream and eventually maybe another horse or two. We want to protect her from being bullied. We'll see how she progresses, like you would with a kid."

"That makes sense." He started massaging her other foot.

"*God* that feels good. I can't believe you've been hiding this skill from me for all these years."

He worked his way up her calf. "We haven't exactly had a hands-on relationship until recently."

She took another drink and set her mug on the end table. "I'm glad we have one now." She cocked her head with a curious expression. "I had you pegged as an acts-of-service love-language guy, but now I'm thinking physical touch might be your love language."

"My love language? Have you been reading Birdie's magazines again?"

She laughed. "I'm never going to live that down, am I?"

"You made everyone at the dinner table take a quiz called How Single Are You?"

She rolled her eyes. "That was at least three years ago. Let it go."

He held up his hands in surrender. "Consider it gone...for now."

"Whatever. Have you always been a touchy person? I know you've always loved on Gus, but I mean with other people?"

"Not really. You know how my dad is. He loves me, but there's never been a lot of outward affection there."

"What about your mom? Was she a hugger?"

"I think she was when I was little. I have memories of being hugged and told she loved me, but after things got bad between her and my dad, I think it changed."

"When did that start changing?"

"I don't know. Maybe when I was ten or eleven. After she left, a lot of those happier feelings got buried beneath hurt and anger."

"That's understandable. I know you don't have a relationship with her now, but did she ever try after she left?"

"Not really." He met her gaze, glad his hands were busy. "She reached out six months after she moved to tell us she'd gone to Greece and was staying with her parents. Honestly, I didn't want anything to do with her at that point. It wasn't until a few years later, when I went through therapy with your mom, that I started to deal with those emotions."

"I'm glad my mom was able to help."

"Me too. She changed the way I viewed everything. She helped me see that people are flawed and that I had a right to be hurt and angry, but if I didn't want to carry that into future relationships, I needed to deal with it. And I did. It was tough, and it took a while, but we got through it."

She shifted her feet off his lap and scooted closer, taking his hand. "Is this too hard to talk about?"

"It's a little uncomfortable, but given our relationship, you should know what I've been through."

"Thank you for trusting me. How did you deal with it? I mean, other than talking to my mom."

"She got me writing letters to my parents that I never sent, to get all those bad feelings out of my system. There was so much fury and vitriol on those early pages, it's no wonder I was a mess."

"You weren't a mess. You were brokenhearted, and rightly so. I've known enough people who have gone through that to understand how it affects everything else in your life."

"That's true, but I was still a mess, and I'm okay with admitting that. Hurt, anger, confusion, feelings of not being worthy of my mother's love. That's pretty fucking messy, babe. I'm sure it bothers you to hear it, but let's deal with reality."

"It doesn't bother me. It makes me sad that you felt that

way and mad that your parents put you through it."

"See? *Messy*." He leaned in and kissed her. "But over time I crawled out of the mess. I began to understand my feelings better, and what I wrote shifted from blame to seeking answers."

"What kind of answers?"

"What you'd expect. Why did my mother leave? Why didn't she stay nearby and have a relationship with me? Why did my father get even more closed off? But I didn't have answers because my father wouldn't talk about it. When I went away to college, I was sidetracked, but those questions were always there, and your mom and I kept in contact by video sessions, and of course I was back here during the summers."

"I remember. I looked forward to seeing you all year."

"You weren't alone in that. I couldn't wait to see you, either."

"Really?" Disbelief shone in her eyes.

"Yes, really. School was stressful. I mean it was fun and there were parties and girls and all that, but it was like I saw all of that as a chaotic tunnel, and you, and this place, were the light at the end of it."

"I don't even care if you're making that up." She cuddled closer. "I love hearing it."

He laughed. "I'm not making it up."

"That makes it even better. So, did you ever get your answers?"

"I had to. I realized if I was ever going to help others through personal issues, I'd better get my arms around my own. It was the summer after my sophomore year. That's the first time I really made an effort to talk to my father about it."

"How did he respond?"

"Like you probably imagine. He said he didn't want to talk

about it and wouldn't talk about the details or the divorce. He said he did his best and couldn't go back and change things or change himself, and that was that. I tried a few more times, but he continued to refuse to talk about the past. He shuts down."

"It must be too painful for him, but it doesn't sound like he gave you any answers."

"He didn't, but my mother did."

Her eyes widened. "You talked to her that summer?"

"It took me a little longer to get up the nerve to call her, but I did a few months later."

"Wow. What was that like after so long?"

He thought about that for a minute, remembering how strange it was to hear his mother's voice. "It was weird. I was nervous but not overly so. I remember going through scenarios in my head before I called. Like, what if she didn't want to talk to me or was upset with me because I was so rebellious after she left. That kind of thing. But then I remembered what your mom had said when I told her I was going to reach out to my mother."

"What did she say?"

"She said before I made the call to look in a mirror and remind myself how far I've come since my mother left. She said to remember that back then, my mother had the power to turn my life upside down because I was a child, and as an adult, I was in control, and she couldn't hurt me unless I let her. She said to consider the source before opening the door to the pain. That was big, hearing that I had a choice in who I let hurt me. People don't usually think that way when it comes to their parents. But she also said sometimes people who have been through that kind of abandonment will revert to feeling like a hurt kid all over again when that wound is reopened. And if that happened, that was okay, too. She'd be there to help me through it."

"That sounds like my mom. So, did you revert to a hurt child?"

"No. It was strange, but when I heard my mother's voice, it was like talking to someone who I knew in my head I had known and loved at one point but who I had also hated for a while, and by the time I made that call, I didn't feel much of anything other than the desire to get answers from the only person who could give them to me."

Compassion shimmered in her eyes. "Oh, *Ez*. That realization must have hurt."

"It didn't. It was actually cathartic. As I was asking the questions, I realized it didn't matter what her excuse was. She was a mother who had left her son behind. Good or bad, in my eyes, that told me who she was. At that point I just wanted to know why so I could close that door."

"What did she say?"

"Not a lot. She said she wasn't getting her emotional needs met by my father, which came as no surprise, but she had to know he was like that before they got married. And she said she didn't want to get caught up in a messy divorce or try to win custody to take me overseas. In her head, she was making my life easier by leaving me with my father. But that's a rationalization, and a bad one. She remarried a year after she left us, and she made no effort to remain in my life."

"I don't know how a parent can do that to a child. To walk away like they don't exist?"

"That's because your love guides you. I think for my mother, there's a level of selfishness and weakness that guides her."

"Like Tina?"

"In a way. The thing is, humans are flawed, and hate can eat away at a person. All I could do was accept what she did and decide if I wanted her in my life or not."

"Does she know about Gus?"

"I don't know. I never reached out to tell her about him. I wanted to protect him from becoming someone who didn't mean enough to his grandmother to warrant a visit or a birthday card or…"

She snuggled into his side. "I love how you love and protect Gus with everything you have. It's amazing to me that you can be so affectionate when you didn't grow up with that type of open affection."

"That's because of Tina and Gus."

"Tina brought that out in you?" she asked with surprise. "I guess she was good for something other than bringing your adorable little boy into the world."

He scoffed. "*No*. Touch is definitely *not* her love language. I don't think she has a love language. *Gus* brought it out in me because of her inability to mother. I think Tina might have suffered from undiagnosed postpartum depression in the weeks after Gus was born. She was tired all the time, and she never got up to feed him at night. I tried to talk with her about it, but she said it was normal to be exhausted after childbirth. Two months later, her energy and her personality came back, and she was all about getting back into shape. The minute I got home from work, she'd head to the gym or out with friends, so from the time Gus was a newborn, he and I had a lot of one-on-one bonding time. I used to put him on my bare chest when I'd rock him. When he was an infant, I worried a lot about making sure he felt loved."

"You still do."

"Yeah. I don't think that ever goes away."

"Well, rest assured that you do a great job of loving him. In fact, I think your love for Gus encompasses all five love languages, and he's learned from that, because he meets them all. He's affectionate, definitely not afraid of physical touch, and he's thoughtful and says sweet things."

Hearing her talk so lovingly about Gus made his heart feel full. He pulled her closer and kissed her. "So, Miss Inquisitive. What's your love language?"

"That's a good question. With the horses, I think it's words of affirmation and physical touch."

"Don't sell yourself short. You do acts of service for them and give quality time on a daily basis."

"True. So do you, for Gus and for your friends."

"This isn't about me. What's your love language with people?"

"That depends on the person. I've been hooked on you for so long, I'm pretty sure I held back showing any real affection to the guys I went out with."

Selfishly, he'd like to believe he was the only guy she'd ever been with, but that wouldn't be healthy for her. "If that's true, I'm sorry, because you have a big heart, Bo Peep, and a lot of love to give. I hope I didn't rip you off from enjoying yourself."

"Oh, I enjoyed myself. I just didn't share my true affections. But now that I'm with you…" She straddled his lap and put her arms around him. "I want to explore all the love languages. Quality time, like we did tonight, and words of affirmation. I love the way you communicate and listen." She kissed his lips. "And physical touch." She ran her fingers over his pecs, lingering on his nipples. "Lots and lots of physical touch."

"That's good, Bo Peep, because I love touching you." He pushed his hands under her shirt, fondling her breasts. He rolled her nipple between his finger and thumb, earning a sexy little gasp. "Give me your mouth, sweetheart."

"I was just getting to that." She reached between them, tugging open the button on his jeans. "I believe it's time for acts of service."

"Damn, baby."

She climbed off his lap, and they stripped off his jeans and boxer briefs. He reached for her, but she pushed him down to the couch and lowered herself to her knees, fisting his rigid cock. Her eyes remained trained on his as she slid her tongue around the broad head and proceeded to lick his length until it was glistening. Then she lowered her mouth over his shaft, her eyes locked on him.

"You're so damn sexy with your mouth on me, baby. Take your shirt off. Let me see your tits." She pulled off her shirt, and her hair tumbled over her shoulders. "Fucking gorgeous."

He leaned forward, kissing her deeply.

"Let me love you," she whispered.

Her words sank into his bones as she went back to stroking, licking, and sucking. To be loved by this incredible woman would be a dream come true. She stroked him faster, tighter, and sucked the crown into her mouth. His thoughts fell away, and a growl rumbled out.

She grinned victoriously. "I love the noises you make."

"Hearing you say that makes me want to drive my cock down your throat. Not to hurt you, just…that's how turned on you make me. I want to fuck all of you."

"You mean like this?" She lowered her mouth over his length, taking him deep, then drew him out slowly and took him deep again, squeezing as her fist chased her lips along his dick.

"Fuuck. Yes."

She quickened her efforts, the head of his cock hitting the back of her throat time and time again. He cursed at the pleasure gripping him. When she moaned around his cock, his hips shot up. She gagged and released him from her swollen lips.

"Shit. Sorry, babe. I didn't mean to hurt you."

"You didn't. It just surprised me. Now that I know what you like, I'll be fine." She dragged her tongue along the head. "Don't go easy. I want you to fuck my mouth like you love it."

His cock jerked with that green light. "How could I not love it, baby? It's *you.*" He leaned forward, taking her in another passionate kiss. "Do you want me to pull out? Or can I come in your sexy mouth?"

Heat flared in her eyes. "Don't pull out. I want you to think about me swallowing your come every time you see me." She lowered her hot, wet mouth over his cock, as if she hadn't just blown him away. Her eyes bored into him as she teased and stroked so fucking perfectly, pleasure burned through his veins, pulsing beneath his skin like an animal clawing for release. It didn't take long before he was gritting his teeth to stave off his orgasm. She took him to the back of her throat, faster, *harder,* taking him deeper. *"I fucking love your mouth."*

He buried his hands in her hair, pumping his hips as she sucked and stroked, her hand tightening exquisitely around his shaft, driving him out of his goddamn mind. He wanted to last, to feel her mouth wrapped around his cock for hours. *Days.* But he couldn't slow down. It felt too good. "I'm close, baby," he warned. She teased his balls with her other hand and tugged. Heat shot down his spine, and her name flew from his lungs in a thunderous roar as he came.

She stayed with him, taking everything he had to give, riding out the very last aftershock. Her gorgeous eyes sought his as she released his cock, looking like the prettiest naughty angel he'd ever seen. Her tongue swept across her glistening lips, and he gathered her in his arms.

"I think we found your superpower." He kissed her passionately, possessively, earning a sinful moan. "I want you naked, baby." He helped her to her feet and took off her shorts. Holding her gaze, he slid his fingers between her legs. "*Mm.* Your pussy is begging for me."

Her cheeks pinked up as he sat on the edge of the couch, guiding her closer, and leaned in to lick her arousal. She sucked in a sharp breath, clinging to his shoulders.

"Your come is so sweet." He licked and teased and sucked and pushed his fingers inside her as he took her clit between his teeth, earning a loud pleasure-filled moan. He found that hidden spot inside her that made her rock and moan. Pleasuring Sasha had become his greatest desire, and he couldn't get enough. He continued fucking her with his fingers, earning gasps every time he stroked that magical spot and teasing her clit until her breathing came in fast spurts, and "*Ohgodohgod...Ez—*" burst from her lungs. Her fingernails carved into his skin, her hips bucking as he devoured every drop of her arousal.

Fucking perfect.

When she went lax, he laid her on the couch and came down over her. Her eyes fluttered open. "Is this heaven?" she whispered.

He laughed and kissed her, his cock nestled against her slick pussy. "My cock is jealous of my tongue. He wants to be inside you."

"Then what are you waiting for?"

She lifted her hips, and as their bodies became one, "*Sash*" fell from his lips as "*Ez*" fell from hers. There was something magical, something bigger than life between them, and he wanted to live in its arms forever. As their mouths came together and they found their rhythm, beyond the pleasure enveloping him, one thought played through his mind. He needed to figure out how they could be together without hiding sooner rather than later, because there was no way in hell he was giving her up, and whatever this was between them was too big to be contained for long.

Chapter Seventeen

"STAY STILL, BUDDY," Ezra said as he helped Gus into his neon-yellow paintball suit.

"I wanna see who wins," Gus said, turning to watch Dare and Cowboy dicking around with Rebel and Hyde. They were seeing who could walk on their hands the longest as the rest of the guys cheered them on. Hyde fell, then pushed Rebel over. Rebel chased him toward Dare and Cowboy, and they ended up on their asses, too. The four of them were shouting and running around like fools, while everyone cracked up.

Never a dull moment.

It was Friday evening, the week before Dare and Billie's wedding, and as the sun went down, ground lights illuminated the paintball field where the bachelor/bachelorette party games would soon begin. Between the Whiskeys, the Mancinis, Dwight and the ranch hands, and the ranch's residential clients, more than two dozen people were milling about in camouflage clothing, waiting for the girls to arrive so the game could begin. Paintball was serious business in the Whiskey family. The field looked like a warzone, with sandbag bunkers, stone walls and barrels, enormous upright tires that were pinned to the ground, dirt barriers, and several other obstacles.

"Where the hell are the girls?" Rebel asked.

Gus tugged on Ezra's jeans. "*Dad*, Rebel said the *H* word."

"Yeah, I heard him."

"Why do girls always take so damn long?" Taz said.

"Taz said the *D* word!" Gus tattled.

"What the hell's wrong with the *D* word?" Hyde asked with a smirk, inciting more tattling.

"Really, guys?" Ezra stifled a laugh and shook his head as they cracked up.

"*Whoa*. I need to come to more paintball games," Kenny pointed across the field toward the main house, where the girls were filing out of the main house wearing bathing suits. Wynnie, Alice, and Sully wore one-pieces, while the others wore bikinis.

Ezra's body flamed at the sight of Sasha strutting toward them in a tiny turquoise bikini and combat boots. In his mind, he heard "Pour Some Sugar on Me" and saw her moving in slow motion as she flipped her long blond hair over her shoulder, hips swaying, gorgeous eyes locked on him. His cock noticed. *Fuck.* He tried doing mental math to stop his dirty thoughts in their tracks.

Taz and Hyde whistled and cheered, sparking the same from some of the ranch hands. Ezra ground his back teeth against the urge to throw a blanket around Sasha so they couldn't look their fill.

"Dad, are we going swimming, too?" Gus exclaimed.

"No, buddy. We're playing paintball."

Gus ran to Sasha. "Sugar! Why are you wearing your bathing suit?"

She scooped him up, a radiant grin blooming across her beautiful face as his little boy threw his arms around her. It had been a week and a half since that rainy evening when he and Sasha had spent all night wrapped in each other's arms. That was the best damn night. He'd had Gus last weekend, and they'd had lunch with his father on Saturday. His father had been totally focused on Gus, and Ezra had spent that time wishing Sasha were there with them. Tina had begged out of taking Gus again Tuesday night, and Sasha had watched him while Ezra had been at church. After Gus had gone to bed, he and Sasha had made love. They'd snuck in a few private moments here and there since then and had been working together on their talk for the networking dinner while Gus played or watched television, but it wasn't nearly enough. Ezra was greedy when it came to Sasha. He wanted more time with her alone and with Gus.

He wanted it all.

Tina was supposed to have Gus tonight, but Ezra had kept him so Gus wouldn't miss out on playing paintball. He was dropping him off with Tina in the morning, and although he'd never wish away his time with his son, he couldn't wait to get Sasha in his arms again.

"Damn. Look at my old lady rocking that swimsuit," Tiny said proudly.

"I'm too busy looking at mine," Manny said.

"My future wife is a smoke show," Dare said.

"Not as hot as mine," Cowboy said as he headed for Sully.

"I'm on *their* team, and I skinny-dip!" Taz announced, and whipped off his shirt. He reached for the button on his jeans.

"Me too!" Kenny exclaimed, and started to take off his shirt.

Ezra and the other men glowered at them, but it was Tiny's gruff voice that stopped them in their tracks. "If you boys take your pants off, it'll be the last time you use those hands."

"Sorry, Pres. I got a little carried away." Taz put his shirt back on.

"Idiot." Rebel masked the word with a cough as the girls joined them.

"Are you ladies trying to start a riot?" Doc crossed his arms, staring down his sisters.

Birdie planted a hand on her hip. "Ever heard of psyching out the other team?"

"Not when the other team includes your brothers," Doc said gruffly.

"You're not *all* our brothers," Sasha said, carrying Gus over to Ezra with a playful look in her eyes.

Ezra ached to pull her into his arms and let everyone there know that she was his and he was damn proud of it.

"Loosen up, Doc. They're only bathing suits," Wynnie said.

"You're not afraid of a little skin, are you, Doc?" Alice asked.

"We like skin," Hyde said as he and Taz circled Bobbie.

Bobbie rolled her eyes.

"You don't hear my man complaining." Billie strutted over to Dare, and he tugged her into a kiss.

"See? They know how to have fun," Birdie exclaimed.

"A'right, girls, you've had your fun," Tiny said loudly. "Get your clothes on."

Sasha set Gus on his feet, and he ran over and took Wynnie's hand. "Wynnie, can the boys wear bathing suits next time?"

Wynnie smiled down at him. "I don't see why not."

Ezra turned his back to the others, whispering to Sasha, "You are absolutely gorgeous, but did you have to wear the turquoise one?"

She looked down at her barely there bikini. "What's wrong with it?"

"It's *smaller* than the pink one. Do you have any idea how hard it is to keep my hands to myself right now?"

"Good. I just wanted to make sure I stayed on your mind tonight," she said sassily.

"Woman, I think about you so much, it's a wonder I can think of anything else."

HE WAS STILL thinking about her in that damn bikini an hour later. The game was in full swing. The sounds of people running, paintball guns shooting, laughter, and shouts filled the air as Taz shot at Ezra. Ezra dove behind a tower of tires, avoiding being hit. He heard Gus giggling and turned just in time to see him running alongside Dare as they snuck up on Simone. They shot her in the back, and she spun around as Dare picked up Gus like a football under his arm and took off running.

Ezra spotted Alice and Manny kissing in a bunker and ran by, shooting both of them.

"What happened to the brotherhood?" Manny hollered.

"All is fair in love and war!" Ezra laughed as he dove behind a metal barrier. He peered out, spotting Sasha peeking out from behind a stone wall as Bobbie darted across the field. Doc popped out of a bunker and shot Bobbie in the chest.

"Darn it, Doc!" Bobbie complained.

Doc sprinted by, cracking up, and Dwight appeared from behind a barrier and shot him. Doc feigned his death, dramatically falling to the ground. Sasha stepped out from behind the wall, shooting Dwight in the back, and yelled, "Loser!" as she sprinted away.

Attagirl.

A shot rang out from behind a cement cylinder, and Wynnie hollered, "Darn it, Tiny!" Tiny's deep laughter filled the air, and Cowboy yelled, "Way to go, Dad!"

Ezra saw Sasha crawling G.I. Joe–style out of a bunker and around the side of a stone wall. He stealthily made his way over, slipping behind one obstacle after another. He heard Gus holler, "Gotcha!"

Kenny shouted, "Oh man! Shot by a peewee!"

Ezra sprinted out from behind a tower of tires and ran behind the wall where Sasha was hiding. She spun around, her gun aimed directly at him. Her camouflage pants and vest were covered in dirt, and her hair was trapped beneath her eye mask. She looked fierce and competitive and so fucking sexy he wanted to ravage her right there. He held his finger up in front of his mouth, and they both looked around. His heart raced as he closed the distance between them. "Hey, sweetheart," he whispered. "I think we're alone."

"I didn't see anyone."

Adrenaline coursed through him as he pulled her into a kiss, feeling like he needed that connection to feel fully alive—and lately, he did. He wanted to take the kiss deeper but knew he couldn't risk it and reluctantly drew back. Her sweet smile and lustful eyes nearly took him to his knees. "Come see me tonight after Gus is asleep," he whispered.

"Okay," she whispered.

Their eyes remained trained on each other as they walked backward toward opposite ends of the wall. He never even realized she'd lifted her gun until the paintball nailed him in the stomach, and by then she was already gone, her laughter trailing behind her like the wind.

LONG AFTER THEIR epic paintball game, which turned into several epic games with a few stolen kisses, Sasha was sitting by the bonfire playing her guitar, as laughter and conversations went on around her. Her parents were holding hands between their chairs, talking with Alice, Manny, and Dwight. Birdie had wrangled Billie into wearing her bride-to-be sash, and now she was pushing for her to wear the crown. Dare was trying to convince Birdie that his beautiful fiancée didn't need a crown, and at the same time, he tried to convince Billie that she'd be the hottest crown-wearing bride-to-be ever to exist.

He was going to be a great husband.

Gus had chocolate all over his fingers as he and Ezra made s'mores while they chatted with Doc. Taz and Hyde were flirting with Bobbie and Simone. There was a lot of eye-rolling going on from the girls, and Kenny was having fun teasing Taz and Hyde about that. Cowboy and Sully were talking among themselves, kissing between conversations. *Sigh.* They were so in love. These were the moments Sasha loved most. When she was surrounded by the people she cared about and love and friendship hung in the air. She only wished she could express her love for Ezra as openly as her siblings were able to for their significant others.

"I'm not wearing a crown," Billie insisted.

"It's tradition," Birdie insisted. "Every bride wears a crown at the bachelorette party."

"We have no traditions yet. We're the first to get married in our families," Billie reminded her. "Our tradition can be *no* crown."

"Speak for yourself, sis," Bobbie interrupted as she roasted a marshmallow. "When I have my bachelorette party, I'm wearing a crown and a sash."

"So am I," Birdie said. "We like crowns, right, Sasha?"

If Sasha were marrying Ezra, she wouldn't care what she wore. "I guess, but I think Billie should wear whatever she wants. It's her bachelorette party."

"Birdie, Billie doesn't have to wear the crown because *you* like the tradition," Dare said. "But I'll happily wear it on her behalf so your tradition will remain in place."

"That works for me." Birdie put the crown on Dare's head and went back to her seat with a bounce in her step.

"You know, if you'd made her a bedazzled cowgirl hat, she probably would have worn it," Bobbie said.

"And it would have made more sense for our family's tradition," Alice said.

"That's a great idea," Birdie said. "What do you think, Sasha? Do you prefer a crown or a cowgirl hat?"

Sasha stole a glance at Ezra, who was licking chocolate off his fingers, and the sinful look in his eyes sent her heart into a wild flutter.

"Sasha, crown or cowgirl hat?" Birdie urged.

Flustered, she said, "Um…Another s'more," and got up to get a marshmallow from the table. The bag was empty. It was just as well. She could use a distraction. "I'm going inside to get more marshmallows. I'll be right back."

"I can get them," Dwight offered.

"It's okay. I've got it." Sasha headed for the big house. A minute later she heard heavy footfalls, and Bobbie and Birdie flanked her, linking their arms with hers.

"Someone's been keeping secrets from her besties," Bobbie said with hushed urgency.

"What are you talking about?" Sasha opened the kitchen door, and they headed inside. "You're the one flirting with Taz and Hyde."

"I am *not*. They're flirting with me," Bobbie insisted. "They're like dogs in heat."

"Hot dogs in heat." Birdie laughed. *"Hot dogs!"*

"Focus, Birdie. Okay, Sasha. Give it up," Bobbie said. "We saw the sexy looks you and Ezra have been giving each other all night."

She was dying to tell them the truth, but she'd made a promise to Ezra that nobody would find out. "You guys are nuts. I'm not giving him sexy looks." She grabbed a bag of marshmallows from the pantry.

They gave her deadpan looks.

"I work at a bar. I know the difference between the looks two people who are fucking give each other and the look of two people who *want to be* fucking." Bobbie narrowed her eyes. "What you and that Greek god are doing is definitely the former."

Holy cow, are we that transparent?

"And you've been way too happy lately," Birdie said.

"Did it ever occur to you that I'm happy because Posey is doing well, and I was worried about her?" It was a viable reason.

Now that Posey was more comfortable and trusting of Sasha and had bonded with Dream, she was settling in nicely. Sasha continued to put them in adjacent pens when she turned them out, giving Posey a schedule and a friend she could anticipate and count on.

"Yes." Birdie leaned forward, whispering, "But you look *orgasm* happy. Not horse happy."

"Unless Ezra is hung like a horse," Bobbie added excitedly.

"Good point. Is he?" Birdie whispered conspiratorially.

Yes, and he drives me crazy with that particular body part, and with his hands and mouth, and everything. She thought about the way he gazed deeply into her eyes when they made love, and her insides clenched. But it was so much bigger than that. He talked and listened and he was thoughtful and loving and would give his own life to protect his son.

She couldn't tell them any of those things, but as she looked at the sister and friend she'd trusted with many of her secrets, she didn't want to lie. "*If* we were hooking up, you know I wouldn't talk about it anyway because it's against policy to date other employees."

"Now you know why I don't work here. You never know when a hottie is going to show up and sweep you off your feet." Birdie's eyes widened. "*Wait.* Does that mean what I think it means?"

Sasha tried to stifle her smile.

"Yes!" Bobbie exclaimed. She and Birdie squealed and hugged Sasha. "I'm so happy for you. But you'd better stop looking at him like you want to eat him for dinner unless you want everyone to know."

"That won't matter. She's always looked at him like that," Birdie said.

"Then why did you say you could tell we were hooking up because of how we were looking at each other?" Sasha asked.

"I didn't. Bobbie did. I said you look orgasm happy, but that wasn't how I knew about you two either. I saw you guys kissing when we were playing paintball."

Sasha's stomach seized, and panic flared in her chest.

"Don't worry. I stood guard. Nobody else saw you, and if they would've come close, I'd have shot them," Birdie reassured her.

"Are you *sure*? Why didn't you tell me? We got carried away and thought we were alone each time."

"Yes, I'm sure, and I didn't say anything because I wanted to see if you'd come clean first."

"It's not like I can talk about it, and you can't either, or he could lose his job and have to move. It would be awful for him and Gus, and Mom and Dad would never trust me again. Promise me you won't say anything."

Birdie took the bag of marshmallows, tossed it on the counter, and clapped two times. Then she clapped her hands against her thighs, eyeing them mischievously.

Sasha and Bobbie exchanged happy glances and joined Birdie in their secret-sister swear.

They clapped twice, clapped their hands against their thighs, then clapped one hand to each of the other girl's in a repetitive pattern, chanting, "Sister, sister, I declare, I'll keep your secrets and never share. Sister, sister, trust me true, my loyalties lie with each of you." They held up their pinkies, hooking them to one another's, and added the parts they'd made up as they got older. "Forever in my heart, forever in my soul. Always your alibi, the shoulder on which you cry, and when you're in trouble."

"I'll bring the shovel," Sasha said.

"I'll bring the booze," Bobbie said.

"I'll bring the bail money and my kick-their-ass shoes," Birdie said.

They hugged and laughed, and when they headed back to the fire, Sasha felt a little lighter inside.

"Aren't you and Ezra going to that networking dinner together?" Birdie asked.

"Yes. So?" Sasha asked.

"We need to go shopping and get you a sexy dress," Birdie said. "Something irresistible."

"It's a professional dinner," Sasha reminded her.

"You can be professional and sexy," Bobbie said.

"I know the perfect place to shop," Birdie said.

They made plans to go shopping the week after Dare and Billie's wedding and went to join the others by the fire.

"Oh good, you're back," her mother said.

"Did you miss us?" Birdie asked, flopping into a chair beside Doc, who snagged the bag of marshmallows from her.

Gus was snuggled on his daddy's lap, and Sasha sat in the empty chair beside them.

"We were just talking about how busy things are going to be over the next few weeks, with the wedding and Festival on the Green and the Reindeer Ride," her mother said.

"I'm gonna practice being the ring boy for Billie and Dare's wedding when we decorate," Gus said.

"Ring bearer," Ezra corrected him, and kissed his forehead.

"That'll be fun." Sasha tickled Gus's belly, earning an adorable giggle. "You'll be so handsome in your suit." *Just like your daddy.*

"I wanna sit with you, Sugar." Gus tried to wriggle off Ezra's lap.

"Give her a minute, buddy," Ezra said. "I think Sasha went to get marshmallows because she wanted to make a s'more."

"I'd much rather have a wiggly boy in my lap." She reached for Gus.

"Would you like me to make you a s'more?" Ezra offered, but his gaze offered so much more, stirring flutters in her chest.

She thought about how Bobbie had read their glances and forced herself to tear her gaze away. She cuddled Gus. "Thanks, but I've got all the sweetness I need right here."

"When are we decorating?" Doc asked as he roasted a marshmallow.

"Friday afternoon," Dare answered. "The wedding tent will be delivered and set up Wednesday afternoon, and the tables and chairs and such are arriving Thursday."

The ceremony was taking place in the big barn, where Billie had first kissed Dare when they were kids. Since there would be close to one hundred and fifty attendees with their extended families and Dare's fellow Dark Knights, the reception would be held in an enormous wedding tent on the grounds.

They talked about wedding preparations, Dare and Billie's honeymoon, Festival on the Green, and when the conversation turned to the Reindeer Ride, Ezra reached over and rubbed Gus's back, his dark eyes holding Sasha's. Her heart squeezed, but she was careful not to look at him for too long.

"I started making my elf costume," Birdie announced. "It's super cute."

"You're making yours?" Bobbie asked.

"I want to be the cutest elf, so *yeah*," Birdie said.

"I have news for you, Bird," Sasha said. "I'm going to be the cutest elf."

"You wish. Have you seen my legs?" Bobbie asked.

"I'd like to get a closer look at them." Taz winked.

"Y'all are all wrong. The cutest elf is going to be riding on the back of my bike." Cowboy leaned over and kissed Sully.

Gus's head popped up. "I wanna be an elf. Can I be an elf, Daddy?"

"You sure can," Ezra said.

"We'll make you the cutest costume, Gusto," Sasha promised. She loved the idea of making costumes together and dressing like a sexy elf for Ezra. Even if he was the only one who would know she was doing it for him.

"I'm gonna be the cutest elf!" Gus exclaimed, making everyone laugh.

"I think we should have a contest for the best elf costume," Alice suggested.

"Yes!" Birdie exclaimed. "I love that idea."

"Me too. Is it okay if I do it, too?" Simone asked.

"Of course," Wynnie said. "You're one of us."

"I'm in! How about you, Billie?" Bobbie asked.

Billie tossed her long dark hair over her shoulder and said, "I'll be baddest elf you've ever seen."

Hyde held up his beer. "I would like to offer my services to judge this contest."

"I think we need more eyes than just yours. I would be happy to be a judge," Rebel said.

"I'm in, too, but fair warning," Taz said. "We might need to do some hands-on judging."

"My ass you will," Manny said.

"Manny said a bad word," Gus announced.

"Sorry, little man," Manny said. "Sometimes you've got to use a bad word to make a point."

"*Oh*," Gus said, and rested his head on Sasha's shoulder

again.

"Hey, girls, do you want to make our costumes together?" Sasha asked.

"It's a *contest*," Birdie said, as if she'd asked a dumb question. "Nobody's seeing my costume until the day of the ride."

Sasha rolled her eyes. "Fine, but just so you know, Gus and I are going to win. Right, Gusto?"

"Yup!" He nodded against her shoulder.

"Dream on," Bobbie said. "Sorry, Gus, but I'm going to win."

"My ass you are," Gus said sleepily.

"*Gus*," Ezra and Sasha said in unison as everyone else tried to stifle their laughter.

"Honey, you can't use bad words like that," Ezra said.

"Sometimes you gotta make a point," Gus said. "Right, Manny?"

Sasha's father barked out a laugh. "Someone's in big trouble."

They joked around and talked about the ride, and as the night wore on, Gus fell asleep on Sasha's lap. Ezra pushed to his feet and stretched. "I think it's time for me to put my sleepy boy to bed. This was the best bachelor/bachelorette party I've ever been to. Thanks for including us."

"You're family, bro," Dare said. "We're glad you and the little man could join us."

Ezra reached for Gus, but Gus clung to Sasha and said, "Can we sleep with Sasha?"

The din of conversation silenced, all eyes turning to Sasha and Ezra, as Bobbie choked on her drink and began coughing.

Taz patted her back. "Do you need mouth to mouth?"

"Not from your petri dish of a mouth," Bobbie said.

Ezra's brows were slanted as he met their curious gazes. "Gus has been on a slumber party kick for weeks, begging her to sleep over."

"I feel ya, buddy. I've been on one for years," Hyde said, and laughter rang out around them.

Sasha ran her hand over Gus's curls. "I'm sorry, Gusto, but I can't have a slumber party tonight. It's late, and you don't want to be tired when you see your mom tomorrow."

"But you *promised* we could camp out sometime," Gus whined.

"And we will, but slumber parties are a big deal. We need time to plan and make sure we have wood for the campfire and the right snacks, and we have to pitch a tent." She wanted to offer to read him a story tonight, but she didn't want to raise eyebrows or reward him for whining. "Be a good boy for Daddy tonight, and we'll figure out a time for our slumber party."

"*Okay*," he relented, and reached for Ezra.

Ezra mouthed *Thank you* as he gathered him in his arms.

She watched them leave, wondering if anyone could tell how badly she wanted to go with them.

Chapter Eighteen

SASHA LAY IN Ezra's arms, watching the clock on the nightstand change from 3:14 a.m. to 3:15 a.m. She'd had an amazing day with the horses, and they'd had fun playing paintball and at the bonfire, but these quiet moments when it was just her and Ezra, with Gus sleeping safe and sound in the other room, were the best of all. She'd been there for hours. It should be enough to hold her over until the next time they could carve out some privacy. She should get up, get dressed, and go home happy with the time they had together. But all she wanted was to stay right there in his arms until the sun came up. She longed to hear Gus's sleepy morning voice and share in their morning ritual, which she was sure was loud and chaotic, but that sounded perfect to her.

She snuggled closer to Ezra. "I wish I could stop time so we could have hours of this."

"Me too." He kissed her temple and rolled onto his side, facing her.

He had that intoxicated look he always had after sex. She loved that look as much as she loved all of his others. Like the look of pure joy when Gus laughed and the way he looked at her lately, like she made his whole day better. She loved the way Ezra had a constant smile when he was joking around with the guys, and she loved that serious look he sported so often, like he was trying to solve the world's biggest problems. That was the look that was currently taking over his handsome face. "What are you thinking about?"

"How much I want to spend time with you out in the open. I hate pretending like there's nothing special between us. I wanted to reach for you and kiss you a dozen times tonight."

"That makes two of us."

His hand slid to her bottom, pulling her tight against him, and he kissed her. "Come with me on a bike ride tomorrow."

"Someone might see us."

"So what? Everyone knows we're friends. They're not going to care."

"Everyone also knows what it means to ride on the back of a biker's motorcycle," she pointed out. "We've never been the kind of friends who took motorcycle rides together, and I haven't exactly been secretive about my crush on you the last couple of years. What if someone puts two and two together like Bobbie did?" She'd told him about both of those incidents, and they'd both agreed to be more careful. She decided to keep Birdie's eagle eyes to herself, so as not to freak him out.

His jaw tightened, and he rose up on his elbow. "Then we'll meet out of town. We can meet at Clayton Field and leave your truck there."

The field where we first met. Her throat thickened with emotions.

"We'll stay off the main roads, drive into the mountains or to another town. I don't care where we go or what we do. I just want to spend time with you without worrying about whether I want to hold your hand, kiss you, or look at you and touch you like you're mine."

She tried not to let herself get carried away with his words, but excitement bubbled up inside her, and she sat up. "That sounds incredible. Are you sure?"

"Surer than I've ever been. I'm dropping off Gus with Tina at ten. What time will you finish with the horses?"

"I can be done by then and meet you around eleven? I'll bring my helmet."

"Perfect." He kissed her again, grinning like he'd won the lottery. "We're going to have a great day."

"I can't wait, but how am I supposed to get any sleep when I'm this excited?"

"I don't know, but you need to sleep, Bo Peep. I don't want you falling off my bike."

"You'd never let that happen."

SATURDAY BROUGHT CLEAR, sunny skies and the promise of a perfect day. Gus was in a great mood as he scrambled into his booster seat with two tiny action figures. Ezra tossed his backpack onto the floor and leaned in to help him with his seat belt.

"I can do it," Gus insisted, struggling to pull the seat belt far enough.

Ezra gave him a little help, and Gus latched it in place. "Great job, buddy."

As he closed Gus's door, his phone rang. He cursed when he saw Tina's name on the screen and put the phone to his ear.

"Yeah?"

"Hi, it's me. Sorry to call so late, but I can't take Gus today. I have to drive to—"

"Are you fucking kidding me?" He stalked away from the car. "How can you do this to him again?"

"I can't help it if I need to get my car fixed."

He closed his eyes, trying to rein in his anger. "You couldn't have gotten it fixed any other day this week?"

"They just called and said they could fit me in today. I need my car. It's not like I can go without one. I'll take him on Tuesday without fail. I promise."

He'd believe it when he saw it. He ended the call, pissed off for Gus *and* for himself. He'd dedicated his entire life to Gus and to his career. All he wanted was a few hours to be a normal guy and spend time with the woman he adored. He didn't want to let Sasha down, either, even though he knew she'd understand if he did.

He looked at Gus, happily playing with his action figures. On any other day, Ezra wouldn't think twice about putting off his plans to be with his son, but not today. He knew damn well if he did, he'd be a bear to deal with, and that wasn't fair to Gus. Today he was going to give himself what he hadn't in too many years to count. A few hours to do as *he* pleased.

He didn't like pawning Gus off on anyone, but as he called his father, he knew he, and Gus, would love to spend some one-on-one time together.

"Good morning, Ezra."

"Hi, Pep. Sorry to bother you, but Tina can't take Gus today, and I've got plans. Think you can take him for a few hours?"

"You bet. Bring him over. We'll have a great time. You need

me to keep him overnight?"

Yes was on the tip of his tongue, but he wasn't quite that selfish. "No. A few hours will be great. Thanks."

After he ended the call, he climbed in behind the wheel and turned to Gus. "Hey, buddy. Your mom had some car trouble, so it looks like you'll be spending the day with Grandpa."

"Okay! Do you think Grandpa will take me to the park? Last time we fished in the pond, and we got to pet a big black dog named Rascal…"

Gus gabbed the whole way to his grandfather's house and ran up to the front door just as Pep opened it. "Grandpa!" He launched himself into Pep's arms, clutching one action figure in each hand.

Pep's entire face lit up as Gus hugged him. "How's my boy?"

"Good. Can we go fishing at the park and get pizza for lunch?" Gus asked as Ezra joined them on the stoop.

"I think we can do that." Pep set Gus down.

"Can we go see your friend Debbie at the ice cream shop? She always gives me extra sprinkles." Gus didn't wait for an answer. He threw his arms around Ezra. "Bye, Dad!"

"Have fun, buddy. I love you."

"Love you, too!" Gus ran into the house.

Ezra arched a brow at his father. "Debbie?"

Pep grumbled something about kids and their big mouths and reached for Gus's backpack. "You let me know if you want me to keep him overnight."

He wondered what that was about but didn't want to push it. If his father was seeing someone special, then he was happy for him. He only hoped Pep wouldn't shut him out of that part of his life, too. "Thanks. I really appreciate you taking him today."

"My pleasure. Go do your thing, and don't worry about Gus. He's in good hands."

"I know he is. Thanks for being here for me today. I'd love to take you out to lunch sometime to thank you, just the two of us." He didn't know why he couldn't let it go, but he had a feeling he'd still be trying twenty years from now.

His father's brows slanted. "Nobody's got time for that."

"I'll make the time," Ezra offered.

"How about we have dinner with Gus one night? That'll be nice."

"Sure, Pep. Thanks again." He turned to leave, then glanced back. "Tell your friend I said thanks for giving my boy extra sprinkles."

His father *almost* smiled and waved a hand dismissively. "Get outta here. We have fishing to do."

EZRA CRUISED DOWN the secluded country road toward Clayton Field, the roar of the motorcycle competing with the anticipation of riding with Sasha and a rush of youthful, rebellious memories.

Sasha's truck came into focus at the edge of the field. She was standing with her back against the driver's door, her long jeans-clad legs crossed at the ankles. He parked beside her, took off his helmet, and climbed off his bike. "Hey, gorgeous."

"Hi. Did Gus get off okay?"

He raked a hand through his hair. "Yeah. Tina couldn't take him, so he's with my dad."

"I'd really like to give that woman a piece of my mind." She pushed from the door, looking as fine as diamonds in a black T-shirt and matching leather boots. "Why didn't you tell me? We could have gone riding on a different day so you could be with Gus."

"Because I wanted to see *you*, and I wasn't going to let her fuck it up." That earned one of those slightly bashful smiles he loved.

"Thank you. That means a lot to me." Her gaze swept over his black leather vest and T-shirt. "I was hoping you'd wear your vest."

"Oh yeah? Why?"

"Because I'm secretly sleeping with a badass biker, but I only ever get to experience the other amazing parts of him."

He drew her into his arms. "Then it's fitting that we're here, where it all started."

"How does it feel to be back here?"

He looked around the overgrown field. "This is where I escaped to too many times to count. It was easy to bury my feelings about my family when I was with a bunch of teenagers whose deepest thought was *What kind of trouble can we get into tonight.*"

"Is that bad?"

"No. I think I needed to go through it all to become who I am now. And being here with you feels like a second chance." He brushed a kiss to her lips. "You brought out something visceral in me back then. I wanted to protect you, but I also wanted to *have* you. And now you're the only person who brings that rebellious kid out in me."

"Are you saying I turn you into a troublemaker?"

"No, Bo Peep. You make me feel young and rebellious and want to take risks. But in a good way. What about you? How does it feel to be here?"

"I feel fifteen years old again, sneaking off to this field. Only it's more exciting this time, because I knew I'd be meeting you here."

"You caught my attention when we were kids, all gorgeous and innocent eyed. But now?" He whistled. "I've got half a mind to toss you in the back of your truck and make up for lost time."

"I've got half a mind to let you," she said sassily. "But I've been thinking about warming your back all morning, so that'll have to wait." She pressed a kiss to the center of his chest. "Play your cards right, and maybe you'll get to christen the bed of my truck *after* our motorcycle ride."

"That's so much better than you running off scared, Bo Peep." He lowered his lips to hers. "I've been waiting years for this moment. Let's get you on the back of my bike."

She grabbed her helmet from her truck, and he helped her climb onto his bike. He took a moment to drink her in. "*Mm-mm.* Now, that's a sight worth waiting for." He straddled the bike in front of her, and she draped herself over him like a second skin, resting her cheek on the back of his shoulder, and sighed. That sigh was so full of relief and contentment, his chest constricted. She felt so good, so fucking *right*, he didn't want to start the bike, much less put on their helmets and drive away.

"You've waited years," she said softly. "But I feel like I've waited a lifetime for this. Can we just sit here for a minute?"

She was undoing him, one sweet sigh and one mirrored sentiment at a time. He knew he'd never forget this moment, but he pulled out his phone and took a picture of them from the side, wanting to cherish the memory. Her eyes were closed, her lips curved into a smile as contented and lovestruck as his own.

Chapter Nineteen

SASHA WASN'T NEW to riding on the back of a motorcycle. But riding with friends and siblings was completely different from riding with Ezra. She'd dreamed about riding with him ever since he'd started riding a motorcycle. But no dream could come close to the thrill of feeling his muscles flexing beneath her hands and against her chest, his body heat burning between them as they drove along back roads, and the warm wind whipping over her arms. She didn't even *try* not to get carried away by how good it felt to be together out in the open. The minute she'd seen him drive up to the field, straddling his shiny black bike, all sexy and badass, in his black leather vest and biker boots, she'd known it would be a futile effort. Everything about him was different today, too. From the way he looked at her to the way he carried himself.

Like a man who had nothing to hide.

They stopped for a late lunch at an out-of-the-way dive far from Hope Valley. Ezra helped her off the bike and drew her into his arms, kissing her right there in the parking lot, bringing a whole new type of thrill. They sat in a corner booth in the back, eating burgers, sharing fries, chatting, and kissing like a real couple. Just when she didn't think she could fall any harder for him, he took pictures of them with his arm around her, with her head resting on his shoulder, and even of them kissing. This less-guarded version of Ezra was utterly intoxicating.

Later that afternoon, they were cruising along back roads. She didn't know where they were or where they were headed, and she'd never been happier in her life. He turned onto a winding mountain road and eventually onto a steep, narrow dirt road. When they reached the crest of the hill, the land leveled out, and the road came to an end. Ezra cut the engine and pulled off his helmet as he climbed off the bike, running a hand through his thick, dark hair.

Sasha took off her helmet and shook out her hair. "Where are we?"

He helped her off the bike. "Someplace we can be alone and enjoy the views."

He took her hand, leading her through the trees and brush to the top of a hill overlooking meadows and mountains as far as the eye could see. "This is beautiful. How did you find this place?"

"When I found out Tina was pregnant, I got on my bike and went for a ride to try to clear my head. This is where I ended up. I've been here quite a few times since." They sat on the grass, and Ezra put his arm around her, pulling her closer.

"It's your thinking spot."

"I guess you could call it that."

She leaned against him. "Why are we here now? What are you thinking about?"

"That I'm not ready to go back to pretending yet." He looked at her. "Is that okay?"

"It's more than okay. I'm not ready either. Thank you for making time for us, but I hope you know you never have to give up time with Gus for me."

"I know, and I love that about you." He kissed her. "He and Pep have a big day of fishing and ice cream planned."

"Sounds like fun. It really bugs me that Tina didn't take him again. Can I ask you something about her?"

"Go ahead."

"I know she was pregnant when you got married, but were you in love with her? I keep trying to reconcile who she is with who you are, and even what I knew about her back then, and it just doesn't make sense to me."

The muscle in his jaw bunched, and he held her a little tighter. "When we were dating, we had fun. She was a great distraction from school and work and…other things I couldn't deal with at the time. We'd never even talked about having a long-term relationship, much less having kids. I got married hoping to give Gus a stable family life, and I figured I'd learn to love her. But it never happened. Once she started to show, she did everything she could to hide the pregnancy. That should have tipped me off about where her mind was, but I was so focused on the idea of giving our baby, and myself, a family, that I ignored all the signs. I told myself it was hard for her to lose her figure, and when Gus was an infant and she went out partying, I told myself she needed the freedom because being a full-time mom was stressful. But the truth is, I was chasing a dream that couldn't have existed with her."

"Do you think she wanted to get married? Or do you think she did it for Gus, too?"

"I've asked myself that a lot over the years. I don't think she did it for Gus. I think she did it for herself."

"What do you mean?"

"I think she saw the marriage as a way to prove to her parents that she was lovable. Her parents were always giving her a hard time. I used to think they were too harsh toward her, but I realized after we were married that she was so self-centered, she took advantage of them every chance she got."

"And now she takes advantage of you."

"Live and learn, right? I never should have married her. I didn't feel one-tenth of what I feel for you toward her."

Her heart turned over in her chest. "Really?"

"Yes, Bo Peep," he said low and sexy. "I think she knew how I felt about you back then, too. She was always jealous of you."

"Why? She had you. I didn't."

"Yes, but not really. I think she sensed how I felt about you. I felt bad about that. I gave our marriage everything I could, but you can't fake love when it's not there." He was quiet for a second. "You got your sweet claws into me a long damn time ago, and you've had some kind of hold on me ever since."

"Lucky me." She giggled.

"No, babe. I'm the lucky one."

His lips came coaxingly down over hers in a slow, sensual kiss that quickly turned hungrier and hotter, until they smoldered like molten metal. She wound her arms around him as he took her down on her back, his big, hard body pressing deliciously against her as they devoured each other. He rocked his hard length against her center, drawing a moan from the needy well inside her.

He drew back, eyes blazing. "I want more of this, babe. More time together. More of *you*."

She'd give him anything and everything. "Then *take* more."

He reclaimed her mouth with a lustful growl, shifting his

weight as his hand roamed over her body. "Too many fucking clothes," he rasped against her lips. They stripped off their boots and clothes between a fury of white-hot kisses and greedy gropes, and he buried himself to the hilt in one hard thrust. They both cried out, but they didn't slow down. She met every hard thrust with one of her own. She was vaguely aware of the rough ground at her back, but her senses whirled and skidded. When he pushed his arms under her and his hands gripped her shoulders, pushing her body down as his hips thrust deeper, a long, surrendering moan sailed from her lips. "*Again*," she begged, clinging to him as he pumped faster and thrust harder, catapulting them into ecstasy so vast and bright, it felt other-worldly. Impossible. But there they were, on a high so beautiful and intense, so real and true, she was sure no two people had ever achieved such a blissful state.

They lay in each other's arms for a long time afterward, as naked as they'd come into the world, the late-afternoon sun warming their intertwined bodies.

"God, babe. I love being with you. We feel so connected. It's unlike anything I've ever felt."

"I feel it, too."

"We need more time alone when we're not hiding in our bedrooms."

"We can stay overnight together at the hotel when we go to the networking dinner and spend time there the next day without hiding."

"As much as I'd love that, I don't want to be that far away from Gus when he's with his mother. I don't trust her."

She felt a spear of disappointment but knew he was right.

"But we'll figure something out." He brushed his nose along her cheek. His hand skimmed down her waist, and he grabbed her butt. "You're supposed to be a friend with benefits, and you're consuming all of my thoughts. What am I going to do with you?"

Love me. Marry me. Have babies with me. Let us be the family you've always wanted. "I can think of a few things."

Chapter Twenty

EZRA TRIED TO keep his emotions in check as he stood on Tina's front stoop with Gus Tuesday afternoon, reading a text she'd just sent.

Tina: *Sorry, but I'm still tied up. Can we swap for another night?*

He gritted his teeth. She'd texted him an hour ago asking if he could pick up Gus after camp and bring him over because she was shopping with her girlfriends and couldn't get there before they closed. Now this? He had church tonight, which meant he had to find someone to watch Gus, and if Tina thought he'd give up a single night with his son for her, she was dead wrong.

"Daddy, I'm hungry," Gus whined. He'd had a big day at camp, and he'd fallen asleep on the ride over.

"I know, buddy. I'm sorry, but it looks like your mom isn't going to make it tonight."

"I don't *care*. Can we go home and eat at the big house with everyone?"

"We sure can." He was becoming increasingly concerned

about Gus's apathy toward his mother and made a mental note to speak with Wynnie about it.

Gus was quiet on the drive back to the ranch, but when they got there, he ran into the dining room in his tiny cowboy boots and shorts, calling out hellos as he raced by the tables. Ezra didn't know if Gus had gotten a second wind, or if he was just thrilled to be back among people he could count on, but when his little boy made a beeline for Sasha as she stood at the buffet, filling her plate, he was happy to follow.

She looked cute in shorts and a T-shirt. He fought the urge to slide his arm around her and pull her close. He couldn't stop thinking about last weekend and craving more time with Sasha, when they didn't have to hide their feelings. Seeing Gus run to her made him want to share those feelings with Gus, too. He wanted his son to know how much he cared about her and to see him giving and receiving affection from a woman they both adored.

"Hi, Sugar." Gus pushed up on his tippy-toes to see the buffet. "Did Cowboy eat all the good stuff?"

"Nope. There's plenty left." She gave Ezra a curious look.

"Grab a plate, buddy." Gus went to get a plate, and Ezra lowered his voice. "Tina got hung up shopping with her girlfriends."

She rolled her eyes.

Gus squeezed between them. "Dad, can I have chicken wings?"

"You sure can. Broccoli, carrots, or peas?" Ezra began filling Gus's plate.

"Trees!" he exclaimed.

"Hey, Gusto. Do you want to work on our elf costumes tonight?" Sasha asked.

"Yeah! Can I, Dad?" he asked hopefully.

"Sash, if you had plans—"

"I was going to work on my costume." She ruffled Gus's hair. "Now we can do it together."

He handed Gus his plate. "Carry this carefully over to the table, and I'll get you a drink."

After Gus walked away, she said, "Are you okay? You don't look happy."

"I'm just sick of this shit with Tina and worried about how it's affecting Gus."

"Was Gus upset when you told him?"

"No. That's what worries me. Thanks for watching him tonight while I'm at church. I owe you one." *More like a million, but who's counting?*

"I'm sure you'll think of a way to pay me back," she said with a seductive twinkle in her eyes, and sauntered away with an extra sway in her hips.

He could think of about a dozen ways and looked forward to doing each and every one.

When he got back to the table, Sully and Sasha were talking about Posey, and Gus was looking at one of Sully's sketches. "What are you looking at, buddy?"

"A picture Sully drawed of me and Sasha and Posey." Sasha had introduced Gus to the sweet mare last week. He had asked dozens of questions, and Sasha had patiently answered each and every one of them.

"Sully *drew* not drawed," Ezra corrected him, admiring the sketch of Sasha in cutoffs and barn boots, her hair trailing down the back of her tank top. She was petting Posey's cheek with one hand and holding the lead in the other. She wore a careful, loving expression, which was trained on Gus, who was standing on his tiptoes in shorts and cowboy boots. His face was tipped up, his curls falling away from his chubby cheeks. His eyes were at half-mast, and his mouth was closed but curved into a smile as Posey sniffed him. Every wayward curl looked so real, it was as if he could reach out and touch them.

He looked across the table at Sully. "I can't get over how lifelike this is. You're really talented."

"Thanks," Sully said. "It's not quite as good as Gus's drawings, but I'm getting there."

"Did you draw it for anyone in particular?" he asked. "Because I'd love to hang it on my wall if you didn't."

"I'm glad to hear that, because I made it for you and Gus."

"You did? Thank you!" Gus exclaimed.

He glanced at Sasha, who looked as happy as Ezra felt about that.

"Dad, this is where Posey's eye should be." Gus pointed to the concave recess on Posey's face. "The doctor took it out because she got a *fection*."

"*Infection*," Sasha corrected him.

"*In*-fection," Gus repeated. "Am I gonna get a *in*fection?"

"No, honey, but if you ever did, I'd get you to the doctor right away," Ezra said. "The person who owned Posey didn't take her to the doctor fast enough when her eye got sick. That's why they had to take it out."

"Maybe Doc could give Posey a new eye," Gus suggested.

"If I could, I would," Doc said from beside Sully. "Unfortunately, I don't think that's possible."

"Oh." Gus stared at the picture for a minute. "Guess we'll just have to give her extra love."

"That's right, Gusto." Sasha put her arm around him, hugging him against her side and sharing an emotional glance with

Ezra.

"If we have kids, I hope they're exactly like him," Sully said.

"If his father is any measure of what he'll be like as a teenager, you might want to reconsider that," Cowboy teased.

"Why?" Sully asked. "Ezra's wonderful."

"Thank you, Sully, but you didn't know me back in my troublemaking days," Ezra said.

"You don't have to worry about that, Sul," Sasha said. "You're marrying the biggest Boy Scout of them all. The worst thing your kids will probably do is boss around all the other kids on the playground."

"I could tell you some stories about Cowboy," Doc said.

"But you know my stories about you are just as bad, so shut your trap," Cowboy warned, and Doc laughed.

"It's always the quiet ones," Billie said, eyeing Sasha.

"Why are you looking at *me*? Dare got into way more trouble than I ever did, and he is anything *but* quiet," Sasha said.

"I seem to remember a dip 'n dash scenario that we had to handle the summer after your junior year, Sash," Doc said.

"Really?" Ezra raised a brow at Sasha, imagining the teenage good girl sneaking into a pool to go skinny-dipping.

Sasha rolled her eyes. "*Please.* That's nothing compared to all the stuff that you guys did. I still can't believe Dad sent you guys to get us."

"I thought Cowboy and Doc were going to rip those boys' heads off," Dare said.

"There were boys involved?" Ezra asked.

"Not for long," Cowboy said.

"What's dip 'n dash?" Sully asked.

"Skinny-dipping," Sasha said. "I went with Bobbie and a few friends."

"Oh." Sully shrank back in her seat, her cheeks flaming.

Billie barked out a laugh. "If that's not a guilty face, then I don't know what is."

"Cowboy might have caught me skinny-dipping once." Sully buried her face in Cowboy's chest.

Cowboy rubbed her back. "That's one of my favorite memories."

"Don't be embarrassed, Sully. It's a rite of passage around here," Billie reassured her.

"What's skinny-dipping?" Gus asked.

"It's when you go swimming naked," Ezra explained.

Gus giggled. "I don't wanna do that."

Not yet anyway.

Gus was his typical happy self throughout dinner, chatting with everyone about everything and anything and asking a million questions. There was so much goodness around the dining room, it was almost enough to make Ezra forget that Tina had blown Gus off again.

AFTER EZRA LEFT for church, his living room became costume central. First Sasha and Gus drew pictures of their costumes. Many, *many* pictures. Then they picked out their favorites and colored them in. Because how could they make costumes unless they knew what color everything should be? Then they got to work, and now there were pieces of green, red, and black fabric spread over the coffee table, and littering the floor were yellow pom-poms, more fabric swatches, and hand-drawn stencils. Christmas music streamed from Sasha's phone, and she and Gus sang along as they worked. Sasha had used the stencils and a Sharpie to mark the material for Gus to cut, and he was hard at work cutting out red cuffs that would go around his wrists.

"Do you think I'll win the contest?" Gus asked, brows knitted in concentration as he cut the material. He was cutting miles away from the lines she'd drawn, but he was so proud of himself, Sasha let him run with it.

"Yup. Nobody else will have a green elf vest with a Dark Knights logo on the back."

Sasha was in love with the elf costumes they were making, but she was even more in love with the process of making them with Gus. She'd worried that he might get bored after a few minutes, but he'd been excited about coming up with ideas, and he'd helped her draw the stencils and trace them onto the fabric. She wished Ezra were there to see how happy his little man was, but she was taking plenty of pictures.

"Should we make Daddy a green vest?" Gus asked.

"I think he'll want to wear his leather vest, but we can make decorations for his motorcycle."

"Can we put reindeers on it? And lights and *orments*?"

"Ornaments?"

"Yeah! *Ornments*. I have to pee!" He dropped the scissors and fabric and ran into the bathroom, leaving the door open.

Sasha heard him singing "Rudolph the Red-Nosed Reindeer." When he flushed the toilet, she said, "Wash your hands."

"I know." She heard the water running. "One, two, three…" The camp counselors were teaching the kids to wash their hands for ten seconds. Gus usually made it to five.

He ran into the living room and dove onto the couch, accidentally kicking over his chocolate milk. "Oops!"

"Shoot. I forgot to put the top on your sippy cup." Sasha righted the cup and ran into the kitchen for a dishcloth and paper towels.

Gus scrambled off the couch. "Hurry. It's getting all over everything!"

"It's okay." She dropped to her knees by the coffee table and began mopping up the mess.

"Did I ruin our costumes?"

"No. It's just a little milk. We'll wash the material that got dirty." She finished cleaning up the mess and hand-washed the pieces of fabric that had milk on them.

"Now what are we gonna do?" Gus asked.

That was a good question. She wanted to keep him off the rug while it dried. "Why don't we run over to the holiday shop and see if they have a Santa hat for your dad to wear on the Reindeer Ride? Maybe we can find something to decorate his motorcycle with while we're there, and if you're a good boy, we might even find something for you."

Half an hour later, they were heading into the holiday shop, when Tina walked out of the yoga studio two doors down. She was wearing yoga pants and an exercise bra, and she was irritatingly gorgeous. A knot formed in Sasha's chest, but she pushed past it for Gus's sake, instinctively holding Gus's hand a little tighter. "Look, Gusto, there's your mom."

"Uh-huh," he said, and continued walking toward the store.

Surprised by his lack of enthusiasm, she tried to figure out how to handle it, but in those few seconds of indecision, Tina saw them and headed their way. *Shit.* "Come on, Gus. Let's go say hi."

The Selfish Witch of the West narrowed her eyes at Sasha but quickly put on the charm for Gus. "Hi, baby," she gushed, crouching to hug him.

"Hi, Mom. Guess what? We're making elf costumes for the Reindeer Ride, and we're gonna get Daddy a Santa hat and stuff for his motorcycle."

"How fun." She eyed Sasha. "Looks like Ezra's getting everything he wants."

"I didn't know he wanted a Santa hat," Sasha said. "But if he does, then he definitely deserves it."

The Selfish Witch made a half-laugh, half-scoff sound.

"We should be going. We have a lot of *shopping* to do." Sasha knew it was petty to throw that back at her, but she couldn't help it. "Say goodbye to your mom, Gusto."

"Bye, Mom." He reached for Sasha's hand.

She'd expected him to hug Tina, and she waited, giving Tina time to initiate an embrace, but she just said, "See you next Tuesday, honey," and walked off.

Sasha wanted to yell, *Hey! You're not going to see him for a week. Don't you want to hug your kid?* Instead, she smiled down at Gus and said, "Santa hat, here we come."

They found a Santa hat for Ezra, and Gus loved it so much, she bought one for each of them. They found battery-operated string lights for Ezra's bike and an extra set of lights to put around Gus's bedroom window. Gus asked for everything from toys to candy, and Sasha agreed to buy one pack of peanut M&M's that they could share. Gus was happy with that.

"Gus, what do you think about these to go with your costume?" She picked up a pair of children's knee-high red-and-white striped socks.

"I like 'em."

"That was easy." She tossed the socks into the basket with the other things they'd found.

Gus pointed to a bin of small stuffed reindeer. "Can we get a reindeer to put on Daddy's bike?"

"That's a cool idea. Maybe we can tie it to the middle of his handlebars. Why don't you go pick one out?" She watched him looking through the bin as if they weren't all identical.

"I want this one." He held one up.

"That one's missing an eye. Why don't you choose another one?"

"But I like this one. It's a Posey reindeer."

She melted a little inside. "You're right. It's perfect."

Gus carried the reindeer as they went up and down more aisles. When they came out of the last aisle, Gus's eyes went wide, and he pointed to a display of artificial Christmas trees in the corner of the store. "Can we get one of *those*? *Please?* Daddy loves Christmas trees. He says they make everything happier."

I love them, too.

She knew Ezra enjoyed the holidays, and she loved seeing Gus's face light up when he helped them decorate the Christmas tree in the main house every year. But she wasn't sure if Ezra would be a fan of having a tree in his cabin in July, or if Gus would expect Santa to bring presents.

"Gus, you know it's not really Christmas, right? Santa won't be bringing presents in July, even if we put up a tree."

"I know. *Please*, Sugar?" He bounced on his toes, big brown eyes pleading. "I promise I won't ask for presents."

Those hopeful eyes tugged at her heartstrings. "If we get a tree, you know what it means?"

"That everything will be happier?"

She tapped the tip of his nose, hoping she wasn't making a mistake. "It means we have to hurry up and get it home so we can decorate it before bedtime."

"Thank you!" Gus threw his arms around her, hugging her tight.

They bought a midsize tree that Sasha could carry on her own, and since she didn't know where Ezra kept his holiday decorations, they bought lights and tinsel and stopped at her cabin to get her tree stand and tree skirt.

The rest of the night was a blur of Christmas music, Gus's constant and adorable chatter, making ornaments out of construction paper, crayons, and ribbons, and decorating the tree. They wore their Santa hats and made a big yellow star for the top of the tree out of three layers of construction paper. Sasha threaded a ribbon through the top of the star and one near the bottom and tied them loosely in the back, forming loops to slide over the top branch.

She was lifting Gus up so he could put the star on the tree when the front door opened and Ezra walked in. *Shoot!* She'd lost track of time! It was also way past Gus's bedtime, and the living room was covered in tinsel, scraps of paper, ribbons, and their costume materials, which they hadn't put away before starting to decorate the tree.

As Gus exclaimed, "Dad! We got a tree—" and wriggled out of her arms, she panicked and began rambling. "How did it get so late? I'm sorry Gus isn't in bed and the place is a wreck. We spilled milk on our costumes and went to get a few things at the holiday shop, and we got carried away."

"Dad! Hey, Dad!" Gus was jumping up and down, tugging on Ezra's leather vest. "Do you like it? Are you happy?"

Ezra looked around the living room, then down at Gus, and finally at Sasha.

She wrinkled her brow. "I'll clean everything up, and if you'd rather not have a tree, we can move it to my place. Gus was so excited, and that got me excited, and…I'm sorry time got away from me."

"I'm not." He laughed as he scooped up his little boy, settling him in one arm, and drew her against his other side.

"I told you he'd be happy!" Gus exclaimed. "Dad, do you like our hats? We got you one, too, and a reindeer and lights for your bike, and…"

As Gus went on about all the things they'd made, bought, and done, Ezra turned an unstoppable grin on Sasha and said, "Thank you."

"For messing up your cabin?"

"For making it feel even more like a home."

Chapter Twenty-One

EZRA HEADED DOWN the hall to Wynnie's office Wednesday afternoon, hoping she could help him figure out what to do about Tina and trying to ignore the twinge of guilt eating away at him about Sasha. That guilt had become a constant companion, but until he figured out his next step, he had to keep that guilt to himself. Gus's well-being was at stake, and after what Sasha told him last night about the run-in they'd had with Tina, he was even more concerned.

Wynnie's door was open. He knocked, and she looked up from whatever she was reading on the computer and smiled. "Hi, Ezra."

"Is this still a good time?"

"Yes. Close the door and make yourself comfortable." She stood and pressed the intercom button. "Maya, can you please hold my calls?"

"Will do," Maya answered as Ezra closed the door, and sat on the couch.

Wynnie came around the desk, looking sharp in a cap-sleeve

magenta blouse and jeans. She sat on the other end of the couch. "How's your day going?"

"Good," Ezra said. "I had productive sessions with Paul and Mike, and my other clients."

"That's always good news."

"Yes. It is. I wanted to speak with you about Tina. I know you can't give me any answers, but I value your opinion, and I'd like to hear your thoughts about what's going on, unless it makes you uncomfortable."

"Why would I be uncomfortable? I haven't been your therapist for almost two decades. We're well past any professional obligations."

"I know." *But I'm secretly seeing your daughter, and that's messing with my head and making me uncomfortable. Projecting much?* "I just wanted to throw that out there."

"Well, I appreciate that. But I'm happy to give you my opinion. What's happening with Tina?"

"She's still blowing off Gus, but she's doing it more often, and he's becoming apathetic about spending time with her."

"Are you seeing any other behavioral issues? A difference in how he treats you or anyone else?"

"No, but you see him every day. You know how excited he is to see everyone. I was worried that I might be reading too much into his lack of enthusiasm about seeing his mother, or even projecting my own feelings about my mother onto him. But Tina blew him off last night to go shopping with her friends, and when Sasha took Gus into town while I was at church, they ran into Tina coming out of a yoga studio, which pisses me off, but that doesn't matter. The thing is, Sasha had to prompt Gus to go over and say hello to her."

"And did he?"

"Yes, and Sasha said he was okay with her, but when they left, Gus and Tina didn't hug goodbye, or anything. I don't like how things are progressively getting worse between them. Two weeks ago she asked me to come get him Sunday morning instead of keeping him for the whole weekend, and then she bailed again last Saturday. If it was only once or twice, that would be one thing, but you know the history. She's consistently putting her boyfriend and his family ahead of Gus, and while that's nothing new, Gus is getting older, and I'm concerned he might be on the road to developing attachment issues like I did."

"That's understandable, given what you went through. It sounds like Tina isn't making much of an effort toward him, which is a shame. What are you thinking about doing at this point?"

He shifted uncomfortably. "I'm wondering if she's doing him more harm than good, and you know that's not an easy thing for me to consider." He pressed his hands into his thighs. "I was hoping you could take a pulse on the situation. Do you think I'm projecting?"

"I can't say for sure, but if his apathy toward her is noticeable to Sasha or anyone else, then he could be heading in that direction. Thankfully, we're not seeing it toward others yet." Her expression softened. "Ezra, you know how big a decision it would be to cut Tina out of Gus's life, and there are a lot of variables. As your friend, I can't tell you what to do, or what would be best for Gus. But you're a smart man, an excellent father, and a skilled therapist. I know how much you love Gus, and I am confident you'll figure out what's best for him if and when the time is right."

He inhaled deeply and blew his breath out slowly. "Now I

know what my clients feel like when they come to me asking for advice and solutions."

She smiled. "You know the best resolutions usually find themselves."

"I know, but it's hard to bide my time when it affects my son." It was just as hard to bide his time with regard to his and Sasha's situation. But that was not a subject that was up for discussion. He pushed to his feet, and she stood as well. "I appreciate you listening."

"I'm always happy to listen. Come here, honey." She opened her arms. He stepped into her embrace, soaking in the maternal comfort she gave so willingly. "You're a wonderful father, and you're doing a great job with Gus. I'm proud of you."

"Thank you." He stepped out of her arms. "I learned a lot from you and Tiny, but this is a rough one. I wish I knew the right thing to do."

"Nobody said parenting would be easy, but you'll get through it. You always do."

"I don't need easy." He reached for the door. "I just need to know my son won't pay the same price I did."

Chapter Twenty-Two

AFTER A WHIRLWIND week of busy days spent working with the horses and helping with wedding preparations, fun-filled evenings of costume making with Gus, and stolen midnight hours with Ezra, Dare and Billie's wedding day finally arrived. They were blessed with a perfect clear, warm evening. The barn looked magical. Cowboy and their father had built a beautiful altar, and Sasha and the girls had decorated it with drapes of white silk, red and white roses, and twinkling lights. More lights sparkled from around the rafters and support poles. The aisle was lined with barrels overflowing with red and white flowers and greenery, and the chairs along the aisle had red bows tied to the sides.

Sasha stood at the altar with Birdie, taking it all in. She'd never seen Dare as excited as he was last night, when they'd met some of their out-of-state cousins and friends at the Roadhouse. He hadn't been able to keep his hands off Billie, and she'd eaten up his attention, the two of them going on about how excited they were to go on their honeymoon to Spain, where they were going to watch the running of the bulls. But that was nothing compared to how elated Dare was tonight, standing at the altar with Doc and Cowboy, as handsome as could be in their black leather vests and dress shirts with jeans, boots, and cowboy hats. Dare looked like he was going to jump out of his skin if Billie didn't walk down that aisle soon. Cowboy was looking lovingly at Sully, who was sitting in the audience with their parents, and Doc appeared as stoic as he had all day. He'd been in a foul mood and had been short with Sasha when she'd done rounds that morning. She didn't know what was going on with him, but no matter how much she tried, she hadn't been able to get him to loosen up.

Birdie nudged her, drawing her attention to Bobbie as she walked down the aisle in her mint-green dress. "She looks gorgeous." Her blond hair was fashionably styled in an updo, with tendrils framing her face. She wore a similar sleeveless, knee-length dress to Sasha's and Birdie's, although Sasha's was peach and Birdie's was lilac.

"So do you," Sasha whispered, her gaze catching on Ezra crouching in front of Gus at the end of the aisle. He was straightening Gus's dress shirt beneath the little black leather vest Ezra had bought him, so he'd look like all the Dark Knights today. Her heart beat faster every time she saw them.

Birdie nudged her again, nodding to Hyde and Taz slipping out the back door. "Where are they going?"

"Who knows?" Sasha said as Bobbie joined them at the altar, smiling brightly.

Her thoughts fell away as Gus walked down the aisle, beaming proudly, carrying a small white pillow with the rings and a red rose tied to it. They'd practiced walking down the aisle earlier in the day, and he was doing such a good job of not walking too fast.

"Look, Grandpa! I'm the ring boy!" he said as he passed Pep.

Laughter rose around them.

God, she loved him.

When Gus reached the last row of chairs, he ran straight to Sasha. "I did it, Sugar! I went slow!"

"You were perfect." She put her hand on his shoulder, choking up as her gaze found Ezra's, who looked even prouder than Gus.

The "Wedding March" began, and the din quieted as everyone turned in their seats, anticipating Billie's arrival. But the song ended abruptly, and the Spice Girls song "Wannabe" came on as Hyde and Taz danced in through the back doors, carrying metal buckets and tossing rose petals. They danced their way down the aisle, thrusting their hips and tossing more rose petals out at the guests. Everyone cracked up as they winked at the women and caressed the backs of a few male guests' heads. Their videographer, Hawk Pennington, another Dark Knight, was discreetly catching it all on film. Leave it to those two to ad-lib something like that.

They danced onto the altar, dirty dancing around Sasha, Birdie, and Bobbie and tossing rose petals, making everyone laugh even harder. When the song ended, they took a bow, and as they headed back to their seats, the "Wedding March" began again.

Billie appeared at the end of the aisle, looking absolutely radiant on her father's arm. Manny was handsome in his leather vest, with a prideful gleam in his eyes, as they started down the aisle. Billie's dark hair hung in loose waves over the thin straps of her stunning, sleeveless lace bridal gown. It was sexy, elegant, and perfectly Billie, with a plunging neckline and a slit up either side of the skirt, revealing her cowgirl boots.

Billie's eyes were locked on Dare, and his eyes dampened. It was hard not to be a little jealous of the love thrumming between them.

Sasha teared up as Billie joined him on the altar, and Treat Braden, one of their father's oldest friends, officiated the ceremony. The ceremony was beautiful, and she glanced at Ezra as Dare and Billie exchanged vows and found him watching her with a loving expression. Her heart stumbled. It had been doing that a lot lately. It was hard to believe they'd been together for only a month. It seemed like forever.

"You may now kiss your bride," Treat said, drawing her attention back to the main event.

"Get over here, wifey." Dare hauled Billie into his arms and kissed the heck out of her, dipping her low as cheers and applause rang out.

He kissed her for so long, Sasha wondered if they'd ever come up for air.

THERE WASN'T A dry eye in the tent when Dare announced, "This one's for Eddie," before he and Billie danced their first dance as husband and wife to "Good Riddance (Time of Your Life)." Sasha stood by the dance floor with Birdie and Bobbie, watching longingly as Dare and Billie gazed into each other's eyes, whispering and kissing, wishing she could dance like that with Ezra. She could tell by Ezra's furtive glances that he was wishing the same thing.

An hour later, the tent was buzzing with joy as couples

drank, danced, and mingled. Sasha still hadn't danced with Ezra, but they were being extra careful. On the other hand, she had fun dancing with the girls and with Flame when he'd asked her to. She was glad there were no hard feelings between them.

As she came off the dance floor with Birdie and Simone, Birdie said, "How are your elf costumes coming along? Mine is so cute."

"Not cuter than Gus's," Sasha said, catching sight of Gus dancing with two other little kids, while Ezra watched on. Ezra glanced over, his dark eyes smiling back at her.

"I mean cute as in hot," Birdie said, drawing Sasha's attention back to their conversation. "Gus will definitely win the little-kid cuteness award."

"My costume is cute as in *cute*," Simone said. "Does it have to be sexy?"

"Definitely not," Sasha reassured her. "We're delivering presents to children."

Birdie put a hand on Simone's shoulder, leaning closer. "You can't help but be sexy with your wild curls and killer body."

"I definitely have wild hair." Simone glanced at their mother and aunt heading their way and lowered her voice. "But I don't have a killer body."

"Yes, you do," Birdie said.

"Hello, girls," Sasha's mother said.

"What are you doing over here by yourselves when there are so many good-looking young men here?" her aunt Red Whiskey asked. Red looked like a young Sharon Osbourne, with short hair and wise eyes. Like Sasha's mother, she was as strong as she was loving and had been wrangling ornery bikers forever.

"We're related to most of them," Birdie pointed out.

"No, you're not," their mother said. "Only the Wickeds and the Whiskeys."

Birdie crossed her arms. "That's true, but did you forget about my three brothers who sneer when any male comes near me? My life would be a lot easier if you had all daughters."

"Oh, honey. We've all been through that," Red said. "You've got to learn to fly under the radar."

I've got that covered. Sasha stifled a grin.

"Let's not encourage that," their mother said. "I'm the one who has to deal with your brother when they get caught."

"You can take Tiny." Red lowered her voice conspiratorially. "Besides, you're way behind on the grandchild race. Your kids could use a little nudging in the right direction."

Her mother laughed softly. "I'm not going to rush my kids into having babies. Let them enjoy their new loves for a while. Besides, I can come visit your grandbabies."

As they talked about grandchildren, Sasha looked around for Red's kids, her cousins from Peaceful Harbor, Maryland. Bones was wrangling his brood with his wife, Sarah. Bullet and Bear were holding their little ones as they stood by the bar talking with Doc and Rebel's brothers Denver and Dallas. Her cousin Dixie was heading to the dance floor with her husband, Jace, her adorable baby bump leading the way. Sasha felt an unfamiliar ache and wondered if maybe Birdie was right, and her biological clock was getting louder.

"How about you, Simone?" Red asked. "Do you have a special someone?"

"Not yet," Simone said.

"It'll happen, sweetie," Red said.

"Maybe sooner than you think," their mother said. "I was talking you up to Marshall Dutch a little while ago, telling him how you were on your way to becoming a substance abuse counselor."

"Marshall? Who is he?" Simone asked.

"He's the hot, broody, tatted guy talking with our cousins Zeke and Zander," Birdie said, pointing him out.

"He's a really nice guy," Sasha said. "But he's been through a lot."

"Haven't we all?" Simone said softly. "What's his story?"

"Marshall showed up at the Roadhouse several years ago looking for a fight big enough to end his life after losing his wife and newborn baby," their mother explained.

"That's horrible," Simone said.

"Yes, but as we all know, reality isn't always pretty," their mother said. "He ended up finding the Dark Knights, which was lucky. We gave him the help he needed to realize life was worth living. Now he runs Annie's Hope, an emotional wellness center he opened in Upstate New York to honor his late wife."

"That's amazing, but are you trying to get rid of me?" Simone asked.

"No. He was *admiring* you from across the dance floor, so I filled him in on how wonderful you are," their mother said.

Simone blushed. "Oh."

"Come on, let's go talk to him." Birdie took Simone's hand, dragging her toward Marshall.

Their mother sighed. "I'd better go with them to keep Birdie in line." Her mother went after them, leaving Red and Sasha alone.

"Well, that should be interesting," Red said. "Fill me in on your life, baby girl. I saw you dancing with Flame. He's quite yummy. Is he on your radar?"

My man is yummier—but off-limits. "Flame's just a friend."

Red's brows knitted. "Are you seeing someone else?"

"Are you spying for my mother?" Sasha knew all about their grapevine, and she wasn't about to divulge her secrets.

"No. I'm spying for myself. Now that all of my kids are married, and Diesel and Tracey have set a wedding date, I don't have any good gossip to follow." Diesel had grown up in Hope Valley, and though he'd been a Nomad for years, he fell in love with a waitress at Red's family's bar and had remained in Peaceful Harbor. They were getting married over the winter.

Sasha glanced at Diesel and Tracey, who were chatting with her cousins, as she lied through her teeth. "I'm not seeing anyone."

"Maybe we need to put together the first annual Hope Valley Bachelor Auction. That's how Dixie and Jace got together, and you know he was her forever crush. Now they're starting their own family."

"I don't think a bachelor auction will do the trick for me, Aunt Red. But thanks for trying."

Red looked out at the crowd. "Well, let's see if I can find you a man. How about one of those two cute guys who danced down the aisle?"

"Hyde and Taz? No, thank you."

"Okay. I've got a few more suggestions." She pointed out a few more guys, and Sasha nixed them all. "Sweetie, what are you not telling me?"

"Nothing. Why?"

"You're saying *no* to guys before you look at who I'm pointing at. That tells me someone already has your heart, or you're waiting for a special guy to notice you."

"What are you, the single-woman whisperer?"

"Let's just say I have a lot of experience watching things

evolve."

"Sorry to disappoint you, but there's nothing evolving here." Sasha saw Gus hurrying toward her.

"Sugar, come dance with me and Daddy!" Gus took her hand.

Red arched a brow. "I don't know about that, sweetie. It looks like someone has a special place in your heart."

"This little man stole all our hearts the day he was born. Come on, Gusto. Let's go rock the dance floor."

Chapter Twenty-Three

EZRA COULDN'T TAKE his eyes off Sasha. She was gorgeous in the peach dress that accentuated her curves, but it was the special light in her eyes that only he and Gus sparked that held his attention as she and Gus joined him on the dance floor.

"I understand you need another dance partner," she said.

"My son is the best wingman. He picked the prettiest woman here. You look gorgeous tonight."

"Thanks. You're looking awfully handsome yourself. Almost as handsome as your wingman."

"Watch me, Sugar!" Gus spun in a circle, waving his arms.

"Those are some great moves, Gusto."

"Do it with me!" Gus said.

Sasha spun around, waving her arms. "Come on, Ez. Do it with us."

As Gus led them through a series of ridiculous moves that only a five-year-old would think were cool, Sasha put her all into it, following his lead and adding her own funky moves. They danced to half a dozen fast songs, acting silly and earning endless giggles from Gus.

A slow song came on, and she scooped Gus into her arms. "Do you think we can get your daddy to slow dance with us?"

"You'd have a harder time getting me not to." He took Gus, settling him on his hip, and put his other arm around Sasha as Gus put one arm around Ezra's neck and the other around hers, keeping them close. He had everything he wanted right there in his arms, and he'd give just about anything for the song never to end.

But, of course, it did, and a short while later, the buffet was brought out. They headed for a table, where Rebel, Cowboy, and Sully were settling in. "Mind if we crash your table?" Ezra asked.

"Not at all," Cowboy said.

"Thanks." Ezra pulled out a chair for Sasha.

"You guys were so cute dancing together," Sully said.

"Gusto can make anyone look good," Sasha said.

"I'm a good dancer," Gus exclaimed as he climbed onto the chair beside Sasha. "If you want, I'll dance with you later."

"I'd like that a lot," Sully said.

"You've got a little Romeo on your hands, Moore," Cowboy said.

"Yeah, he's got it all going on. Guess I'm next to you, Rebel," Ezra said as he sat down between Gus and Rebel. "How's it going?"

"I'll let you know in a minute," he grumbled, and downed his drink.

Ezra felt a heavy hand on his shoulder and turned to find Rebel's oldest brother, Denver standing behind him, which explained Rebel's sudden discomfort. "Hey, Denver. It's nice to see you."

"You, too." Denver was about six five and had an easy twenty pounds on Rebel. He had dark hair and a thick beard, and he was as gruff as Rebel was easygoing. "When are you going to get your ass home, little brother?"

"Dad, he said a bad word," Gus said hushed and urgent. "Is he making a point?"

"Yeah, little man, I am." Denver crossed his arms over his chest and lowered his chin. "I asked you a question, Raleigh." Raleigh was Rebel's given name.

Rebel held his steady gaze. "The answer hasn't changed since you asked me last night."

"It's time to cut the BS and come home," Denver said gruffly.

"Get over yourself." Rebel pushed to his feet and walked away.

"Nice going, Denver," Sasha said. "Why do you have to push him all the time?"

Denver's brows slanted. "What did I say? We all miss him. He belongs back home with us."

"Maybe you could've led with missing him," Ezra suggested. "He has a life here, and it would probably be good if you acknowledged that, too."

Denver scrubbed a hand down his face. "Right. Thanks."

As he walked away, the clink of silverware on glasses rang out around them, urging Dare and Billie to kiss. Dare never needed a reason to kiss his new bride. He hammed it up, motioning with his hand for everyone to do it again, bringing rise to laughter and more *clinking*.

Tiny stood to make a speech, and the noise quieted. This was one of the few times Ezra had ever seen Tiny without a bandanna around his head. His gray hair was pulled back and tidily braided, his long beard was groomed, and as he stood before them, holding up a champagne glass, he was looking at Dare and Billie with so much love, it felt tangible. "I'd like to thank everyone for coming out to celebrate Dare and Billie's first anniversary."

Murmurs of confusion rose around them. Ezra looked at Sasha in question. She shrugged and shook her head. Even Wynnie looked confused.

"What're you talking about, old man?" Dare asked. "Are you having a senior moment?"

"No, son, but don't tell me you've forgotten that you and Billie snuck Treat in here last summer and had him marry you in the same barn where you said *I do* tonight."

There was a collective gasp.

Billie winced. "Sorry, Mom."

Everyone laughed.

"How'd you know about that?" Dare asked incredulously.

"I wonder what *else* he knows about," Bobbie said, causing more laughter.

Bobbie's glance at Sasha was not lost on Ezra, or apparently on Sasha, as she lowered her eyes and stole a worried glance at him.

Tiny held up his hand, quieting the guests again. "Dare and Billie have been sneaking around since they were six years old. See this gray hair?" He pointed to his head, then at Dare and Billie. "Your names are written all over it." More laughter rose around them. "I'll never forget the day my little boy came to me wearing his shorts and his cowboy boots and hat, and no shirt, because even at six he'd rather have been naked than clothed. He crossed his spindly little arms and said, *Dad, Billie Mancini kissed me and called me a dummy. I'm gonna marry her one day.*"

A collective "Aw" rang out, and Wynnie put her hand over her heart. Ezra glanced at Sasha, wishing he could tell her that *that* was exactly how he'd felt about her all those years ago.

"Now, I know kids say all sorts of things," Tiny said. "But when a Whiskey sets his heart on someone, that's all they see, and for Dare, it was always Billie."

Cowboy said, "Stalker," masked in a cough, and more chuckles rang out.

"They say when your son takes a wife, she becomes family." Tiny looked at Billie. "But darlin', you've been family since before you were a twinkle in your parents' eyes. There's nobody better suited, no woman strong enough or wild enough to be my son's old lady than you. It is an honor and a privilege to call you our daughter-in-law. All I ask is that you keep one thing in mind." He paused, and a smile lit his eyes. "Wynnie and I have a no-return policy."

Laughter filled the tent.

Cowboy put his arm around Sully and said, "See what you signed up for, darlin'?"

She gazed at him with stars in her eyes. "I wouldn't want it any other way."

Tiny held up his glass. "To Billie and Dare. May their love remain strong, their hearts true, and their babies do to them what they've done to us!"

As more laughter and cheers rang out, Ezra longed to be the one at the receiving end of that welcome. He put his arm around Gus, brushing his fingers along Sasha's shoulder, drawing her eyes to his. It was a good thing he was sitting down, because the emotions staring back at him hit like a lightning strike.

Gus beamed at Sasha. "When I'm big like Dare, will you

marry me?"

"I will always love you, Gusto, but I'm too old for you," Sasha said sweetly. "One day you're going to meet someone who you love even more than you love me. That's the person you should marry. But I'll come to your wedding."

"Maybe you could marry my dad and be my mom instead."

Her eyes flicked to Ezra's, and before he could step in, she said, "How about I just keep being your Sugar?"

As Manny started to make a toast, Ezra decided he was done pussyfooting around. One way or another, he was going to figure this shit out and find a way they could be together.

More toasts were made, dinner was eaten, and the cake was cut. They danced and laughed, and Ezra caught up with some Dark Knights he hadn't seen in forever. As the night wore on, the crowd thinned, and Dare got the guys together for a few rounds of shots by the bar.

"To long, lustful nights that leave you spent," Taz toasted, and they all tossed back their shots.

Ezra put his shot glass on the bar and glanced at Gus, sitting in Pep's lap, about ready to fall asleep. "That's it for me, guys. I've got to get my boy home."

"One more shot. We need to do one for Cowboy." Dare clapped Cowboy on the back as Taz filled the shot glasses. "He's next up in the marriage line."

"How're you feeling about that impending ball and chain?" Hyde asked.

"I'm looking forward to it," Cowboy said.

"Been there, done that. Better you than me," Rebel chimed in.

"You won't see me going there, either," Doc said.

"What about you, mate?" Taz lifted his chin in Ezra's direction. "Think you'll ever do it again?"

Ezra looked across the room at Sasha, who was talking with a gaggle of girls by the dance floor. "If the right girl came along, I do believe I would."

Doc narrowed his eyes. "That right?"

He'd been getting weird vibes from Doc all night. "Yeah, I think so. You really don't ever want to get married?"

Doc scoffed. "Nope. I don't need the headaches that go along with relationships."

"The right girl might change your mind," Ezra said.

"Don't waste your breath," Cowboy said. "Doc's about as anti-relationship as a guy can get. I, on the other hand, cannot wait to get my girl home tonight. So, how about we do that shot?"

They picked up their glasses and Dare said, "Here's to the best thing that can happen to you, bro. To Cowboy's ball and chain."

They all lifted their glasses and said, "To Cowboy's ball and chain," and drank their shots.

"Congratulations, Dare." Ezra clapped Dare on the shoulder and pulled him into an embrace. "If ever there were two people destined to be together, it was you two."

"Thanks, man," Dare said. "And thanks for letting your little guy be our ring bearer."

Ezra said his goodbyes, and as he walked away, Doc sidled up to him and grabbed his upper arm. "We need to talk."

Ezra yanked his arm free as they walked out of the tent. "What the hell, Doc? What do you think you're doing?"

"Stopping you from breaking my sister's heart."

Fuck. He tried to play it cool. "What are you talking about?"

"I saw her sneaking out of your place when I was coming

home last night."

"We—"

"*Save it*," Doc bit out. "I'm not fucking stupid. What are you thinking? Tiny's the president of the club, and you're fucking around with his daughter."

Ezra squared his shoulders, anger rising inside him. "It's none of Tiny's business who I'm sleeping with, and it's none of yours, either. But it's not what you think."

"What I *think* is that you're in there spewing bullshit about marriage while you're sneaking around with my sister like she's some cheap trick."

All of his pent-up anger roared out, and he got in Doc's face. "Don't you *ever* talk about her that way. I care about Sasha, and I'm *trying* to protect my son."

"You're supposed to be loyal to the brotherhood."

"I *am* fucking loyal to the club, but Gus will *always* come first," he gritted out. He saw Sasha watching them from the entrance to the tent. "Listen, I'm trying to figure things out, so I'm asking you, brother to brother, to trust that I would never do wrong by Sasha and to mind your own business. But you do what you need to do." He stalked back toward the tent, feeling like he was going to explode.

Sasha rushed out. "What was that about?"

"He saw you leaving my place last night."

"*Shit.* I thought that I saw his truck."

"He's pissed. He might tell your father."

"Like hell he will." She stormed toward her brother. "Doc!"

Doc turned around, and Ezra went after her, but she was already giving him hell.

"What happens between me and Ezra is none of your business, and if you tell Dad, I'll *never* speak to you again."

Doc's eyes narrowed. "I'm trying to protect you from get-ting hurt. Those rules are in place for a reason. This is *not* going to end well for either of you."

"You know what?" she said with a strangely lighter tone. "Those rules are in place because *you* got your heart broken. I'm sorry things didn't work out for you and Juliette. I know that had to hurt, because you have never been the same. But Ezra is not you, and I'm not Juliette, so stay the hell out of my personal life." She strode past Ezra, right back into the tent, looking like she was going to either punch someone or cry.

It killed Ezra that he couldn't pull her into his arms and tell her everything would be okay.

GUS WAS OUT cold when Ezra tucked him into bed, which was a good thing, because Ezra's thoughts were all over the map. There were too many people around tonight for him to talk with Sasha about what had happened with Doc. Gus had asked to say good night to her, and he'd asked her to read him a bedtime story. Ezra had hoped they'd be able to talk about it then, but she'd gently turned Gus down, claiming she needed to stay at the reception. He knew she was probably just being cautious, but he was worried. He didn't have a solid plan yet, and figuring out their next step would take time. He thought about cutting Doc off at the pass and getting to Tiny first, but there were too many loose ends to put Sasha in that situation.

He sat down at his computer and tapped the keyboard. The talk he and Sasha had put together for next weekend's network-ing dinner was still on the screen. His chest constricted. He'd always been impressed by her, but working together on the talk had given him a whole new level of appreciation for her expertise and professionalism. They'd come up with a joint presentation that flowed seamlessly and felt as natural as their relationship did. He was looking forward to representing the ranch together.

Now he wondered if he'd still have a job by then.

A while later, a knock at the door drew his attention. He strode to the door, squaring his shoulders, readying for a confrontation. He pulled it open and was relieved to see Sasha, but her expression was tentative, her brows knitted.

"Hi. I didn't think you'd come by tonight."

She worried with her hands. "I wasn't sure you'd still want to see me."

"Of course I do." He took her hand, bringing her inside with him, and shut the door.

"Sorry I told Gus I couldn't read to him, but I didn't want to raise any suspicions."

"That's okay. He fell asleep the second his head hit the pillow. Did Doc say anything else to you?"

"No. He avoided me like the plague. Ezra, what are we going to do if he tells my parents?"

"I don't know yet, but if that happens, I'll handle it." He couldn't promise her the world, but he wanted to take away her worries, or at least settle them enough to see her smile before she walked out his door. He took her hand, leading her into the living room. "I don't know if this thing will blow up tomorrow, or the next day, or a month from now, and I don't want to spend the rest of the night playing a what-if game. I just spent the evening watching the woman I adore dance with other guys. So we're not going to worry about our lives imploding or anything else that we can't control right now."

He pulled out his phone, queuing up the song that had always reminded him of Sasha, and dimmed the lights.

A sweet smile pushed the shadows from her eyes. "What are you doing?"

"I'm going to dance with my girl." He hit play and set the phone on the coffee table, drawing Sasha into his arms, and gazed deeply into her eyes as "In Case You Didn't Know" came on, and he whisper-sang the words that he could have scripted just for her.

Chapter Twenty-Four

"THIS STORE IS great. They have a little of everything. How did you find it?" Sasha pulled another dress off the rack at Luxe Looks. It was Wednesday evening, and they were shopping for a dress for the networking dinner.

"The owner goes to my hot yoga class," Birdie said. "I knew you'd love it."

"The owner is a guy? He's got great taste," Bobbie chimed in.

"Yes, he does. He hangs out with *me*, after all." She wiggled her shoulders.

Sasha arched a brow. "Are you seeing him?"

"I wish," Birdie said. "He's everything I like in a guy. Big and beefy, funny, and a little offbeat. But he likes dick and I don't have one, so I'm still on my own. I think I'm going to use the dating profile I made you on Cowboy Cupid."

"Seriously?" Sasha asked.

"Why not? I used a fake name for you." She patted her hair. "Don't I look like a traveling ranch hand named Samantha to you?"

"Didn't you have to put a picture on the profile?" Bobbie asked.

Birdie smirked. "I used a black-and-white cartoon picture, so there's no hair color."

"That's weird, but why'd you say I was a traveling ranch hand?" Sasha added.

"I was keeping you safe. There aren't many horse rehab therapists around here, which means you'd be easy to find."

"That's brilliant," Bobbie said. "But I doubt that profile will get much interest without a real picture."

"You'd be surprised," Birdie said. "Guys are like puppies. They want treats, but they're not particularly picky about who they get them from. Give them a trail of goodies, and they'll keep their noses to the ground until they find them."

"*Ew.* I don't want you with guys like that." Sasha wondered if she needed to keep a closer eye on her little sister.

"I didn't *say* I'm doing it."

"You better not, or I'll tell Cowboy," Sasha warned.

"Forget I said anything. You're such a party pooper." Birdie held up a shiny pink dress that was sleeveless on one side and off-the-shoulder on the other. The skirt gathered at the waist and had a ridiculously high and wide slit on one side. "What do you think of this one?"

"It's not really my style," Sasha said.

"Really?" Birdie admired the dress. "I think you'd look good in it."

"Sasha, you'd look hot in this one." Bobbie held up a black minidress with white cuffs and a white collar.

"She's trying to turn her man on, not show him how to use his library card," Birdie said.

"I bet tons of guys fantasize about women who don't feel the need to flaunt their assets," Bobbie said. "You know, *lady in the streets, freak in the sheets.*"

Sasha laughed. "I totally agree about all that, but I think I can go a little sexier since my man already knows I'll be anything he wants in the sheets."

"Finally, some details!" Birdie hurried over to Sasha, pushing a shopping cart, which was already full of dresses. "What's he like in the bedroom?" she asked hushed and urgently. "I bet he's got a dominant side. Is he good at finding the doorbell? He must be, because otherwise you wouldn't risk pissing off Mom and Dad."

"I think you've got that backward," Bobbie said. "*Sasha* must be phenomenal in bed for *him* to risk everything for her. Especially after what Doc said at the wedding."

Sasha's stomach twisted. She'd been so upset after that confrontation, she'd confided in them about it. "I still can't believe he saw me leaving Ezra's that night. We fully expected to walk into breakfast the morning after the wedding and have our asses handed to us, but everyone acted normal. Well, everyone except Doc. He's been giving me the cold shoulder, and I hate it."

"That must be uncomfortable since you work so closely with him," Bobbie said empathetically.

"It's awful. When we meet in the mornings after I do rounds, I swear he looks like he can't stand the sight of me. I keep thinking about what he said, and I know he's worried I'll get hurt. But why punish *me* for it?"

"Is he punishing you? Or worried about you?" Bobbie asked.

"I don't know, but it feels like a punishment since he's so mad at me."

"Maybe he feels like he got punished for falling in love with Juliette," Bobbie said. "You've heard the rumors about Juliette's father saying he was going to destroy him, and you and Ezra are doing exactly what he was doing, only they weren't keeping it a secret."

"You could be right," Birdie said. "But I think it's because he can't control Sasha. He's always had a tight rein on us, and she gave him hell for it. I'm proud of you, sis."

"I'm proud of myself, too, but Doc and I have always been close, and I hate that he's so angry at me."

Bobbie pulled out a dress and looked it over as she said, "Do you think he's hurt that you shut him out? Or didn't trust him enough to tell him?"

"Why would I *ever* willingly tell Doc who I'm sleeping with?"

"You wouldn't." Bobbie put the dress back on the rack. "I don't know what I was thinking."

"You weren't thinking. We'd be nuts to tell any of our brothers about our private lives," Birdie said.

"I don't know what to do," Sasha admitted. "I'm afraid Doc's going to say something, which has me on edge, and I hate lying to Mom and Dad. But most of all, I want to be close to Ezra all the time, and I can't. I can't hold his hand or touch him or anything."

"That has to be hard, but where can you go from here?" Bobbie asked.

"That's what I'm trying to figure out, and I know he is, too, but I don't want to push him. It's not like he can quit and move off the ranch without disrupting Gus's entire life." A painful knot lodged in her chest. "I can't talk about it anymore. Let's just focus on finding a great dress."

"Hey, did Ezra change his mind about staying overnight in Colorado Springs?" Bobbie asked. "At least you guys can have that night together."

"We're driving together, but I haven't asked him about staying overnight again. I want to, but with everything that happened with Tina lately, I didn't want to push it. I'm kind of hoping he'll bring it up, because having a whole night of freedom would be amazing."

"You can always get a hotel room for a few hours, have great sex, and *pretend* you have all night, even if you don't stay all night." Bobbie draped another dress over her arm.

"How is staying at a hotel any different from staying at your cabin together?" Birdie asked. "Nobody knows what you do inside your cabin. I know Doc saw you leaving, but it's not like he has cameras inside your cabin."

"I know, but we won't have to worry about every little thing. We won't have to hide or sneak back to our own places before morning, and we can have breakfast together in public and walk through town holding hands if we want to. I never realized how much those little things meant, but I really want to do them with him."

"Have you lost your mind?" Birdie looked at her incredulously. "I bet most of the people who are going to that dinner are going to stay for the weekend, and you guys are giving a talk, which means they'll all know you and Ezra work together. You know how well connected Dad is. I swear he has eyes and ears everywhere. It's not like you can be smooching and holding hands without word getting back to him and Mom. I would not risk it if I were you."

Sasha looked up at the ceiling, her shoulders dropping in disappointment. "*That's it.* I'm going to pack up Ezra and Gus and move to Upstate New York. Ezra can join that Dark Knights' chapter and work at Annie's Hope, and I'll find a job working with horses at one of the ranches in the area."

"And cry yourself to sleep every night because you'll miss me," Birdie said as she put another dress in the cart.

"Give it up, Sash. You'd miss the heck out of me, too." Bobbie flashed a cheesy grin.

"I hate when you guys are right." She sighed. "Guess I'm stuck secretly having great sex with the man of my dreams forever."

"At least you'll look good. Come on. Time for a fashion show." Birdie grabbed the cart.

Sasha peered into the cart. "How many dresses do you have in there?"

"Enough to find one that the pickiest girl on the planet will like. Don't worry." Birdie pushed the cart toward the dressing room. "They'll all look amazing on you. I have excellent taste."

"I saw her put that shiny pink dress in there," Bobbie whispered.

"*Great.*" Sasha's sarcasm earned a glare from Birdie, making her and Bobbie laugh.

Birdie had Sasha try on so many shiny, sparkling, and colorful dresses, Sasha was losing hope of finding anything that said professional and sexy without looking like she was trying too hard.

"Try this on." Bobbie pushed a dress through the dressing room's curtain. "It has long sleeves, but banquet rooms are always kept cool."

Sasha held up the burnt-sienna wrap dress. "This is gorgeous, and it's as soft as butter, but I've never worn this color before. I hope it doesn't make me look washed out." She tried it on and was shocked by how great it fit and how elegant she felt in it. She opened the curtain, and Birdie and Bobbie gasped.

"Wow," Birdie said. "You look amazing."

"Ezra is going to lose his mind," Bobbie added.

She inhaled deeply, unable to suppress her grin. "That's the hope. Does it show too much cleavage?"

"No. Just cinch it a little higher. I'll show you." Bobbie untied the knot Sasha had tied above her hip, pulled the fabric a little tighter and higher, and retied it. She turned Sasha toward the mirror. "See? But you'll need a plunge bra."

"They sell them down the street at Heidi's Lingerie," Birdie said.

Sasha's heart skipped as she turned, admiring the way the dress hugged her in all the right places. "I don't think I've ever felt this beautiful before."

"That's because you're a weirdo," Birdie said. "Dresses don't make you beautiful. They just amplify your natural hotness. You're always gorgeous. We all are."

"You should've been a cheerleader," Bobbie said.

"*Pfft.* And follow the crowd?" Birdie waved her hand. "No thanks."

"Birdie would've rewritten every cheer. Right, Bird?"

"That's right. *Let's go, Sasha.*" She clapped, emphasizing each word like a cheer. "*Pay for the dress, because your sister is the best, and she needs a margarita.*"

Sasha and Bobbie laughed, and Bobbie said, "Well, that's a first."

"What? Her cheer?" Sasha asked.

"No. That I was actually wrong about something," Bobbie said.

"Sounds like I need to remind you about that time you told

me if we got our periods it meant we were vampires," Sasha said.

Birdie snort-laughed, and as they took a hilarious walk down memory lane, Sasha took a picture of herself in the dress and texted it to Ezra.

Sasha: *Thought you might like to see what I'm wearing to the networking dinner.*

Ezra sent three flame emojis.

Ezra: *How am I supposed to speak coherently about anything other than stripping that dress off of you with my teeth?*

Yup. It was the perfect dress.

Chapter Twenty-Five

THE HOTEL BANQUET room was packed with people dressed to the nines, sharing insights and information and vying for connections at the networking event. Ezra stood at the bar, waiting for his drink, watching Sasha chatting with a handful of other attendees. She was stunning in a deep orange dress that accentuated her curves and had him salivating to get his hands on her. Their talk was well received, and he'd enjoyed giving the presentation together. They'd fallen into sync as comfortably as they did in the bedroom, finishing each other's sentences and inciting interesting questions and even a few laughs from the crowd. Everything about them was harmonious, making him want a future with her even more than ever before. But getting from here to there meant walking barefoot through fire on a bed of glass, which he'd do in a heartbeat if it didn't mean making Gus do the same.

"Here you are, sir." The bartender set his glass down in front of him.

"Thank you." Ezra tossed a twenty on the bar and sipped

his drink as he made his way back to Sasha and the others.

She glanced over, eyeing him seductively, and licked her lips. *You know I want you, baby.* They'd been taunting each other all night, exchanging furtive glances and subtle innuendos that were growing steamier as the night wore on. He was itching to satiate those desires. Sasha had brought up the idea of spending the night together at the hotel, and while he was still nervous about being that far away from Gus, she was weakening his resolve one coy glance at a time.

Several conversations were going on when he joined the group, but all he heard were the silent messages passing between him and Sasha. Her gaze moved over his chest, following his tie south and lingering below his belt. His dick rose to greet the heat in her eyes, and she covered her triumphant smile.

Fucking hell.

As the others discussed the economy and difficulties of growing their businesses, he put his hand on Sasha's back, leaning in close and lowering his voice for her ears only. "Keep looking at me like that, and I'll bend you over a table and take you right here."

Her eyes flamed. "Well, that's one way to capitalize on your surroundings. I think I'd like a drink after all. I'm especially *thirsty* tonight. You don't mind if I take a sip of yours, do you?" She reached for his glass and took a sip. "This is delicious." A surprised little gasp escaped, and she plucked the cherry from his drink, sucking it into her mouth. "*Mm.* What's better than an alcohol-drenched cherry?"

His little vixen knew just how to play him. Now he was thinking about her splayed out on a bed as he licked that drink off her body.

"Have I ever shown you my old party trick?" Ezra took the

cherry stem from her and put it in his mouth, expertly tying it into a knot with his tongue, then pushed it out between his teeth, loving the blush on Sasha's cheeks.

"*Whoa,*" a banker named Joe said. "I bet you got all the girls in college with that trick."

"Don't fool yourself, Joe. That particular skill is much appreciated by ladies of all ages." The attractive brunette offered her hand. "It's Ezra, right?"

He shook her hand. "Yes, and this is my colleague Sasha Whiskey."

"Hi," Sasha said.

"I'm Nora Winkler. I run the marketing division of Skyline Advertising in Denver. I enjoyed hearing about Redemption Ranch. It sounds like a special place."

"Thank you. We'd like to think we're making a difference," he said.

"Nora knows all the new advertising trends," Joe said. "She was just telling me about how TikTok is doing wonders for some of her clients."

"Really?" Ezra asked. "I thought that platform was used for fun."

"It's *too* much fun," Justine, an HR executive, said. "Our employees waste far too much time on it."

"That's why it's good for advertisers. You'd be surprised at the impact a thirty-second video can have on the bottom line," Nora said. "You have to get creative. I find some businesses need to really pound their points home, and others need more finesse, but either way, it's a hot trend you can ride all the way to the bank."

"I'm definitely into getting creative." Ezra eyed Sasha, earning a knowing grin.

"I like TikTok, but it is addicting," Joe said. "Like riding a train with such great scenery, you never want to get off."

"I couldn't agree more," Sasha said. "I'm so busy on the ranch, I appreciate the quickies that I can sneak in, but I find they only whet my appetite." Her gaze flicked to Ezra. "Come midnight, I'm riding that train for all its worth, and it doesn't matter how many times I get off. I always end up going back for more."

Ezra stifled a chuckle.

"Is there extra liability in that type of advertising?" Joe asked.

"There's liability in everything," Nora said. "As with any investment, you should always make sure your assets are covered."

Sasha turned her back to the others, acting like she was looking around the room as she whispered, "My assets are definitely not covered tonight. I forgot to wear panties."

Holy. Hell. Was she trying to kill him?

"My assets are definitely on the rise." Ezra took the glass from her, downing his drink and earning another victorious grin as she turned back to the group.

"If you don't mind me asking, what have you found that's working so well?" Nora asked, looking directly at Ezra.

"Yes, Ezra, please share. What's got your assets rising?" Amusement danced in Sasha's eyes.

A sassy blonde with a killer body and eyes that drive me wild was on the tip of his tongue. "I recently veered away from my typical short-term investments, which weren't doing much for me, and I took a chance on a riskier route with a longer-term strategy. It's paying off triple-fold, but you know what they say. A gentleman never gives away all his secrets."

"I admire that in a man," Sasha said as the band began playing.

"I think that's enough business talk for me," Justine said. "Sasha, I love your dress. Where did you get it?"

"My sister turned me on to this great shop in Allure called Luxe Looks. They have *everything*." She touched her collarbone. "I should've worn a necklace, but I couldn't decide between silver and gold."

"Hm, that is a tough one," Justine said. "Either would probably look great."

Ezra knew he'd probably go straight to hell for what he was about to say, but he couldn't help himself. "I'm no expert on accessories, but I think a pearl necklace would look nice."

The heat in Sasha's eyes was palpable.

"You know what? I think he's right," Justine said. "That's much classier."

Sasha coughed to cover the laugh she was futilely trying to stifle.

"Are you okay?" Ezra rubbed her back.

"Yes. Thank you."

Her pink cheeks were killing him. "If you'll excuse us. I'd like to take my colleague for a spin on the dance floor." He set his empty glass on a table and led her onto the dance floor.

"A *pearl* necklace?" she asked as he drew her into his arms.

"You're the one who taunted me with your pantiless comment." He slid his hand down her back, resting on the curve at the base of her spine. "I've been dying to be close to you all night, Bo Peep."

She smiled. "Me too."

He felt her heart beating faster and lowered his mouth beside her ear. "Do you know how badly I want to taste you right now?"

"As badly as I want you to." She ran her fingers along the back of his neck, the intimate touch making him ache for her even more. "It's after Gus's bedtime. If anything was going to happen, wouldn't we know by now?"

He should be used to hearing her say *we* with regard to Gus, but it struck him deeper tonight. He was wound so tight with restraint, so full of lust and love, one look in her hopeful eyes snapped his resolve. "Fuck it. You're right. Let's get out of here." He took her hand, hurrying out of the banquet room toward the front desk.

It didn't take long to get a room, but every minute felt like an hour. They caught the elevator, and thankfully they were alone on the ride up to their floor. The second the doors closed, Ezra's mouth was on hers, his hands roaming over the woman whose body he knew by heart. Sasha moaned, bowing off the elevator wall and rubbing against him.

He tore his mouth away when the elevator stopped on their floor, and a few rampant beats later he was kicking their hotel room door shut behind them as they stumbled toward the bedroom, stripping off each other's clothes. The second he stepped out of his boxer briefs, she fisted his cock and dropped to her knees, taking him into her mouth. "*Fuuck*, baby." Their eyes locked. "You're so fucking beautiful, taking my cock." He pushed his fingers into her hair as she stroked and sucked, driving him out of his mind. Engulfed in pleasure, he was dangerously close to coming. He withdrew with a primal growl and lifted her to her feet. "You're *too* good at that, baby. I don't want to come yet." He kissed her swollen lips, loving the feel of her naked body against his as he lowered them to the bed.

"I need to taste you." He lowered his mouth to her breast,

teasing her with his teeth and hands. She arched beneath him, and he lavished her other breast with the same attention. She made the sexiest moans and gasps as he loved his way down her body, every sound fueling his need for her. He lifted her legs over his shoulders and devoured her.

"Ezra." She clawed at the sheets, rocking against his mouth. He slicked his tongue over her clit and pushed two fingers inside her, homing in on that magical spot, earning more gasps, moans, and whimpers. *"Ez.* Ohgod…" Her hips shot off the mattress, her sex clenching around his fingers as a stream of erotic noises flew from her lips. He held her at the peak, enjoying every drop of her arousal, every quiver and quake of her body, as she gave herself over to the pleasure.

When he finally loved his way up her body, slowing to lick and suck all her oversensitive spots, she panted out, "I need *you.*"

He was so far past *need* and *want*, he couldn't even think straight. "You've got me, Bo Peep. I've been yours since our very first kiss." He lowered his lips to hers, entering her slowly, savoring the feel of her tight heat swallowing his cock inch by inch, until he was buried so deep, he felt her in every iota of his being. Like every other time they made love, he was over-whelmed anew with the surge of emotions that came with their coupling, but this time felt even stronger. Knowing they had all night without worry of being discovered unleashed a new type of freedom that magnified everything.

He wanted their night to last forever and took his time, loving her from every position, letting their passion lead their way. He took her fast and deep and slow and shallow, giving her one magnificent orgasm after another. There was no greater pleasure, nothing more beautiful, than seeing his girl in the throes of passion and knowing it was all for him. When she panted out, "*Come with me*," the love in her voice severed his restraint, and his release crashed into him like a freight train. He gritted out her name as waves of pleasure engulfed him, taking her right back up to the peak of ecstasy with him, making his climax that much sweeter.

SASHA LAY IN Ezra's arms, pulse racing, body vibrating, and her heart bursting with so much emotion, she wanted to scream *I love Ezra Moore* from the rooftops. She struggled to hold that love in. "Am I dead? Is this heaven? I must be dead, because nothing on earth has ever felt this good."

Ezra chuckled and kissed her temple, pulling her closer. "You are very much alive, Bo Peep."

"*Whew.* Although orgasmed to death would be a great way to go."

He chuckled. "Yes, it would." He lowered his lips to hers in a tender kiss. "But, baby, I'm not ready to let you go."

He went up on his elbow, gazing down at her with so much emotion, her heart tumbled out. "*I love you*" flew from her lips. "You don't have to say it back. I just can't hold it in anymore. I think I've loved you forever. No, I know I have, and I know we have a lot to figure out and I don't know if you are looking for forever, but I can't help it. I love you and Gus, and I want you to know it."

"*Sash—*" He was interrupted by a shrill, strange ring coming from his cell phone. "That's Gus's ringtone." He bolted out of bed and grabbed his phone. "Gus? Are you okay?" The blood drained from his face, and then all at once, his chest expanded, his jaw clenched, and controlled rage took over. As he put on his boxer briefs, he said, "Listen to me, buddy. Lock the bedroom door. Do it while I'm on the phone. I'm going to look at the app to see where you are, but I'm still here." He navigated to an app on his phone and cursed.

Sasha scrambled out of bed and started getting dressed.

"Good boy. Don't open the door for anyone, okay?" He looked at Sasha. "I need your phone."

She thrust it into his hands. "What's going on?"

He lowered the phone and his voice. "His mother took him to a fucking party, and he can't find her. I've got the location. He's about an hour from here." He put the phone to his ear again. "Gus, I'm going to let you talk to Sasha while I call Tiny, okay? Don't hang up. We're on our way."

Sasha put the phone to her ear. "Hi, Gusto. I'm right here."

"Sasha, I'm scared."

Her heart cracked open at the fear in his tiny voice. "I know, honey. It's okay. We're coming to get you."

"Will you sing to me?" Gus asked.

She started singing "Lean on Me" as Ezra shoved his feet into his shoes and spoke to her father. "I'll text you the address. I don't know what we're walking into."

Twenty minutes later, they were speeding down the highway, Sasha was singing to Gus over the phone, trying not to let him hear the worry in her voice, while Ezra white-knuckled the steering wheel, cursing under his breath, and mumbling, "This was a mistake. A big fucking mistake."

It was all she could do to continue singing, telling herself he couldn't be talking about them.

Chapter Twenty-Six

THERE WERE DOZENS of high-end cars parked in front of the massive stone house where Gus was holed up in a bedroom. Ezra threw the truck into park. "Stay here. I don't want you getting hurt." He flew out the door, and when Sasha did the same, he knew it was a futile battle to get her to wait behind. The rumble and roar of motorcycles were closing in on them, but he had tunnel vision as he tore up to the front door and stormed inside with Sasha on his heels.

There were dozens of people milling about with drinks, sitting on couches smoking, and doing lines of cocaine on mirrors and coffee tables. "Stairs!" Sasha pointed to the stairs, and he took them two at a time. They threw open every door, checked every bedroom, and didn't find Gus.

"Gusto," Sasha said into the phone. "Are you upstairs or downstairs?"

"I don't remember," Gus said with tears in his voice.

"He's not sure," Sasha said to Ezra. "There's got to be more bedrooms."

"Fuck." Ezra ran downstairs, nearly barreling into Tiny and Cowboy on their way up. "He's not up there." He saw two more Dark Knights manning the door, and in the living room, Hyde and Taz were opening doors and checking closets.

"Ezra!" Doc shouted as he came out of another room, tugging Tina by the upper arm.

Ezra closed the distance between them, seething through gritted teeth, "Where's my son?"

"Why are you acting like a crazy person?" Tina asked, glassy-eyed. "I put him to bed downstairs."

"You're a fucking mess, and this shit is done. You'll be hearing from my lawyer."

"Ezra!" Sasha ran toward another set of stairs at the other end of the living room, where more Dark Knights, including Pep, were heading. Into the phone, she said, "We're coming, Gus. We'll be right there."

The staircase led to another wing of bedrooms and dens. They threw open each door, interrupting a naked couple in one who cursed them out. Ezra twisted another doorknob, and it was locked. Blinded by fury, he kicked it in. "Gus?"

Gus peered out from the closet, tears spilling down his cheeks. "Dad!" He ran into Ezra's arms.

Ezra held him tight, struggling against his own tears. "I've got you, buddy. You're safe."

Sasha rubbed Gus's back, tears raining down her cheeks. "We've got him. He's safe. Let's get him home."

Cowboy and Doc walked ahead of the three of them, and Tiny and Pep took up the rear as Ezra carried Gus out of the house and put him in the truck. He put him in his booster seat and took his little face between his hands, his heart breaking for the trauma his boy suffered. "I love you, Gus. You'll never go through anything like that again."

"I did emergency right?" Gus asked.

"Yes, buddy. You did it perfectly." He hugged him and kissed his forehead before buckling him in.

"I'm going to sit with Gus." Sasha climbed in beside Gus in the back seat and reached for Gus's hand.

As Ezra closed the door, Doc said, "I'll check him out at your place if you'd like."

Touched that Doc was there and willing to help after everything that had happened between them, he said, "Thanks, man. That would be great." He looked at his father standing back with the other guys and nodded in acknowledgment of his being there. For the life of him, he couldn't understand why his father wasn't running over to give his grandson a hug.

"The cops are on their way," Tiny said. "I'll leave a few men here to deal with them, and the boys and I are going to follow you back in case your ex sends anyone looking for trouble tonight."

Ezra's head was spinning with anger, relief, and guilt. "Thank you."

HYDE AND TAZ hung back to guard the entrance of the ranch, though Ezra wasn't worried about Tina retaliating, and the rest of the guys followed Ezra home. Wynnie was waiting for them when they got to his place. The worry in her eyes was as palpable as it was in Ezra's heart. "Thanks for being here."

"I needed to see that he was okay with my own eyes." Wynnie brushed her hand over Gus's back. "We love you, sweet boy."

"Love you, Wynnie," Gus said sleepily from Ezra's arms.

"Doc's going to check you out, buddy, okay?" Ezra said, and Gus nodded. On the drive there, Gus told them his mother had put him to bed and he'd woken up scared and had gone looking for her. But there were so many people, he'd gone back to the bedroom and had called Ezra. Ezra was fairly certain nobody had gone near him, but it wouldn't hurt to have him checked out.

As they headed inside with Doc, Gus said, "Sugar."

"I'm right here, Gusto." Sasha followed them inside.

Doc gave Gus a once-over. "He's in good shape."

At least physically he was. Ezra knew the trauma of the night and what was yet to come were going to take an emotional toll, but he was ready for it. "Thanks for checking him out."

After Doc left, Sasha kissed Gus good night and whispered, "I love you, Gusto. You're safe with Daddy." She looked at Ezra. "I'll be in the living room if you need me."

Ezra lay with Gus, listening to the even cadence of his breathing as he fell asleep, thinking about all that had happened. When he'd seen Sasha's family and the other Dark Knights swarming the house, searching for his son, it all hit home. His family, the brotherhood, the Whiskeys. They were everything to him, and he was lying to every one of them. He couldn't play this game anymore, telling himself he wasn't hurting anyone, when he knew damn well it was a lie.

This farce needed to stop before anything worse happened.

He flicked on the holiday lights he and Sasha had hung around Gus's window and prayed for the best as he climbed out of his son's bed and headed into the living room.

Sasha pushed to her feet from the couch. "Is he okay?"

"He will be. Is everyone still outside?"

"Just my family."

He headed for the door. "Good, we need to put an end to this."

"*What?* And end to *what*?" She followed him outside.

Tiny and Wynnie were sitting on chairs on the porch, and Doc and Cowboy were talking in the yard. He wished Dare were there, but he was on his honeymoon. He'd have to be the last to know. They all turned around. "Thank you for being here for us tonight."

"You're family, son," Tiny said. "Is our boy okay?"

"He will be. I'm going to speak to an attorney about getting sole custody."

"I think that's smart," Wynnie said. "We'll all help him through the transition."

"I appreciate that. But before you make that offer, you need to know that there are more changes on the horizon. From the moment I found out I was going to be a father, I have spent my life trying to do the right thing by Gus. And in doing so, I mistakenly hurt us all. Tiny, Wynnie, I'm sorry, but I've been lying to you for a while, and I'm not proud of it, but I couldn't see another way around it. I am madly and passionately in love with your daughter, and I have been since we were teenagers."

"*Ez...?*" Sasha's jaw dropped.

Cowboy said, "*Oh shit.*"

Ezra looked at Sasha. He was filled with so much love for her, he couldn't hold back if he'd wanted to. "I've wanted to tell you a million times, but how could I promise I would do anything for you if I couldn't stand behind it? I'm ready, baby. I love you, and I'm standing behind it right here and now, and every day forward." He looked at her parents. "I came to this ranch when I was a kid without putting up a fight because I knew Sasha lived here, and when I went off to school, it was to become a better man for *her*. When I got my master's, I thought I'd finally done it. I was finally worthy of being with your daughter, and I was going to tell all of you how I felt. But that night I found out about Gus, and I made the wrong choice. I will find another job, and Gus and I will move off this ranch, but I will *not* make the wrong choice again and give up the woman I love. Tiny, if you want me to turn in my club patches, I'll do it."

"*What* are you talking about?" Sasha stomped over to him. "You're not quitting or moving! If anyone's going anywhere it's me."

"I already put feelers out for a new job."

"But you *can't* quit. You love this place as much as I do," she insisted.

"Yes, but I love you *more*," he insisted.

"I love you, too, but Ezra, I put out feelers, too. I spoke to someone tonight about opening my own consulting business. Then I won't work for Mom and Dad anymore, and we can both stay."

"Whoa, darlin'," Tiny said. "Slow down."

"*No*, Dad," she barked. "This is Gus's home, and I'm not going to let you make him leave. If we can't be together if we both work here, then I quit."

"Sasha, you're not quitting," Wynnie said.

"*Yes*, I am," she fumed. "I've always been the good one who did the right thing. I have given my life to this ranch, and now I want to do something for myself. I love Ezra and Gus, and I'm not letting you and Dad stop us from being together over some stupid rule."

Doc strode up to the porch, eyeing their parents. "Don't punish them because of my fuckup. You put that rule in place because I fell for someone who had a psycho father who was dead set on fucking me over. Don't make them pay the price for my mistake."

"Honey, we put that rule in place to protect everyone, not just you," Wynnie said. "What happened with you and Juliette was an eye-opener."

"The rule makes no sense," Sasha snapped. "You and Dad are sleeping together, and you both work here."

"That *is* a little hypocritical," Cowboy said.

Tiny narrowed his eyes. "Well, hell, son. We're married."

"Are you saying if we're married, we can both work here?" Sasha turned to Ezra with a spark in her eyes that was equally rebellious and loving, matching the feelings in his racing heart. She said, "Ezra, will you marry me?" at the same time he said, "Tiny, if you'll give us your blessing, I'll marry Sasha right now."

Sasha's eyes widened. "You will?"

"You stole my heart at seventeen, Bo Peep, and we both know I'm never getting it back."

She laughed softly.

He reached for her hand. "If this last month has proven anything to me, it's that we're meant to be together. You're my forever, baby. You're the only woman I have ever truly loved, and I would give anything to wake up next to you every morning and hold you in my arms every night."

Sasha's eyes teared up.

"*Damn,*" Cowboy said. "I want to be pissed about you lying to us, but you have my blessing, dude."

"Let's slow down here," Tiny said.

"*Dad*, give him your blessing!" Sasha snapped.

"Every father wants his daughter to be with someone who will burn the world down for her, darlin'," Tiny said. "If I didn't believe that was Ezra, I would've stopped you two from sneaking around a month ago."

Shocked, Ezra said, "You knew about us?"

Tiny scoffed. "Son, a fly can't take a piss on this ranch without me knowing about it."

"Well, you could have clued *me* in," Wynnie said. "I sent them to that dinner to nudge them along without you knowing what I was really doing."

"What?" Sasha said incredulously. "You mean we've been sneaking around all this time and we didn't have to?"

"I've always known you and Ezra had a thing for each other," Wynnie said. "But when you started skipping mealtimes, and I saw you that day on the boulder, you looked as devastated as you did the morning after you and Bobbie snuck out to that damn party when you were kids."

Sasha's jaw dropped.

Cowboy eyed Ezra. "You were lucky I didn't pound the shit out of you that night."

"You were there?" Ezra asked.

"Of course my boys were there. Do you think I didn't notice my little girl wanting to grow up? But that night, while she was out wagging her tail, she showed me she could make good decisions and respect herself," Tiny said. "My boys were there in case she wasn't respected back."

Sasha shook her head. "I feel like I'm in the Twilight Zone."

"I couldn't've tried any harder than I did at the wedding to get you fools to come clean," Doc said. "But Ezra was determined to get his ducks in a row first."

Ezra looked at Tiny. "Why didn't *you* call us out?"

"Because that wasn't my call to make," Tiny said. "You're adults. You needed to decide once and for all how much you were worth to each other. As much as I hate the way you two snuck around, I respect you for trying to protect Gus and Sasha, and yourself, and figure things out first. I couldn't ask for a better man for my daughter. You have my blessing, son, but I'm not keen on this behind-my-back shit."

"I'm sorry, Tiny. It weighed heavily on both of us every day. We're done with that, but what about the rule?"

"Can we nix that fucking rule, please?" Doc asked. "It's a constant reminder of a really hard time."

Tiny glanced at Wynnie, and she nodded with a small smile. "Consider it nixed," Tiny said.

"So, am I hustling up to the house to get a bottle of champagne or what?" Wynnie asked.

"I don't know." Sasha looked tentatively at Ezra. "Is she? Or were we being hasty?"

Ezra pulled her into his arms. "Oh no, Bo Peep, you're not getting away that easy."

Laughter rang out, and Tiny said, "Bring out the champagne!"

Ezra brushed his lips over Sasha's. "Now you're really stuck with me."

"That's all I've ever wanted."

Chapter Twenty-Seven

EZRA FINISHED TAKING down the tent in the backyard where he, Gus, and Sasha had spent the last two nights and put it away in the shed. His little boy had loved camping out so much, he was already making plans for their next night in the tent. The last six weeks had been bittersweet as they'd tiptoed through transitions, finding their way to a new normal. Ezra had filed an emergency motion to restrict parenting time from Tina, and two weeks later he was issued a permanent protection order. Tina hadn't fought him on it, and as much as it still worried him for Gus, he knew it was best. His son hadn't been unscathed by what had gone down with his mother. Gus had been clingier and had climbed into bed with Ezra many times during the first few weeks after that dreaded night. He'd stuck close to Ezra and Sasha at Festival on the Green and around the ranch, but he'd been more like his confident little self lately. He'd learned to ride a bike last weekend and had even tried to push the envelope, asking if he could ride over to Cowboy and Sully's cabin by himself. Ezra wasn't quite ready for him to do that, but he was thankful Gus was coming into his own again.

As he headed up to the front door, he gave his motorcycle a once-over. They'd decorated his bike with lights and had strapped a stuffed one-eyed reindeer to the handlebars for the Reindeer Ride today. They'd decorated Sasha's truck, too, since she'd be riding with Gus.

He headed inside and was greeted by the sound of Gus giggling in his bedroom, where he and Sasha were putting on their elf costumes. They'd been careful not to thrust too many changes on Gus at once and had slowly shown more affection toward each other in front of him. The more they showed their love, the more Gus seemed to thrive.

He glanced at the Christmas tree that was still standing in the living room. They'd added more homemade ornaments over the last few weeks. He'd miss it when they took it down, but the tree would be moving to Sasha's house with them in the coming weeks, along with the sketch of Sasha and Gus that Sully had made and he'd framed, and all their other belongings.

Their lives were finally coming together in the way Ezra had always dreamed.

Gus's bedroom door opened, and Sasha and Gus burst out holding hands. Ezra's heart nearly stopped at their gleeful laughter.

"Look, Daddy, we're elves!" Gus wore green shorts and a red shirt that had two big white buttons on the front, a jagged red felt collar and matching cuffs, a black-and-gold felt belt with candy canes tucked into it, red-and-white striped socks, red sneakers, and a green vest. "Look at my patches!"

He spun around, showing off the patches Sasha had made that read ELF CHAPTER and DARK KNIGHTS on the back of his vest. Ezra's heart swelled. "You look awesome, buddy."

He came around the counter, and Gus ran to his side as Ezra admired Sasha in a red skirt with white fur trim, a cap-sleeved shiny green top with white trim, belted around her waist, and red-and-white striped thigh-high socks with her white cowgirl boots. She wore a green choker with a tiny red heart around her neck and looked sexy and gorgeous.

"And you, Ms. Whiskey, are looking mighty fine, too."

"You like it?" She glanced down at her outfit.

"I love it." He took Gus's hand. "What do you think, Gus?"

"Sugar looks pretty!" Gus said. "Tell her to spin, Dad."

Ezra laughed softly. "You heard the boy. How about you give us a spin, babe?" He held up his finger, making a *turn around* sign.

"A spin it is." She turned in a circle, and when she faced them again, her jaw dropped at the sight of Ezra and Gus down on one knee. "*Ezra …?*" she asked softly.

"We got you a ring!" Gus announced.

Sasha covered her mouth, her eyes tearing up.

Ezra laughed. "I wanted to do this right, but someone's a little excited."

Gus jumped to his feet. "Show her the ring, Dad!"

Ezra opened his palm, revealing the solitaire canary diamond engagement ring with a horseshoe of white diamonds around it. "So much for doing it right." He rose to his feet, gazing into her tear-brimmed eyes. "Sasha, I loved you before I even knew what the word really meant, and I will love you long past my dying days. Will you do me and Gus the honor of becoming my wife and his stepmother?"

"*Yes!* Of course I will!" She threw her arm around him, pressing her lips to his.

"She said yes! Give her the ring!" Gus jumped up and down,

hugging them both.

Ezra took her hand in his, and as he slid the ring on her finger, he said, "I love you, Bo Peep. I may not be able to give you the world, but I promise to give you and Gus my all for the rest of our lives."

Tears spilled down her cheeks. "Don't you know you and Gus *are* my world?"

"You're ours, too, baby." As he lowered his lips to hers, Gus exclaimed, "We're getting married!"

SASHA WAS STILL smiling when she and Gus followed Ezra in her truck to the Dark Knights' clubhouse to get ready for the ride. The parking lot was packed with motorcycles and other vehicles that belonged to the Dark Knights' families. All the bikes were decorated with lights and ornaments. Some of the men wore Santa hats, like Ezra, some wore colorful shirts beneath their vests, and others had on holiday costumes. Hyde and Taz were dressed like reindeer. The women were dressed as elves and in other green and red festive outfits. Guys were loading presents into a massive, high-sided trailer that had been decorated for the event.

As Sasha parked the truck, she spotted her parents, dressed as Santa and Mrs. Claus, talking with Ezra's father and a handful of other men. Pep was wearing a red shirt beneath his vest and a ring of colorful lights around his neck.

As soon as she cut the engine, Gus scrambled out the passenger door and hollered, "Sugar's gonna be my mom! We're getting married!" causing an explosion of cheers and congratulations as Sasha climbed out of the truck and Ezra climbed off his bike.

Ezra took a step in Sasha's direction, but the girls converged on her. She went up on her toes, trying to see Ezra, and he blew her a kiss, scooped up Gus, and headed over to the guys.

"About time he put a ring on your finger!" Birdie grabbed Sasha's hand. "Let me see!"

"Wow, that's beautiful," Simone said.

"Isn't it gorgeous?" Sasha beamed.

"It's absolutely stunning. You win in the ring department, but I'm still the cuter elf," Birdie said. She was wearing a headband with two stuffed candy canes sticking up like ears and an off-the-shoulder short red dress with three white-and-green hearts along the bottom and white fur trim along the hem, a thick green belt, and striped suspenders. She wore elbow-length, red-green-and-white striped fingerless gloves, and red platform boots.

"You do have a flair for costumes," Bobbie said, looking great in a green minidress with red trim, red, white, and green ribbons braided into her hair, and green booties.

"I still can't believe we missed all the drama while we were on our honeymoon," Billie said. She was wearing black leather shorts and a red-and-white tank top that had DARE'S NAUGHTY ELF across the chest.

"I can't believe Dare really didn't run with the bulls," Sasha said. Dare and Billie had come to see them after they got back from their honeymoon. They told them all about Spain and how happy they were for them. Having their support meant the world to Sasha and Ezra.

Billie smirked. "If I told you what he got instead, you'd believe it."

"I don't want to know." Sasha shook her head.

"I want all the details," Simone said. "Not about you and Dare doing dirty deeds, but about Ezra's proposal. How did he give you the ring? Did he get down on one knee?"

"When is the wedding?" Sully asked.

Sasha filled them in on every little detail, getting choked up as she talked about it. "We haven't set a date yet. We won't wait too long, but we want to make sure Gus is settled with the move and at his new school for kindergarten, and, well, with us." She lowered her voice. "I can't believe I'm going to marry the man of my *dreams*!"

They crushed her in a group hug, and then everyone talked at once about weddings and dresses and happiness and everything in between. Birdie kept them entertained with news about her latest mission—finding a guy to be her plus-one for Cowboy's and Sasha's weddings. It didn't seem to matter that they hadn't chosen their wedding dates yet. Bobbie was all too happy to be Birdie's wingwoman.

Birdie pointed at Billie and Sully. "It's your jobs to keep Dare and Cowboy busy so they don't find out we're scoping out guys."

"That's like leading a child to candy," Billie said proudly.

"What about Doc?" Sasha asked.

"I've got a few women in mind to keep him busy," Birdie said.

A little while later, after catching loving looks from her man, who was now talking with her parents, Sasha finally made her way over to them.

"There's your beautiful bride-to-be," her mother said.

"I love the sound of that." Ezra slid his arm around Sasha's waist and kissed her temple.

"Me too." Sasha put her arm around him, feeling happier than she ever had. The last few weeks had been amazing, not having to hide their feelings for each other. But being there, among the Dark Knights and all their families and friends, brought a whole new level of elation. She looked at her parents and hoped she and Ezra would be as happy as they were thirty-plus years from now. "You guys missed your calling," she said to her parents. "You make a perfect Mr. and Mrs. Claus."

"And you and Ezra make a perfect couple," her mother said. "I can't believe my baby girl is getting married. May I?" She lifted Sasha's hand, admiring her ring. "It's beautiful. Were you surprised?"

"Completely surprised. You should've seen how excited Gus was."

"I think everyone here knows how excited he is," Wynnie said.

"I told Gus before breakfast that I was going to propose, and I'm surprised he lasted as long as he did. Leave it to a five-year-old to blow my cover," Ezra said.

"He didn't blow it. It was a perfect proposal." Sasha caught sight of Gus in Pep's arms and warmed all over. "I love that Gus was part of it. It made it even more unforgettable."

Tiny clapped Ezra on the shoulder. "You did good, son. Now, we need to get a move on. I'm sweating under this outfit." Her father turned to the group and announced, "A'right, let's get our bikes lined up and get this show on the road!"

Ezra slung an arm over Sasha's shoulder as they headed for her truck. "I wish you could ride on my bike with me, but I guess I'll see you and Gus at the hospital when we deliver presents."

Sasha looked around. "Where is your bike? Did you move it?"

"No. Why?" He looked over to where he'd parked it, and it was gone. "What the hell?" He patted his vest pocket. "My keys are gone. *Shit.* Who'd steal a bike with all of us here?"

The old firehouse alarm in the Dark Knights' clubhouse went off, and they looked over just as the bay door to Rebel's auto shop opened, and Dare drove Ezra's bike out of it, with Cowboy on the back and Doc sitting in a shiny black sidecar. Rebel jogged behind them, all four of them whooping and cheering as applause rang out, and all eyes landed on Ezra and Sasha.

"What the hell is this?" Ezra asked with a laugh as the guys climbed off the bike and out of the sidecar.

"You can't go on a Reindeer Ride without your girl and your little man," Dare said.

"Are you shitting me?" Ezra shook his head. "You did this for us?"

"It was your old man's idea," Rebel said as Pep walked over holding Gus.

"*Dad*, is that your bike?" Gus wriggled out of Pep's arms and ran over to Ezra. "Can I ride in that?"

"Yeah, buddy, you can." Ezra was looking at his father with disbelief. "You did this?"

Pep looked at him with more emotion than Sasha had ever seen between them. "I was never very good at being a father, but watching you with Gus has taught me a thing or two. I know how important family is to you, son, and I don't want you to miss out on a second of yours."

Tears welled in Sasha's eyes.

Ezra embraced him. "Thanks, Dad. You can't imagine how

much this means to me."

"I think I can," Pep said. "If the offer is still good, maybe we can have that lunch sometime. Just the two of us."

Ezra blinked several times, and Sasha knew he was struggling to keep his emotions in check. "I'd like that."

"Grandpa! Look at me!" Gus waved his hands from within the sidecar as Dare tried to settle him down and put a helmet on him.

"If we don't leave soon, I'm going to strip off this Santa suit and wear my birthday suit," Tiny said, and everyone laughed.

Ezra thanked her brothers and Rebel, and Sasha noticed something different in the way he carried himself. He kept glancing at his father, as if he were trying to put the pieces of the man who had just crawled far outside his comfort zone and offered an olive branch together with the man Ezra had known all his life.

Once they got Gus strapped in and settled, Sasha climbed onto the back of Ezra's bike, and he straddled it in front of her. He reached back and put his hand on her leg, glancing down at Gus, then looked at her and said, "This is going to be the best ride ever."

He gave her leg a squeeze, and they put on their helmets. As they fell into line behind the other motorcycles driving out of the clubhouse lot, Sasha knew she'd finally found her needle in a haystack, and he was worth every painful poke it had taken to get there.

Ready for More Whiskeys?

Get ready to fall hard for the mysterious Seeley "Doc" Whiskey and the one woman he never thought would walk back into his life, in LOVE, LIES, AND WHISKEY.

More Books By Melissa Foster

STANDALONE ROMANTIC COMEDY
Hot Mess Summer

LOVE IN BLOOM BIG-FAMILY ROMANCE COLLECTION

SNOW SISTERS
Sisters in Love
Sisters in Bloom
Sisters in White

THE BRADENS at Weston
Lovers at Heart, Reimagined
Destined for Love
Friendship on Fire
Sea of Love
Bursting with Love
Hearts at Play

THE BRADENS at Trusty
Taken by Love
Fated for Love
Romancing My Love
Flirting with Love
Dreaming of Love
Crashing into Love

THE BRADENS at Peaceful Harbor
Healed by Love
Surrender My Love
River of Love
Crushing on Love
Whisper of Love
Thrill of Love

THE BRADENS & MONTGOMERYS at Pleasant Hill – Oak Falls
Embracing Her Heart
Anything for Love
Trails of Love
Wild Crazy Hearts
Making You Mine
Searching for Love
Hot for Love
Sweet Sexy Heart
Then Came Love
Rocked by Love
Falling For Mr. Bad (Previously *Our Wicked Hearts*)

THE BRADENS at Ridgeport
Playing Mr. Perfect
Sincerely, Mr. Braden

THE BRADEN NOVELLAS
Promise My Love
Our New Love
Daring Her Love
Story of Love
Love at Last
A Very Braden Christmas

THE REMINGTONS
Game of Love
Stroke of Love
Flames of Love
Slope of Love
Read, Write, Love
Touched by Love

SEASIDE SUMMERS
Seaside Dreams
Seaside Hearts
Seaside Sunsets

Seaside Secrets
Seaside Nights
Seaside Embrace
Seaside Lovers
Seaside Whispers
Seaside Serenade

BAYSIDE SUMMERS
Bayside Desires
Bayside Passions
Bayside Heat
Bayside Escape
Bayside Romance
Bayside Fantasies

THE STEELES AT SILVER ISLAND
Tempted by Love
My True Love
Caught by Love
Always Her Love
Wild Island Love
Enticing Her Love

THE RYDERS
Seized by Love
Claimed by Love
Chased by Love
Rescued by Love
Swept Into Love

THE WHISKEYS: DARK KNIGHTS AT PEACEFUL HARBOR
Tru Blue
Truly, Madly, Whiskey
Driving Whiskey Wild
Wicked Whiskey Love
Mad About Moon
Taming My Whiskey

The Gritty Truth
In for a Penny
Running on Diesel

THE WHISKEYS: DARK KNIGHTS AT REDEMPTION RANCH
The Trouble with Whiskey
Freeing Sully: Prequel to For the Love of Whiskey
For the Love of Whiskey
A Taste of Whiskey
Love, Lies, and Whiskey

SUGAR LAKE
The Real Thing
Only for You
Love Like Ours
Finding My Girl

HARMONY POINTE
Call Her Mine
This is Love
She Loves Me

THE WICKEDS: DARK KNIGHTS AT BAYSIDE
A Little Bit Wicked
The Wicked Aftermath
Crazy, Wicked Love
The Wicked Truth
His Wicked Ways
Talk Wicked to Me

SILVER HARBOR
Maybe We Will
Maybe We Should
Maybe We Won't

WILD BOYS AFTER DARK
Logan

Heath
Jackson
Cooper

BAD BOYS AFTER DARK
Mick
Dylan
Carson
Brett

HARBORSIDE NIGHTS SERIES
Includes characters from the Love in Bloom series
Catching Cassidy
Discovering Delilah
Tempting Tristan

More Books by Melissa
Chasing Amanda (mystery/suspense)
Come Back to Me (mystery/suspense)
Have No Shame (historical fiction/romance)
Love, Lies & Mystery (3-book bundle)
Megan's Way (literary fiction)
Traces of Kara (psychological thriller)
Where Petals Fall (suspense)

Acknowledgments

I wrote this book over the holidays when I was with my family and sick with COVID. While writing about Sasha, Ezra, Gus, and the whole Redemption Ranch cast was a joy, I had a rough few weeks, and luckily, some very special people pulled me through and kept me sane. First and foremost, a huge thank-you goes out to my assistant and friend Lisa Filipe, who not only never let me jump off the ledge but also reminded me how magical my books were. When I was ready to give up, she made me take a break. When I didn't think I could write another word, she reminded me how capable I was. Yes, it was a low point. COVID was worse than sucky, and Lisa was my hero on a daily basis. Thank you, Lisa, for being you. Heaps of gratitude also go out to the rest of my girl squad, who stuck by me, cheered me on, listened to me bitch, and picked me up with endless love and support. Sharon Martin, Amy Manemann, Natasha Brown, Sue Pettazzoni, and Missy Dehaven, I truly appreciate each of you. To my developmental editor, Kristen Weber, who happily read the first hundred pages while I was still writing to make sure COVID hadn't blurred my ability to write well, thank you for always being there to help and encourage me. You are a pillar of positivity and knowledge, and I am so lucky to have worked with you for so many years. I look forward to many more. Lastly, to my soul sisters Toni and Kate, oh what fun we had brainstorming funny, flirty conversations! Thank you for our chat over the holidays. I love you, ladies, and can't wait to see you again.

The horse named Posey in this story has a special place in my heart. In researching horse rescues, I spoke with Susan Pierce, the owner of Red Bucket Horse Rescue. Susan works tirelessly to save horses, and she was kind enough to share several stories with me and answer my endless questions. My avid readers will understand why, when Susan told me about a horse named Rosey, whom she'd buddied up with another horse named Juju, I felt we were destined to meet, and I *had* to feature Rosey (whose name I changed to Posey to avoid confusion with my characters) in this story. If you've just started my books and would like to understand why this is, please check out THE WICKED AFTERMATH (The Wickeds: Dark Knights at Bayside).

I continue to be inspired by my fans, many of whom are in my fan club on Facebook. If you haven't yet joined my fan club, please do. We have a great time chatting about the Love in Bloom hunky heroes and sassy heroines. You never know when you'll inspire a story or a character and end up in one of my books, as several fan club members have already discovered. To stay abreast of what's going on in our fictional boyfriends' worlds and sales, like and follow me on social media.

Facebook Fan Club: MelissaFosterFans
Facebook Page: MelissaFosterAuthor
Instagram: MelissaFoster_author
TikTok: MelissaFoster_author

Sign up for my newsletter to keep up to date with new releases and special promotions and events.
www.MelissaFoster.com/Newsletter

As always, loads of gratitude go out to my incredible team of editors and proofreaders: Kristen Weber, Penina Lopez, Elaini Caruso, Juliette Hill, Lynn Mullan, and Justinn Harrison.

Meet Melissa

shop.melissafoster.com

Melissa Foster is a *New York Times*, *Wall Street Journal*, and *USA Today* bestselling and award-winning author. Her books have been recommended by *USA Today*'s book blog, *Hagerstown* magazine, *The Patriot*, and several other print venues. Melissa has painted and donated several murals to the Hospital for Sick Children in Washington, DC.

Visit Melissa on her website or chat with her on social media. Melissa enjoys discussing her books with book clubs and reader groups and welcomes an invitation to your event. Melissa's books are available through most online retailers in paperback, digital, and audio formats.

Shop Melissa's store for exclusive discounts, bundles, and more.

Printed in Great Britain
by Amazon